Pan's Flute

BY THE SAME AUTHOR

Pan's Flute
and Other Stories

by
J.-H. Rosny *aîné*

Translated, annotated and introduced by
Brian Stableford

A Black Coat Press Book

TABLE OF CONTENTS

Introduction

La Flûte de Pan, here translated as "Pan's Flute," was first published by Borel in 1897; *Amour Étrusque* ("Etruscan Amour") was issued by the same publisher in 1898, and *Les Femmes de Setnê* ("Setne's Women") was first published by Ollendorff in 1903; all three initially appeared under the pseudonym Enacryos, although all three were subsequently reissued under the author's more familiar pseudonym, J.-H. Rosny aîné. His baptismal name was Joseph-Henri Boëx (1856-1940), and his appellations are further confused by the fact that he shared the pseudonym J.-H. Rosny for some years with his younger brother Justin (1859-1948), and when they abandoned the pretence that they wrote in collaboration they distinguished themselves as J.-H. Rosny aîné and J.-H. Rosny jeune.

Joseph was by far the more prolific and more enterprising of the two brothers, and he developed a considerable reputation writing in several fiction genres. Having been taken under the wing of Edmond de Goncourt when he first arrived in Paris in the early 1880s with the intention of building a career as a writer, he was initially allocated to the Naturalist camp of which Goncourt had long been a pillar, but his work was very various, and he is nowadays best known as a significant pioneer of what Maurice Renard called "scientific marvel fiction," a kind of imaginative fiction that had affinities with British scientific romance and the fiction that eventually acquired the label "science fiction" in the U.S.A. Almost all of his

7

work in that vein is translated in a seven-volume set issued by Black Coat Press in 2010, consisting of *Navigators of Space and Other Alien Encounters, The World of the Variants and Other Strange Lands, The Mysterious Force and Other Anomalous Phenomena, Vamireh and Other Prehistoric Fantasies, The Givreuse Enigma and Other Stories, The Young Vampire and Other Cautionary Tales* and *Helgvor of the Blue River and The Giant Feline*. (A detailed overview of Rosny's career can be found in the introduction to the first of those volumes.)

As the use of a different pseudonym implies, the three Enacryos stories are, in a sense, further removed from the supposed canon of Naturalistic fiction than Rosny's scientific romances, but the nature of that apparent removal has more to do with their context than their content. In the 1890s, Naturalism, which had became a significant literary movement in France in the 1870s, was widely seen to be in a contest for prestige with the more recent Symbolist Movement, based on the literary theories of Stéphane Mallarmé. The contest was largely illusory, and very few of the writers categorized by commentators as belonging to one or other movement wanted to be pigeon-holed, let alone strait-jacketed, by any such classification. Even so, it presumably seemed convenient and politic to Joseph Boëx at that time to issue his nakedly Symbolist fiction under a distinct pseudonym, and that is why the three works in the present volume were initially signed "Enacryos."

La Flûte de Pan bears a strong resemblance in its content and narrative strategy to a series of mythological fantasies written by the Symbolist writer Pierre Louÿs (1870-1925) commenced with "Leda, ou la louange des bienheureuses ténèbres," (tr. as "Leda; or, The Praise of Blissful Darkness") which first appeared as a booklet from Libraire de l'Art Indépendant in 1893 and was subsequently reprinted with similar items in *Le Crépuscule des nymphes* (1925; tr. as *The Twilight of the Nymphs*). If there were any doubt regarding Louÿs' influence, it was dispelled when Rosny followed up the short story with the short novel *Amour Étrusque*. Louÿs had followed up his short story with *Aphrodite, moeurs antiques* (1896; tr. as *Aphrodite*), a fervent study of erotic obsession, which is one of the great Symbolist novels, and became the best-selling novel of its era. *Amour Étrusque*, a similarly fervent study of erotic obsession and ancient mores, was by no means as successful commercially, but it is nevertheless a very striking exercise in extended Symbolist fiction, and deserves more credit in that regard than it obtained at the time or has accumulated since.

Les Femmes de Setné marked a change of direction in the brief career of Enacryos, although it is certainly a further story of ancient mores as they could be perceived at the end of the nineteenth century, with the aid of contemporary archeological and anthropological endeavors and a forceful imagination. It retains a strong Symbolist element, but it adds a far more robust plot, similar in many ways to J.-H. Rosny's endeavors in imaginative fiction—and, in fact, "Setne's Women" would not have been entirely out of place in the earlier set of translations of Rosny's scientific romances. Its most striking feature, however, is its further development of the most distinctive aspect of *Amour Étrusque*, which is the protagonist's erotic obsession and, more particularly, one idiosyncratic feature thereof.

It is virtually taken for granted throughout the extraordinarily prolific literature depicting the psychological operations of amour that erotic obsession is essentially singular. There is a widespread acceptance of the fact that erotic obsessions tend to be temporary and replaceable, so that the most common development of amorous careers tends to involve a series of relationships rather than the unique lifelong passion that is often held to be ideal, but the conventional phrase representing that pattern—"serial monogamy"—still asserts emphatically that obsession is typically, and perhaps necessarily, exclusive. Rosny's two novels are, therefore, highly unusually in setting out to describe and explore the psychological predicament of simultaneous erotic obsession.

It is by no means unusual, of course, for literary representations of amour to feature erotic conflicts of interest; indeed, they are typically summarized by the phrase "the eternal triangle." Almost invariably, however, such situations are represented as matters of agonizing choice and melodramas of jealousy. Such triangles are acute because the fundamental assumption is that they essentially unstable and cannot—or, at least, ought not to—endure. They are very frequently seen as aspects of the transitions of serial monogamy, in which one relationship is dying and another burgeoning, inevitably moving toward a resolution that can leave only one intact, if any. The relationships depicted in Rosny's novels are not like that. Dionys in *Amour Étrusque* and Setné in *Les Femmes de Setné* are both simultaneously obsessed with two women, Dehva and Flavia in the first instance, and Gaïla and Aoura in the latter, and although both heroes suffer a certain agony by virtue of being unable to make a choice between them, there is never any possibility of their making such a choice. They not only want both, but feel that they literally cannot do without both, even if it seems impossible that they could ever have both in the long term, by virtue of the pressure of social expectations and the fury of female jealousy.

It is worth noting that Symbolist fiction is, in general, not replete with conventional "happy endings." The vast majority of Symbolist fictions are *contes cruels*, although they range in length and tone from epic tragedies to curt black comedies. Unlike generic love stories, which tend to be drawn irresistibly toward a climactic monogamous commitment, pretentious accounts of great amours—Naturalist, Symbolist or whatever—are far more likely to end in disaster and death than happy marriage. That is particularly true of love stories in which social circumstances are adverse; although princes routinely marry shepherdesses in artificial fairy tales, serious fiction tends to take a much dimmer view of the likelihood of such outcomes. The angles of eternal triangles become even sharper as their sides acquire additional social distance, and those in which Dionys and Setné are involved each have a particularly awkward social geometry, enhancing their excursions into literary *terra incognita*. Given that, the bizarre aspects of Setné's incidental journey to military glory are perhaps not as out of place, symbolically speaking, as they might seem.

Le Flûte de Pan is a straightforward exercise in erotic symbolism whose elements are inherited. Like Pierre Louÿs, Enacryos embeds the myth-based story within a frame narrative, in which the teller employs it deliberately as an erotic stimulant—emphasizing its symbolism in the process—and provides the story-teller with a lyre, in order that he can illustrate the essential eroticism of music. Dionys, in *Amour Étrusque*, inherits Pan's reed flute and employs it in the same way, as a powerful erotic magnet, which helps to captivate both of the women whose beauty captivates him. Setné, however has no artificial aid of that sort, and has to rely on a different kind of magic to enhance his personal charisma. Although the period of history in which he is operating is more remote than that in which Dionys is supposedly living, it is actually further removed from the "fabulous times" of Pan's Syrinx in terms of cultural distance. Its magic is essentially fake, in spite of being lent considerable force by credulity, and the same is true of its emblems of Fate—which helps to explain the very different outcomes of the two novels, and the estimation of their intended and actual psychological effects.

Amour Étrusque is not unique within the canon of the author's work; it has affinities with this prehistoric fantasies, and exhibits the same fascination with the employment of the literary imagination to build coherent images of human life based on scanty archeological evidence and speculative anthropological theory. As its title implies, it really is an attempt to construct a representation of a specifically Etruscan amour, albeit viewed from the perspective of a partial outsider, whose Syracusan mores originate from a distinct and markedly different part of Magna Graecia. In that regard, it is an endeavor parallel to J.-H. Rosny's attempt to depict Lacustrian society—including Lacustrian amour—in *Eyrimah* (1893), and to Enacryos' subsequent attempt to model ancient Egyptian society in *Les Femmes de Setné*. Nor is its focus on unorthodox erotic obsession out of keeping with a thread that ran through all of Rosny's works, extending in his scientific romances even to love affairs between humans and aliens, and members of *Homo sapiens* and those of purely hypothetical species.

In the latter regard, the essential triangle of *Les Femmes de Setné*, like that of *Amour Étrusque*, is relatively moderate; although Gaïla belongs to a different race—she is described, somewhat enigmatically, as a "Bedouine"—she is not so very different culturally from the Egyptian Setné. The later novel does, however introduce the exotic character of the Queen of the Waters, a member of a distinct human species with whom one suspects that Setné, had his quota of duplicate erotic obsessions not been already complete, might have been willing and able to extend the brief sexual relationship that he forms for political reasons.

The Queen of the Waters and her people, as well as their geographical proximity to exotic monsters seemingly left over from the fabulous times of paleontological science represent another enduring preoccupation of Rosny's, with which he apparently had considerable difficulty. Prior to writing *Les Femmes de Setné* he seems to have started and aborted two novels in which enclaves of such exotic survivals were to be explored. The early chapters of one were disguised as a novelette in "Nymphée (1893; tr. as "Nymphaeum), while "La Contrée prodigieuse des cavernes" (1896; tr. as "The Wonderful Cave Country") and "Les Profondeurs de Kyamo" (1896; tr. a "The Depths of Kyamo") appear to be two fragments of another. *Les Femmes de Setné* was the first complete narrative into which the author managed to include such an interlude, although its presence might well seem to some readers to be grotesquely anomalous. He went on to do it twice more, in the African adventure story *L'Étonnante aventure de Hareton Ironcastle* (1922; tr. as "Hareton Ironcastle's Amazing Adventure") and the Indonesia-set *La Sauvage aventure* (1935; tr. as "Adventure in the Wild"), both apparently modeled on American pulp fiction, and both sternly conventional in their representation of mild erotic obsession. Whether than makes the endeavors in question any more coherent is a matter of opinion, but it certainly does not make them more interesting.

The three Enacryos stories thus show a marked evolution as well as a fundamental commonality. They are all hybrid works, even the brief *La Flûte de Pan*, but the nature and extent of their hybridization changes progressively. Seen as speculative explorations of the nature and possibilities of erotic obsession, they could not, of course, be expected to reach any kind of conclusion, even though the individual narratives are obliged to do so, but that essential inconclusiveness does not detract from their audacity, and the two longer stories certainly look at the question from an unusual angle.

The Symbolists and their fellow travelers brought to a spectacular climax to Romantic literary mythology of the *femme fatale*, and, in particular, to the particular version of the eternal triangle in which a hapless hero is torn between a dangerous but irresistible *femme fatale* and modest but dependable lover. Rosny's triangles break that pattern decisively, not simply because Flavia and Gaïa are uncommonly accommodating exotic love objects, while Dehva and Aoura are far from being modest, but because of the heroes' absolute insistence on not making a decision between the two attractions, no matter how agonizing the conflict of their forces threatens to become.

Audacity and variation have rarely been successful selling points in the marketing of love stories, where formula is paramount, but they have a corollary fascination for connoisseurs and anyone not stuck, so to speak, in a rut. *Amour Étrusque* and *Les Femmes de Setné* certainly have no lack of that kind of fascination, and are uniquely precious because of it. They are fantastic and they are lurid, but in the context or erotic fantasies, those are recommendations, not defects, for any reader possessed of imagination. The three stories included in the present volume thus make up one of the most remarkable of literary triptychs, and one of the most intriguing.

All three translations were made from the versions of the texts reprinted in *Fables Antiques et autres récits érotiques* by J.-H. Rosny aîné, published in 2015 by Bibliogs, compiled and edited by Fabrice Mundzik, whose contributions to contemporary literary archeology are invaluable.

Brian Stableford

PAN'S FLUTE

Dusk was already falling. The beautiful sycamores extended enormous shadows over the river and the tall reeds. The yellow sun was seen setting and the moon rising, as pale as a silver cloud.

Lycaon savored the charming moment when the daughter and son of Latone occupied the edge of the horizon simultaneously. Covered in the dust of the roads, he was carrying a lyre of blackened wood, for he was an aede, having received the education of singers and philosophers under elegant porticoes, and the caresses of painted slaves on ivory beds, in the odor of aromatic plants, amid the harmony of musical instruments. He also remembered, both pleasantly and bitterly, industrious courtesans who knew the art of converting human sighs into gold.

And he was traveling through Hellas of the hundred cities in order to find his chimera. He sang as he went, on the agoras of cities and the edges of villages, and the kindly soil of Achaea gave him hospitality, clothing and amour in exchange. He knew how to relate the legends that please young women and how to draw the instruction therefrom that invites sensuality.

He had arrived at the Ladon of the grassy banks. In the divine half-light, he dreamed about the son of Laertes, the destroyer of ramparts, and Nausicaa with the white arms. How pleasant it would be to see her appear amid the willows of the river, with her semi-naked followers, laughing through their wet hair!

As he was thinking that, exhausted by fatigue, with his heart full of the charm of Eros, he heard silvery laughter that was prolonged amid the song of naiads. He stopped, and looked.

The red sun was about to disappear; the large moon resembled an immense mirror in which a hill was reflected. And among the slender trees, over the reeds and the lotus, he saw nymphs or mortals, scarcely clad in pure wool, who were letting their hair dry. In the crimson and white light they were as brilliant as the daughter of Antinous and her companions.

And one of them, who seemed coiffed in radiance and woven of lilies, made him think that peoples might not have been unready to suffer for her, as for Helen.

Meanwhile, he moved forward. The sparkling young women, finally perceiving him, got to their feet in order to flee across the meadows; but he raised his hands and shouted in a soft voice exercised by music and eloquence:

"Oh! Goddesses or mortals, luminous daughters of the earth, or naiads issued from the waters, have no fear of the solitary traveler. He cannot do you any harm. Rather listen to his voice…for I know stories of the men of old and the songs of good aedes. Would you not like me to relate for you the misfortune of Syrinx, daughter of this river of the transparent gulfs: Syrinx, who could only flee the hairy god with the goat's legs by becoming a slender reed? That story is charming on summer nights, and full of secret lessons."

The young woman who seemed to be coiffed by radiance stopped, and then the others. They all approached the aede with the gestures of curious hinds with large starlit eyes, and one of them shouted: "Tell us the story of the nymph Syrinx, stranger. We will listen to it mingle with the voice of the river. But first take a cup of dark wine, gentle on the heart."

She picked up a goatskin full of wine and poured a cupful for Lycaon. He raised the cup toward the sky, made a small libation to the river, and savored the beverage, the winged soul of which filled him with eloquence.

"Now I will tell you the story of Syrinx, issue of the river Ladon, and the terrible god who, prowling the woods and the meadows, renders the darkness more menacing."

They sat down beside him. He respired the pleasant odor of their flesh, and saw their mouths shining crimson and silver in the light of Hecate. His breast palpitated with sensuality while he tuned his sonorous lyre; the largest of the stars came to mirror themselves in the water and in the eyes of the beautiful young women, and a breath sometimes descended that seemed perfumed with the ambrosia of a god hovering in the crystalline twilight.

Lycaon first made audible the little euphonic nymphs that are captive in the strings of the lyre, and then he spoke.

So, the god Pan was hiding from the gods and from men; that is why old Hesiod did not know him. He hid in the noise of tempests, in the murmur of trees, and in the sudden voices that throw panic into livestock, travelers and armies in battle. He haunted the forests that moaned, he howled with the voice of invisible wolves, the anger of equinoxes and the resonance of the sea.

Now, the nymph Syrinx lived near the river, her father, in the scintillating meadows, on the shady islands and beside tranquil coves. She was tremulous and supple, she glided happily on moonbeams; she disappeared silently into the trunks of willows; she wove her red hair with fresh herbs. There was no immortal more fearful. A leaf curved by the wind caused her to flee; she was afraid of looking at her own image, and the song of frogs in the marsh troubled her dreams.

As soon as dusk fell, she took shelter among the branches; she listened to the darkness while curling herself up. And that was not without pleasure. She knew the little sensualities of the fear that gives a voice to things and brings the stones of paths to live. She did not detest the fact that the smallest insect seemed terrible.

One morning, she heard footfalls following her over the meadow. She turned round and saw nothing. But the next day, as she lay down in the shade of a sycamore, she felt a warm breath on her neck and in her hair. One evening, when she was about to go into a grotto, an invisible obstacle stopped her for some time; she saw the vapor of breath rising.

She uttered a scream, and the obstacle disappeared.

After that, she was followed incessantly. The trees sighed as she passed by, the water uttered a soft plaint in receiving her figure, and she no longer dared to look at her naked flesh, for hidden eyes were looking at it at the same time as her. In spite of her fear of the dark, she no longer bathed except in the secrecy of night.

She understood that a god was smitten with her, and was troubled, like hinds by Autumn. Was it Phoebus, king of light, or the great Zeus, perfumed with ambrosia? She lay down on the moss of the forest or on odiferous grass. She dreamed about the blue flesh of the firmament, and the clouds, the sons of Saturn. She did not know whether she was quivering with fear or desire.

It seemed to her that she would have liked to summon Eros, but that she did not dare. The breath came down; she sensed the invisible god beside her young body, palpitating for the eternal hymen, the objective of being. Sometimes, a soft arm embraced her, with the friction of a torso. She thought that she was about to see, but she saw nothing but a furtive radiance, a fleeing animal, or the slight of a black bird in the sky.

One day, she was arranging her hair with iris flowers and little lively herbs. She was mirroring her golden head in a spring. And she was smiling, vaguely, at her flexible grace, while foliage quivered beside her and began to speak. And it said, in a voice that resembled the murmur of waves:

"It is the god Pan who loves you, nymph issued from the beautiful river Ladon. He wants to create new beings with you, who have no peers on earth. You will give birth to chimerical animals: lion-men and swan-women. You will put into the woods and the meadows figures that are not accustomed to be there. And you will be glorious among the immortals, for nothing is more beautiful than to be the mother of unknown forms."

The fearful nymph only understood what it said vaguely, but she found charm in the voice that quivered in the foliage, and she said, softly: "Has the god Pan no face, then, that he always speaks by means of the trees, the waters and echoes?"

The foliage replied: "The god Pan has many faces, for he is the king of all the beasts and all the satyrs who live among the trees…and who are modeled in his resemblance."

But the nymph with the bright eyes still did not understand. She said in her turn: "What is the point of so many faces, if they cannot make themselves visible?"

As she spoke, the foliage started to laugh.

"Would you like to see Pan, innocent nymph?"

She trembled, but curiosity was stronger than fear.

"Yes."

"Look!"

She saw a reflection, and then a large stag with ten branches. It threw its head back and pawed the grass with its cloven hoof. Its eyes sparkled like the red stars of Ares; ardor elevated its muscular flanks. It came toward the nymph and placed its warm mouth on her shoulder. She sensed the ardor of Eros in that agile guest of the forests, and wanted to recoil. But she found herself pressed against the vast trunk of an oak; the powerful beast caressed her white breast, and her shoulders, comparable to those of silver Hebe. Thus the wild bull on the Phoenician shore mingled its breath with that of the pale Europa.

Syrinx uttered a loud scream of fear. The stag looked at her them with its bright eyes, raised its branched horns and vanished like a cloud.

"You have seen one of the faces of the god Pan," murmured the foliage. "But he can also take on human form."

Syrinx was still shivering. The gaze of the stag was within her, like a fire in a hearth. Eternal life excited her to abandon herself, for the benefit of beings that were to be born in the future. She desired to see Pan in human form, and said so in a whisper to the foliage.

Then, in the blue shade, a human face appeared. It bore a forked beard, and horns on the head; his body was covered with unkempt hair, and his limbs were those of a goat. And his eyes were resplendent with the same red flame that had appeared in the stag's eyes.

"Syrinx, tremulous daughter of the waters and the meadows, your destiny will be as sweet as Echo, to whom I gave Iynx, and Aega, who conceived Aegipan. I am the great god of the future. My descendants will populate the earth when those of Zeus, Poseidon and Phoebus are hidden in sad dwellings and disdained by men. Come, nymph with the beautiful tresses, we shall be happy on the profound moss. We shall unite in order to make the forest more mysterious."

He spoke, but Syrinx disdained his hairy body and his horned head. She rose to her feet nimbly and tried to flee toward the river with the beautiful eddies; but the god barred her route. She raised her hands toward the heavens and prayed:

"Zeus, O Father who reigns from the heights of Ida, very great, very glorious, and you, Phoebus, conductor of light, and you, divine River who gave birth to me, have pity on me; do not let me fall into the hands of this brutal god."

"Your prayer is vain, Syrinx," said the god Pan, "for I am the master of nymphs born of rivers. It is insensate, for you are refusing happiness..."

"Change your face!" cried the nymph. "I cannot abide your goat's feet and your hairy torso..."

"It is the form in which I desire to be a father...there is none more beautiful."

She fled toward the hills. She bounded like a filly that has not yet known the human yoke; he followed her like a proud stallion, the king of herds. They ran over pastures, hills and plains where men live who nourish themselves on wheat. And when dusk fell, and the shadows of the trees were elongated, when they both returned toward the Ladon, whose bend they had cut across, Pan cried:

"Stop, Syrinx. Fear, in fleeing the decree of Eros, running to your doom. The River itself cannot protect you, and for having escaped destiny, you would be similar to a sterile herb."

"I would rather be similar to a reed." she replied, "than be the mother of a satyr..."

As she spoke, the river appeared, all red in the dusk. It appeared for a moment that Syrinx was finally about to reach it, but as she was already throwing herself into the water, Pan extended his arms and touched the fugitive nymph.

He was holding nothing but a long, flexible reed...

The aede stopped speaking; the young women remained silent. They were moved; their breasts were rising gently.

A violet light descended through the branches. The river scintillated among the reeds; the population of frogs sang in a melancholy fashion.

Lycaon went on: "The great god Pan cut the reed and made the amorous flute that it is so sweet to hear on fine evenings. Thus, the nymph who died for not having wanted amour took on the voice of amour, and the flute sings the eternal regret of young women who, like her, die sterile. For they are dead among the dead! It is necessary to love, virgins similar to the Immortals...even if the lover is animal as well as divine. He has caprine feet as well as starry eyes; his body is hairy but his action is magnificent. Those who have scorned him will never be anything but plaintive reeds...

"It is said," he added, "that on beautiful evenings, when the air is tranquil and rivers sleep like living beings, that those who are ripe for Eros hear the sounds of the flute rising on the shores of lakes, rivers or marshes. That is the melancholy Syrinx, who is exhorting them not to be pitiless for themselves, and to savor the felicity of being conquered."

At those words, young ears were directed toward the river. Nothing could be heard but the slight movement of the waves, the noise of the batrachians and quivering foliage, but Agamede, crowned with radiance, turned her beautiful eyes toward the aede and murmured in an emotional voice:

"I can hear the voice of Syrinx..."

She had allowed her veil to fall, and her youthful cleavage was visible in the moonlight. She was listening, attentively, to the faint flute whose moaning she alone could hear.

Lycaon sensed the terrible soft flame for which generations of men live and perish, and which caused the black ships of the Achaeans to depart in order to recover the daughter of Leda from the Trojan horse-tamers.

He said:

"It's the voice of the god, charming young woman. Beware of resisting him..."

"I have no desire to resist him," she replied.

She stood up, happy to be submissive, already letting down her long hair made of light and gold. Her companions did not murmur, for they believed that they recognized the mysterious will that no more permits the disputation of the sacrifice of a young woman than the sacrifice of a dove.

And the aede prayed:

"Be propitious to us, god of the invincible arrows, who reigns ardently over Thespis, you who conducted me to these divine shores. I shall ornament your magnificent altar, in Samos or in Crete…but could I offer you a victim, more superb than this one, a priestess more splendid and better made to celebrate your glorious mysteries?"

The voice and the lyre fell silent. The aede carried his ravishing prey away.

While the aede united his mouth with unknown young lips, behind the willows, in the embalmed shade, where fireflies shone like little mortal stars, the Arcadian chorus sang the light hymn of Aphrodite; and the delicious soul of Hellas, which knew how to make beauty a glory and amour a virtue, floated over the silvery waters of the river, in an atmosphere so diaphanous that it seemed that the sky and all the stars were touching the crowns of the trees.

ETRUSCAN AMOUR

Advertisement

I have placed the setting of this story in an Etruscan village in Campania, under the reign of Vespasian.[1]

There must have been a large number of such villages, but the inhabitants were, in general, ignorant of their origin.

The characters I am putting on stage have kept a few traditions, but no one will expect to find them similar to their ancestors of the times of the Lucumons.[2] They have mixed Etruscan, Greek, Roman and Asiatic legends, customs and rites strangely.

---

[1] Vespasian was Roman Emperor from 69-79 A.D. Campania, in southern Italy, had been colonized by the Greeks in the seventh century B.C., around the city of Neapolis (now Naples), and had been part of what the Romans called Magna Graecia, the region that retained a fundamentally Grecian culture while belonging of the Roman Empire.

[2] According to a fourth-century commentary on the *Aeneid* by Maurus Servius Honoratus, the Etruscans designated their kings as Lucumons prior to their conquest by the Romans. The Etruscan civilization, whose heartland was in northern Italy but presumably extended as far south as Campania before the latter region was colonized by the Greeks, existed for an unknown length of time before 700 B.C., from which its first known inscriptions date, until its conquest by the Romans at the end of the fourth century B.C.—the effective commencement of what was eventually to become the Roman Empire.

Then again, their race is not pure: the Latins as well as Hellenes, and Oriental slaves, have transformed their language, their tastes and their own names to a greater or lesser extent. It is, however, an Etruscan population. The reader who has some erudition will perceive that clearly, but it is easy to please that reader; it is the other that I would like to reach, the one who knows about Etruscans what he has learned vaguely in Roman history. I am addressing this small advertisement to him, in order that he might mistrust memories of school, for the sake of criticism; he must convince himself that he knows nothing about Etruscans. In truth, no one knows any more, but, all the same, in order to appreciate this story, let him make a distinction between his "pure" ignorance and the perverted ignorance of those who have studied the matter at length.

PART ONE

I. The Traveler

The traveler stopped near the Volturne with the tall reeds. It was the terrible hour when the cicadas are glad to be alive and sing in unison their hymn to Phoebus. The black poplars and sycamores were swooning beneath the furnace of the sky, the vast pools, as primitive as the day when they emerged from Chaos, enveloped Veila, quietly asleep on the Campanian soil.

The traveler took off his chlamys and placed his lamentable pilos on a root. He was carrying an olive-wood staff polished by several generations and the flute that Pan drew from the melancholy body of Syrinx, for he cultivated the magical art of sounds. Having left Syracuse in a Phoenician trireme, he had walked from city to city, village to village, with the intention of reaching Rome. He was young and agile, made like the men of Argos or Mycene, his eyes bright, his hair ardent and black. His mind had received the delicate cultivation of philosophers, aedes and courtesans, but, blind fortune having swallowed his patrimony, he lived on his art.

The excess of his fatigue hid the beauty of the landscape from him. He had scarcely slept the night before, in a primitive village, and had been marching since dawn.

His eyes half-closed, he had the chagrined and marvelous vision of his vanished happiness, over the indefatigable sea, where the vessels of Libya, Asia Minor and Gaul sailed. Then, abundance had rendered the nights more voluptuous; the seduction of hetaerae mingled with the joy of cargoes extended on the shore; life had been as easy and luminous as the palpitating waves.

And in the house of Archimedes, all peoples simultaneously poured out gold, admirable guests, slaves clad in the suppleness of lust, rhetors with sonorous voices, sophists, and the harmonious forms of art. But at the written hour, the sea devours riches. Archimedes had opened his veins, and his son was wandering the earth in poverty.

He found no pleasure in it. He was irritated by distracting imbeciles, took the salary of his art with chagrin, and held the brutality of those who provided it in execration.

As he advanced toward Rome, souls became more embittered, ears less delicate. He did not always encounter hospitality, and, disdainful of ruses, he had known odious hunger and reposed the delicate skin of his limbs on the bare ground.

"Hermes, cruel god," he cried, "you have not been helpful to me."

His eyes filled with tears. He sensed the sadness of the world, further embittered for his soul accustomed to luxury. And he had a vision of little blue tables, and meat sliced by a carver. He had touched it with disdainful lips, only taking pleasure in foodstuffs disguised by sharp spices and wine aged in closed vessels. Now, his memory did not retrace for him pheasants' brains or Sicilian eels, but abundant nourishment: pulmentum, speusticus, barley polenta and minced meat.

His suffering was humiliating. He smiled, the ironic smile of a man accustomed to the lessons of sophists.

And gradually, as fatigue overcame hunger, his ideas became confused. He fell asleep.

When he woke up, the shadows had elongated. The entire country had undergone a metamorphosis. A softer charm had descended over the Volturne, over the renascent meadows, over the young springs running from the hills with a rumor that dominated that of the cicadas, and the silvery foliage of the poplars emerged from its silence.

The traveler's body was also less sad, and his soul more courageous. He considered the vines, the olive groves and the rice-fields that enveloped the habitations of the divine village. Potters could be seen turning their wheels, others depositing vases in the sun, and, toward the center, the red mouth of a forge, partly open.

Veila was renowned in Tarente, Capua and Pompeii, all the way to Syracuse and the isles of the Archipelago, for its charming vases, with harmonious contours and subtle paintings. It combined Hellenic grace, Etruscan secrets, the naivety of fabulous times, and the delicacy of imminent decadence.

The traveler exclaimed: "Dionys, son of Archimedes, salutes you, divine Earth, and you, Volturne of the mild abysms; it would be sweet to forget oneself here, like a harmonious shade; but your inhabitants are doubtless malevolent and rude."

An amiable melancholy passed into his heart. It awoke art. He raised his flute to his lips, and sighed his admiration, his youth and his poverty. The soulful sonorities rose and died amid the sound of the waters, like gnats in a storm.

And Dionys sensed something within him that was bitter and charming, proud, tender and courageous. It was beauty, the mother of the gods, the veritable ocean from which Aphrodite emerged. The exile bore a little of its magnificent foam. And the sounds sprang from the flute like contours from the chisel of Praxiteles, like winged words from Homeric lips.[3]

The world was less bitter, the hunger less cruel. Dionys understood the legend, and what monsters Orpheus had tamed.

He fell silent, and heard a quivering in the silence.

Then a voice rose up, which was even sweeter than the flute of the god Pan, as if mingled with crystal and lively water.

"May Selene and Phoebus protect your footsteps, traveler with the beautiful tones! May every door be hospitable to you, and may every encounter be beneficent!"

He turned round and saw a young woman against the thorny hedge, still showing traces of childhood but with the proud lines of a young statue, a voluptuous contour departing from the shoulders to the round waist and mingling the lyre-shaped hip with the loose folds of her garment.

She reminded Dionys of the slim Anadyomene worshiped in Syracuse in a little temple of green marble, not unworthy of the golden goddess.

She was clad in a white woolen stola and coiffed with admirable black tresses, in which violet light ran, a wave of brilliant sensuality like a starlit river. Her eyes contained all the splendor of poems; they were the color

---

[3] The editor of the version of the text from which the present translation is taken adds a note here to record that the final sentence of this paragraph was replaced in the 1931 edition by the line: "Then he sang the nymph Syrinx pursued by the hairy god."

of the Tyrrhenian Sea when it reflected daylight; the lashes, half-lowered, rendered them more mysterious and tenderly redoubtable.

A god had taken pleasure, in that remote village, in sculpting the form of a goddess. Every gesture of the young woman revealed her beauty.

Dionys considered the delicately curved cheeks, the mouth ornamented by fire and snow, the glistening neck that changed shape amorously, depending on whether her face was raised, lowered or turned sideways, and the young bosom that inflated the stola with every respiration. That magnificent presence enchained the traveler's movements. His heart groaned, not with lust or amour, but with the turbulence of art. And he knew that none of the subtle and supple hetaerae who had come aboard his father's ships has been finished by such a proud chisel.

He finally replied: "Your words bring me joy, young woman, for beauty is propitious. Its wishes are granted. Already, the road seems to me to be less rude, the future more exorable."

She smiled, and seemed more child-like. Then familiarly and curiously: she asked "Where have you come from?"

He hastened to satisfy that curiosity, impatient to appear as he was: "I've come from Syracuse. My father had ships at sea, laden with oil, wheat and dark wines. The abyss took everything. I left for Rome, where I hope to find employment for my art. Doubtless the journey seems so harsh to me because I'm accustomed to living without hardship. I shall make it."

She replied, with vivacity: "I am Dehva, granddaughter of Tarao, the master-potter of Veila, whose vases are sought all the way to Syracuse. This village is hospitable. If you desire to rest here, go to the house that you see behind the Wall of the Ancestors. With your fine tunes you will charm the soul of Tarao; there is no man more attached to divine things."

Dionys' bosom filled with freshness. His brilliant gaze enveloped Dehva. It appeared to him to be impossible not to pause in the village.

"I shall obey," he murmured, very softly.

"Go," she said, "and I hope that you will play again, at dinner, what you played to the reeds of the Volturne."

Having spoken, she departed. He listened to the flight of little sandals and the rustle of the stola against the olive branches. Then the elegant figure disappeared around a bend in the path.

And Dionys knew the hope of Jason on the edge of the garden of the Hesperides.

Dionys traversed a field of grass and blue vines. He found himself before the Wall of the Ancestors, a thousand years old, made of blocks of Carrara marble deposited in the cyclopean manner. From there the village could be seen more clearly. In the amber sunlight, in the long violet shadows, the olive groves, the pines, the rice-fields, the fine orchards, the Campanian cattle dreaming in the pastures and the dwellings of humans depicted the image of happiness.

The houses and cabins only emerged part way from the fleece of virgin vines or tall sycamores. They were almost all made of volcanic stone, lava and basalt extracted from ground that had trembled with terrible fires for twenty thousand years. Some, in pietra panchina, seemed to be made of shells, and really were, but shells born before all the ages of man.

In the orchards, before the shady facades, beneath the abundant branches, wheels could be seen turning, chisels fashioning docile clay and brushes poised over black varnish.

A group of young women on a terrace were tracing the ornamentation of vases. Attentively, they were repeating punctiliously some game of fauns, some rustic scene, or simply harmonious lines. And all of them seemed full of grace in their light stolas, among the clusters of grapes that only left them partially visible. One of them, her bare leg raised on a tripod, her hair dangling somewhat, was showing the bright vases of her bosom in a pose both ingenuous and lascivious.

Dionys went around the wall and became visible to everyone. Heads were raised, Etruscan heads with dreaming eyes, graces that had been accustomed to living in that land a thousand years before the foundation of Rome. Suspicious, full of melancholy traditions, they did not smile at the stranger. They seemed to be remembering the misfortune of the ancestors, still full of traditions in a district where Rome had not, as elsewhere, dispersed the people, insulted the sepulchers and annihilated the customs.

The large house appeared, shady with virgin vines and centenarian olive trees. It was built in travertine and the white flint of Tarquinia. Sculpted in a single block, the Etruscan god whose name was lost, who had taught the art of baking clay, was visible over the door. Two fountains were flowing quietly. And before the large open bays, young men and young women were trying to fashion brown or blue clay, to discover the form of a lamp, an urn or a bowl, and to trace figures thereon.

A tall, bald old man was supervising the school. He was passionate, reprimanding or praising ardently. His voice was rough and his gestures nervous. A profound gleam remained in his sunken eyes, the force of life inhabited his wrinkled face and his violet lips; and harsh summers had not curbed his stature.

Dionys considered him with anxiety, for the hunger had returned, with the desire for a halt, a good meal, and the company of men less primitive than those he had frequented on his route.

He raised his flute slowly; he played a hymn that he had composed for the cruel sea and glaucous Poseidon.

At that voice, the old man stopped and cocked his right ear. He did not show any pleasure, or annoyance, but a profound attention. And when the cries of the Syrinx had faded away into the blue-tinted air, he exclaimed: "By the complicit Gods, stranger, you've reminded me the dusty roads of Attica and bright evenings on the Agora. You merit the praise of sages! Tell me where you come from, and who your master was; he must certainly have partaken of an uncommon skill."

"My name is Dionys," he replied, "And I come from Syracuse. My father Archimedes had ships at sea. The sea devoured his wealth, and creditors harsher than the sea. Many masters have taught me the art of sounds. I am going to Rome, where life is vast."

"It is vast, but not gentle," replied the old man. He had come to the doorstep. He smiled, full of memories. It pleased him that Dionys was not a vagabond raised at hazard, for he hoped to be able to dispense a few of the words accumulated within him, which his old age rendered more intolerable not being able to speak. He glimpsed an evening of eloquence, a guest with an attentive ear. He asked with avidity, in the Greek language: "You doubtless knew Hellenic artists, rhetors and sophists in Syracuse?"

"Archimedes took pleasure in seeing them," the Sicilian replied, "and I have savored their words since childhood."

He was not speaking without cunning, for he was aware of the lust that old men have to pronounce speeches, and that they love, above all, those who can listen to them and understand them. He divined that this one had traveled the world and was provided with many anecdotes.

"If it depends on me, Dionys, your sojourn in Veila will be agreeable. It is appropriate that hospitality is mild to those who have received the divine gift...and I want you to taste my Capuan wine, a pike from Lake Bolsena and the thrushes from our vineyards. I am Tarao. I descend from the ancient Rasenas whom destiny sacrificed to the fortune of Rome.[4] My forefathers fought for several centuries. The blood that flows in my veins is that of the last Lucumon, who perished under the legionaries' javelins. He died victorious; he had spread terror for ten years, sheltered in this Ciminian forest, where the consuls feared to tempt the fate of arms.

He spoke like the old Gerenian horseman,[5] full of complaisance in being heard. He adopted a soft voice, very tender, to say: "I've traveled Hellas of the hundred

---

[4] The origins of the Etruscan civilization were a mystery to the Romans, various writers offering different opinions. Among the modern scholars whom Rosny probably consulted—although, as his advertisement makes clear, he felt free to invent—was the German historian of ancient Rome Barthold Niebuhr (1776-1831), who maintained that the Etruscans were a hybrid race resulting from a conquest by northern invaders he called Rasenas, who became the aristocracy of the compound culture.

[5] Nestor, called "the Gerenian horseman" in Homer's *Iliad*.

cities, and I've known the divine sculptors of Corinth and white Athens. I retain a little of their flame; on this earth of clay, I humbly adore imperishable Beauty."

While he spoke, young women and children had slipped out of the school. Potters had abandoned their work and women, their hair sown with fine spirals of silver and gold, were arriving, guided by the curious instinct of their sex and followed by large Rasena dogs with short hair, indolent during the day but as redoubtable as wolves by night are for the solitary traveler.

The men were still suspicious, but the women and girls were not without indulgence for the Sicilian with the large eyes and the lithe figure; and the children regretted not being able, as usual, to throw stones at the traveler. At least the youngest were not deprived of showing the fig, augmented by pantomimes, and slyly exciting the large ferocious dogs.

The old man, looking at the shadow of the gnomon set up before the large schoolhouse, cried: "The sixteenth hour! We can go to supervise the evening meal young man. I have, in addition to you, three guests whom it is agreeable for me to receive."

The dwelling of the master potter Tarao stood four stades from the river, at the top of a gentle slope, in a cheerful atmosphere. It was rectangular, with two gables and shady awnings. Pillars sustained the pitched roof, colonnettes ornamented a pine-wood balcony on which one could savor the pleasure of warm evenings. Air and light entered through a wide low trellised window. A terrace planted with herbs and the odorous flowers of which it was said "that more perfumes come in Campania than from the oils of other countries" separated the house from olive groves, a rose garden and Carthaginian fig-trees.

Sycamores, immortal pines and virgin vines cast a cool shade over the master-potter's abode; and the river could be seen extending its silvery scales, along with the pallid meadows, forests and the pure violet mountains lost in the luminous dust of a great space the color of the sea.

"Here," said the old man, "lived the five generations that preceded me, and those, alas, that will come after me. It is pleasant for me to think that I will close my eyes here."

He opened the arched door, under one of the awnings. A small vestibule led to the atrium. That room was vast, painted in yellow and lazulite, brilliant with the crimsons of Parthenopean carpets, multicolored enamels, vases fired in the kilns of Veila and tables sculpted in Corinth or Neapolis.

In a niche near the hearth and on pedestals, the little family of the Penates could be seen, young or ruinous, dominated by an obscene idol with scaly arms, tubercular legs and the mouth of a lamprey, so old, so cracked and so naïve that it had to date back to the era of the Villanovan potters.[6]

Dionys went to sit down on the ashes and cried: "May the Penates bless you and your generation, dear host, and heap favors on your old age, for having welcomed a traveler generously."

Tarao replied: "The blessing of a guest is the most cherished and the surest; all the gods obtain honored in granting it."

---

[6] The Villanovan culture was the earliest Iron Age culture of northern Italy, predating the Etruscan civilization, named after a village in the vicinity of which the definitive archeological discoveries were made in the 1850s.

They went out through a low door. Dionys crossed the atrium slowly; it was like a great voyage over the profound sea of Time. Men of other ages had worn away those familiar things. They had carried those arms in the legions, in voyages, adventures and hunts. They had drunk at the tables of lemon-wood and ivory, reposed at length on the chairs and beds draped with hides or crimson cloth, loved the old naïve cups, the Attic bowls, the sideboards laminated with gold, nacre or electrum, dreaming about the voyages, wild hunts and fabulous gardens panted on the walls.

Dionys saw the paternal dwelling again, and the treasures dispersed at the whim of sales by auction.

He sighed, and sensed that yesterday is as far away as a century, and youth full of old things. Oh, odorous fountains, gods of Syenite and Paros, standing among the oleanders, little nymphs scintillating in the light of torches, gold apples embalmed around satyrs...!

The creaking of the door, and the soft voice of a woman interrupted his melancholy.

"The water of the bath is hot, traveler."

Dionys followed the slave, and savored, for the first time since he had embarked on the Phoenician trireme, the warm bath that reposes the limbs and pours an appeasing sensuality into the heart.

II. The Banquet

The guests had finished eating the eggs, and the gustatio was being brought in when Foedus, man in his fifties, raised his head crowned with iris to say: "This empire will perish by virtue of laws and taxes. They will envelop every effort of the citizen, to the extent that no one will be able to make a movement without reflection and without anxiety. It is easier to count the stars than the ordinances, and more comfortable to weigh the wind than the caprices of the public treasury."

He was speaking in an ill humor, for he had been able to amass wealth, and feared the voyage of Vespasian to Campania. The vigilant emperor, skillful in extracting tribute even from the bladders of citizens,[7] rarely passed through a province without discovering taxable substances.

Half raised up on the sigma, the master-potter, Dionys, Vimnos the oil-merchant, Aulei, priest of Diana Etrusca,[8] and Verus the Taciturn were listening to Foedus in silence, while Dehva smiled at interior voices.

"Is it necessary to believe," replied Tarao, "that the multitude of laws and taxes will soften men, or that laxity itself creates these laws and taxes? A young people would refuse this excess of shackles, and nothing would serve to constrain them to it; but an old people demands them and draws its security therefrom."

---

[7] Vespasian's name is curiously preserved in the name given to urinals in French and Italian, allegedly because of a tax that he levied on the collection of urine (employed in a process for the production of ammonia).

[8] "Diane-Étrusque" [Diana Etrusca] is the name Rosny uses to depict a goddess whose origins remain unclear, but whose worship appears to have been introduced into Campania when it was part of Magna Graecia; she would then have been named Artemis, whom the Romans fused with their own moon goddess and the moon and the hunt, Diana. Rosny assumes that the Greek Artemis was probably fused with a goddess whose worship was already native to the region, retaining some of her more brutal characteristics—hence the distinctive epithet.

"I don't much like the security of rendering my money to the treasury!" riposted Foedus. "An aureus reassures me more in my coffers than in those of the republic."

The priest of Diana Etrusca raised his cheerful face, aglow with the pleasure of eating, and said: "The treasury sows for your peers, Foedus. Your warehouses would not be overflowing with wealth if Vespasian had not organized Campania so well." He swallowed an anchovy on a slice of turnip in vinegar, and resumed, with a sigh: "Truly, you're too fond of complaining, Foedus, when it would be fitting for you to praise the gods and render them exorable. What's the point of quibbling about fattening a pig or a sheep that will render you a hundredfold profit?"

He looked at both Foedus and Vimnos the oil-merchant. Both lowered their eyes, discontented and troubled.

"But I sacrificed a white lamb on your altar on the nones of May," said Foedus, eventually.

"I brought two doves and a kid," added the oil-merchant."

"Your offerings would be nourished even more," riposted Aulei, "if you had renewed that slight sacrifice."

Desirous of sparing his guests such words, old Tarao intervened. "Venerable priest," he said, "I would like your judgment on these snails..."

They were giant snails nourished on bread, hot wine and figs. The master-potter boasted of their merit: "I obtain them from the parks of Tullius Albus, who sends them all the way to Neapolis, and even Rome. Tullius knows the art of removing the bitter taste that is the only thing that can spoil their exquisite flesh."

"The entire universe is now on tables," said Foedus. "No abyss or mountain can shelter a terrestrial or aquatic animal from gluttony."

"It would be unjust," said Tarao, "for one animal to escape rather than another. I praise the art that has made a delicacy of the vulgar need of feeding oneself."

Aulei was eating silently, but with such joy that it excited the sensuality of the other guests. He contented himself with saying: "Your snails are incomparable, Tarao. All praise to your vigilance and your taste. Cookery is the art of happiness; it is the only one to provide unalloyed sensuality."

And he directed a snail steeped in fish sauce toward his mouth, amorously.

"Unalloyed sensuality," said Tarao, "because it is simple, even in refinement. So too is the amour that only aims at generation. The sensualities of beauty and those of grand amour have something sad about them. They surpass the man who conceives them. He can only realize a part of them; he does not perceive their limits."

"That is true," said Dionys, "but the sadness of the beautiful is so delicious that, for having known it, one can no longer conceive of anything better."

"From which I conclude that it is divine," replied the master-potter, "for it is necessary that an eternal force animates us in order for us to love suffering."

At that moment the pike was brought in.

The monstrous creature was lying among aromatic herbs, with a border of limes, on a large red platter painted with conger eels and dolphins. Its mouth was open; its cruel little teeth were visible; its form exhibited strength, violence and voracity. With a tender smile Aulei addressed these words to it:

"Salutations, guest of Lake Bolena. You have not exterminated carp and monkfish in vain, since it was necessary for you to appear in your glory on this table."

He fixed the pale flesh that Tarao was dividing up with a devouring gaze, and Foedus said: "why must it be that odious old age now forbids me to go and cast harpoons into fresh water? How beautiful life is, Tarao, when the agile boat departs on the morning wind, and the limbs quiver with a blood livelier than this Sicilian wine."

"Ah!" sighed the master-potter. "You're not yet fifty-five years old. You're young, Foedus. You hadn't yet uttered your lament of life when I was already carrying my twentieth year on the vessels with innumerable sails. I knew the night over the resounding sea, the isles, foreign coasts, in the delightful islands of the Archipelago. But nothing is worth as much as having seen divine Athens, for it alone gives reason to the world, which is to search for Beauty and to devote one's life to it. Beauty is the mother of the gods and men. It explains evil, injustice and dolor, which, without it, would render every breath we take dolorous."

Thus old Tarao always returned to the objective. Aulei listened while sprinkling dark wine on the delicate flesh of the pike, but Foedus protested.

"No," he said, "it is truth and justice that govern the World and explain it. The world lives under laws, like men. It is only beautiful by accident. Ugliness inhabits the depths of the sea, the tempests of the sky and the faces of our fellows. In the same way that there is only one beautiful woman in a thousand, there is only one beautiful thing among a myriad. I love beauty, but like one fresh apple hidden among rotten apples."

"I disagree," Dionys interjected. "Injustice dominates justice everywhere—good is a debilitated infant before the colossal figure of evil—but beauty is present in all things. It's only a matter of knowing how to recognize it. Lucretius has seen it amid the fury of tempests. If the monsters of the abyss seem ugly to us, it is because their structure frightens us at first. On looking at them, one discovers a strange splendor in them. Life is dolorous, but so beautiful that one can no longer imagine limits to its beauty. And we name ugliness the beauty that is less beautiful, in order to encourage us to assemble the elements of a superior harmony."

"Those are irreproachable words!" cried the master-potter. "The man who has thought such things has not lived in vain."

A roasted cockerel was brought in, surrounded by thrushes, which exhaled a vapor of spices. The priest, full of tender enthusiasm, said: "It is very just to say that beauty resides in all things, young man. I contend that it is as manifest in these roasted thrushes as it is in the body of a perfect woman."

"Just as," replied Foedus, "the wing is manifest in the chicken as well as the hawk."

Meanwhile, dusk was falling. A magical breeze came in through the window and the open door. The sky was tinted with subtle fires, dark blues and mauves fringed with nacre. The soft plaint of the dying day settled over the guests.

Dehva had risen to her feet. She remained standing in the fragile strength of her beauty. The light of the setting sun surrounded her with a melancholy redness. She seemed to be glory made flesh, the sensible image of all human desire. And the guests looked at her with a secret bitterness, while a tumultuous army swelled Dionys' bosom.

She crossed the room and went out on to the terrace, and as soon as the immense sun was swallowed by the Occident she rang the great clay bell that Tarao had constructed for his dwelling and sang:

Voyager of abysms,
Terror of the eternal night,
Luminous seed that the veiled Gods
Dart into the bosom of Chaos;
Your red twilight is the world's blood,
Which appeared in the dawn of things,
And will vanish in their decline.

Everyone remained pensive as they listened.

When it had disappeared, Tarao had sealed vases brought in for the commisatio and said to Dionys:

"That is the song of the old Etruscans. They knew the primitive gods, the imprecise powers. They knew that, in the beginning, the mysterious intelligences had not put on form, for they were not yet individuals but multitudes. The Rasenas attained the gods of the fabulous night, and transmitted to the Romans the veiled Gods, the Penates, the Lares and the Manes." A great sadness caused his lip to sag and hollowed out his eyes. He added: "Our race is not dead. It will project its beauty over the world. I sense it quivering in future times and flourishing like divine Hellas. Over Rome, dead without having left Roman art, the vanquished sons of the Rasenas will weave the immortal crown."

They drank old wine full of souls. The skiff of Hecate rose over the horizon.. Through the open door the goddess mingled her light with that of clay lamps.

"Let's go refresh out heads," proposed Verus, who sensed too much blood in his temples.

Old Tarao consulted his guests and, having the drinking-bowls filled, he said: "We'll walk as far as the Wall of the Ancestors. Phoebe is enchanting the pathways." He led his guests out on to the terrace.

The land of Campania was casting it perfume to the stars. An extraordinary transparency united distant things with things close at hand. The four men followed their shadows, sometimes elongated over the white path, sometime confounded with the shadow of a tree or a bank.

"Selene," remarked Foedus, "is the enemy of horses. Her face fills them with fear."

"She irritates dogs no less," said Aulei, "but it seems that they stand up to her."

"Unless," said Verus, "they are saluting her and offering her their services for the hunt."

"She is the friend of elephants," said Tarao. "They go down every month to the banks of rivers in Libya, when she is nascent. They worship her and consecrate great reeds to her, which they throw toward her image in the current."

"She is redoubtable," said Dionys. "It cannot be denied that she rules over madness, gives fever and presides over blindness."

"Harsh to men, she seems gentle to monkeys," said Foedus. "They are afflicted on seeing her decrease, and rejoice on her return."

They arrived at the Wall of the Ancestors. The place was as white as the surf. The village was visible, drowsy between the olive groves. The light spilled over the pale walls, over the flowers, over the waters, and mysterious paths appeared and disappeared in the night.

There was a charming and very sad calm, full of a melancholy of eternity, with the taste of death and the subtle potency of a thousand hidden desires.

"Enchant the night, Dionys" said old Tarao. "You will see the festival of slumber spring forth."

The Sicilian's flute launched rapid sounds into space, which seemed to pursue one another from tree to tree and join together in the depths of gardens.

At first, the calm was untroubled. One might have thought that the voice of a light god was passing on a moonbeam. Then, the doors of houses opened, shadows moved in the orchards, and a slight sound of footfalls filled the silence. First, women appeared on terraces, and then somber men, who gradually began to laugh and show their bright teeth. And one sensed an ardor of pleasure rising, the insatiable sensuality of those individuals saturated with the embalmed sunlight of Campania.

Then Dionys played a grave and profound dance, which people practiced from Rome all the way to Syria. A woman mimed it, and then another, and adolescents, in their turn, with exclamations, agitated on the spot. The spectators accompanied the flute with a voice, muffled at first, which gradually grew stronger. And those people with delicate ears, effortlessly, filled the night with a chorus worthy to sing the glory of Priam or the great Atreides.[9]

They became animated. The joy of living spread over their faces, like streams over the mountains in April. One sensed an artistic and sensual race, made to savor the graces of form and become intoxicated on the mere sensation of being in a crowd.

---

[9] Agamemnon, so-called in the *Iliad*.

Eros also impelled them, ever present on those odorous terraces; and brown men slid next to the black hair of women.

A voice cried: "The Arquinian dance!"

That was an Etruscan dance, only practiced in villages. The dancers, mingled in garlands and rounds, alternately going to meet one another or turning in spirals like the gulfs of the sea. It went back to the times of the great glory of the Rasenas and had scarcely spread beyond the peoples of that race, although vestiges of it were still found in Bacchanals. It was voluptuous, complex and variable. It required an exquisite sense of rhythm in the fullest frenzy. In the course of his travels, Dionys had learned the plaintive song that led the dance in question.

"Ah!" said Tarao, as soon as the musician had commenced. "I seem to be hearing my ancestor Farntho. The soul of sounds resides in you, traveler from Syracuse.

The crowd showed by its exclamations that its members approved of that eulogy.

Meanwhile, a woman came forward, followed by a lame old man, whose dazzling visage effaced the beauty of all the others. She smiled at Dionys, and then, in a loud voice, as pure as a silver mirror, passionate, ardent and winged, she accompanied the flute with deft undulations.

Immediately, with an infallible instinct, the crowd supported her in low voices, and one might have thought that one was hearing, from the depths of the ages, an Etruscan tribe celebrating its as-yet-unvanquished glory and its profound instinct of sensuality.

The dance began, grave and slow but full of ardor. The men and the women pressed against one another therein, flesh mingling in a desire rendered stronger by constraint.

Dionys only perceived the woman who was singing alongside him, with such a languorous and penetrating voice. Everything about her was charming, even her shadow. Her face, in accordance with the flexions of her neck, sometimes turned toward the star, sometime toward the shadow, seemed to be made of jasmine pulp or silver silk. Her eyes were as variable as fish-ponds rippled by brightness and clouds. Her mouth smiled in an extraordinary manner, so much did it signify simultaneously sensuality, dreaming, mockery and soft languor. Her red stola, falling in great heavy pleats, rendered her leonine hair even tawnier.

And Dionys mingled the magnificence of that woman with the sinuous silhouette of Dehva. The obscure village obtained a glory therefrom. Like those solitary places in which one finds a temple or an illustrious oracle.

By Kypris! he said to himself, while casting the ancient song into the night. *It's a divine place that bears two such images. Neither Syracuse nor Neapolis can boast of anything comparable!*

And in the Etruscan dance, the tunics, the stolas and the chitons of the women mingled their blue, green, yellow and red waves like colored waters; quivering tresses sowed spirals sparkling with gold and silver pins, and rendered the young woman enveloped in a crimson veil finer and more enigmatic.

Meanwhile, the flute has fallen silent. The ardent multitude still want to dance; it would dance all night. Those dry and passionate beings are on fire. Their eyes and mouths are scintillating with pleasure. The women are blooming. Their skin is more beautiful, their gestures more captivating. They spread the atmosphere of Eros.

And words go from face to face, leaping, rapid, sonorous, enveloping the crowd like another crowd, a more ephemeral, more vivacious, more confused crowd, troubling and stimulating.

But the master-potter, putting his hand on Dionys' shoulder, says: "It is time, my guest, to confide ourselves to the light gods of repose."

Dionys darts and oblique glance at the singer and follows the old man along the clay path.

He asked him: "Who was that beautiful woman? She would adorn the house of Emperors."

"She's an Umbrian," replied Tarao, with a hint of ill humor. "She's a slave of that rich old man, as lame as Vulcan, who has been unable to make use of her for a long time. It's something contrary to divine laws. Beauty is offended by it. Of all offenses, I know of none more sacrilegious."

He walked in silence, and then resumed speaking: "Nature and the gods have nothing comparable to a woman or man of harmonious forms. It is odious that that grace does not make them as free and honored as demigods among their peers. I cannot succeed in understanding it."

The songs of the belated Veilans could still be heard in the distance. Sweet Campania sent her odorous breath toward the stars.

The Volturne shone softly amid the reeds, the willows and the black poplars. The two men had an obscure sensibility of that exquisite hour, and the words of Virgil came to the lips of the old Etruscan:

Qualis in Eurotae ripis, aut pet juga Cynthi

Exerce Diana choros...[10]

III. The Refuge

Veila awoke early. The bulk of the work was done in the shady hours of the morning or at the approach of dusk.

Nowhere, from Rome to Neapolis, was there a more seductive depiction of happiness. For the village united its charming industries, the fecundity of the soil and the grace of its gardens, and did not know odious poverty. Ten generations of artists had created the instinct of the beautiful there without having given birth to suffering. The earnings of the potters were not sufficiently considerable to introduce wealth, and that voluptuous people ardently savored the fruits, the perfumes, the gaiety of the sky and the suppleness of the women.

Dionys got up at Tarao's signal.

On the balcony of the garden a little blue table with twisted feet bore bread from Picenum, milk, honey and figs.

The master-potter and Dehva were waiting for the guest. The air, full of shade, mildly refreshed by the vapors of the river, traversed the garden in short bursts and caused the virgin vines to quiver. There were still dewdrops in the grass, which the sun was gradually drinking. Brightly-clad children, chickens, geese and piglets were running around little farms, among barking dogs. The hills were clad in ardent mist; luminous roses incensed the expanse. The plain, beyond the river, strewn with sycamores, pines, fields of wheat, with pale sinuous

---

[10] Roughly, "As Diana schools the chorus on the banks of the Eurotas or the ridges of Cynthis...."

paths, hamlets of white stone and blue clay amid the olive groves and vines, extended all the way to a horizon dented by cliffs.

Tarao's granddaughter divinized that landscape. She was clad in a turquoise stola that brightened her skin of pearl and petal magnificently. Her long hair, freshly reknotted, spread a mauve and blue light.

The reflections of the sky, the vines, the tunic and the hair agitated over the slender neck, varying at every instant the tone of that dazzling skin. Her arms were half-bare, still moist from ablutions; the young woman emitted an odor of irises, roses and youth, which seemed to be part of her movement. And Dionys admired the line that, descending in delicate rhythms from the shoulder to the knee, brushed the contours of the cleavage, the waist and the loins, incessantly transformed with euphony like the sounds of a perfect lyre.

"Hail, traveler from Syracuse!" cried the masterpotter. "The gods have, I hope, watched over your slumber?"

"They have made it an enchantment," replied Dionys. "Blessed be the host to whom I owe that sweet repose; it has effaced all the baneful days."

Smiling, Dehva served the milk, the honey and the bread. And all three came together in the fresh repast.

Tarao sometimes looked into himself and sometimes at the landscape; and, comparing numerous images, he said: "The river and its trees, the plain and the hills, are such as I saw them on similar mornings when my stature was still growing. And I have not been able to weary of living here. I sense that I could discover unknown things here eternally. The world always has our stature and our age. We are its veritable measure."

For Dionys, however, the measure of the world was then the seductive young woman who was biting into bread of Picenum dipped in honey. She was laughing and full of the joy of living.

She said: "It's good, the morning, the honey, the bread and the milk!"

And those words, like a magic formula, gave a new grace to the repast.

"Yes, Dionys replied, "these placid foodstuffs are sweeter in the youth of the day."

He bit into them with an agile haste; a fluid of well-being seemed to be flowing within him. He seemed to be one of those ancient voyagers tossed from shore to shore, who finally encounters Nausicaa and good King Alcinous. His desire increased to live in that mouth of the Volturne, where the plain almost became an island.

He said: "This land is magical venerable host. The man who has known it cannot quit it with a light heart." His tone had become melancholy.

The master-potter looked at him in silence, and then said: "Can you regret it, having only seen it for a few hours?"

Dionys replied in a low voice: "How could I not regret it, further embellished by the memory of your brilliant hospitality?"

"What care forces you to depart, traveler? Your art can recompense your hosts, and, if it pleases you, a few hours of a potter's labor would deliver you from scruples."

A quiver of repose passed through the weary heart of the exile. He consulted the old man's hollow eyes and the laughing face of Dehva. He saw them full of hospitable promises, and his heart filled with a profound emotion.

"It would have been hard for me," he said, with a smile, "to reenter into exile immediately. I will try, my host, to render my sojourn tolerable."

They remained silent, in a tender softness. A charming bond linked them, the mysterious ardor that mingles with rapidly arisen sympathies.

Dionys added: "In my short terrestrial voyage, your generosity will remain unforgettable, divine Tarao. And this house will always be as sacred to me as a temple."

IV. The Potters

In the large house, under the vines that enveloped it, the young potters toil. Their arms and torsos are naked. The wavy hair of the girls falls back over the nape of the neck and becomes entangled with the eyebrows.

The master-potter teaches with an indefatigable fervor. His old soul cannot weary of desiring beautiful forms, He goes from the one who is holding the chisel to one who is tracing the fine line with a stylus, to those who are applying the pattern to the belly of a urn or the background to an ornament.

"Don't confuse," he said, "this vase, which ought to contain oil, with that one, in which a more generous liquid ought to reside. There is a harmony in things that it is necessary not to break, under pain of rendering life less sweet... Enlarge this girth...and you, redo that line; it is false, like the sound of a poorly tuned instrument... It's necessary to put more brightness into that background, Claudius..."

He took up the fashioning chisel or the stylus himself and corrected the forms. His hand was sure, his eye precise. And while repairing the awkwardness of the pupils, he sought to give some new elegance to the structure of cups, olpes, amphorae, komasts, urns, and even vulgar jars and plates.

The need to create was united in him with that of keeping old models intact, even unskillful ones devoid of harmony. He had children reproduce Villanovan pottery, such as it is found in sepulcher pits, vases in which the reliefs resemble the handles of baskets, which it was once customary to put there, and the first efforts of black earthenware, in which Etruscan art was seeking an original ceramic. Thus, the child followed the groping of humankind and reached the refined and proud forms issued from Greece, after having run through the cycle of the primitive Etruscans, the Phoenicians, the men of Egypt, and the Asiatics of Assyria and Persia.

Tarao stopped near a swarm of young girls on the terrace, in the shadow of a clump of holm-oaks. They were drawing or engraving ornaments of vases of soft clay. Some, with a cylinder, were repeating indefinitely interlacements, chevrons, chimeras, ducks or centaurs. Others, with the aid of molds, were imprinting battles, hunts, amorous scenes, fauns pursuing nymphs, or monsters of the abyss attached to the wake of Poseidon or Amphitrite.

Tarao addressed wise words to them:

"It is necessary to ornament vases with unskillful contours richly, but let your hand be subtle and delicate for admirable forms. The design there should be light to the point that it would only be a short step from appearing to be made of veins or fine incisions. A beautiful vase ought to live on its structure alone, like a living creature."

They listened with mischievous lips. Their eyelashes fluttered, their cheeks defended themselves against the violence of laughter. It was not that the master's discourse seemed ridiculous to them; they venerated him. But every speech and every gesture, reverberating from one to another, stimulated their insouciant youth and their coquettish joy.

"Laughter," said Master Tarao, "is the amiable brother of repose. It swells the heart and gives a gentle strength to the mind. It is fitting that it interrupts toil and recompenses success, and I don't forbid you to laugh, Faustine, for your style has traced pure lines, but you, Albe, have no reason to be cheerful; you have embedded your imprints too deeply, to the extent that the form of your kantharos has become similar to the belly of a hydropic man,"

At those words, Faustine became serious, and Albe could no longer hold back from the perversity of foolish laughter. The master-potter straightened, with a stiff tip, the contours spoiled by the engraving, and traced a few meanders. His skill caused the mischievous to fall silent. Those adolescents, born of generations of artists, admired the old hand full of charming secrets.

Tarao took pleasure for some time in their attentive youth. Before departing he exhorted them: "Fortunate are those among you who attach themselves to their work This humble clay will console them for their troubles and augment their joys. They will feel that they are accomplishing the veritable wish of the Gods, and that their soul is becoming more alive with each new beauty."

Old Tarao was not unaware that he was repeating himself, but, apart from the fact that his age condemned him to that weakness, he knew that the people of Veila, in spite of so many repetitions, had not yet understood his thought.

When he had gone, the girls recommenced laughing, but a little of the sacred light was shining in the depths of their frivolous little souls.

Meanwhile, the master-potter went on his way. He arrived in a gallery where young men were working. At the back, Dionys was attempting to manipulate a stylus and Dehva was advising him in a familiar fashion. The old man blinked in order to see the young folk better. He was pensive. An anxious shadow passed over his face. He drew nearer, and looked at the Syracusan's work. It was Diomedes, King of the Bistones of Thrace, delivered to the man-eating horses. Tarao considered the work momentarily, the figures of which had elegance and harmony.

"Why were you going to seek your bread in Rome?" he cried. "Your divine art would not have saved you from humiliation there, whereas you can find joy and abundance with pride in creating models for our vases!"

Dionys, penetrated by joy, looked at the young woman. The master-potter surprised that glance. He did not allow anything to show.

"It's necessary, Dehva, to resume your work," he said.

When she disappeared around the corner of the gallery, the old man smiled with a hint of chagrin. Then he spoke softly to his guest.

"I have learned, Dionys, that it is bad to let suspicion and anxiety sleep. Words said in good time and promises well made have a superior virtue. Dehva is consecrated to Diana Etrusca until her eighteenth year. Such was her mother's wish, the rupture of which would bring death for her as well as her accomplice. You have sat on the ashes of my hearth and you would not want to betray it. I therefore have confidence in you. Good faith is more reliable than guards and walls."

Dionys had no precise morality. Syracuse, by virtue of passing through the government of all peoples and subjected to hazards, had lent the most accommodating humor to its gods. Life there was soft and uncertain, embellished by civilized vices and benevolent perversities; and the act of the flesh was not held to be a sin—a misdemeanor, at the most, when it violated a proprietary right. But the young man understood the profound virtue that attached a guest to a host. He felt that he could not betray Tarao.

He replied with a sincerity that the love of the beautiful has caused to grow in his heart: "I will not betray the confidence of my host."

Dehva was dangerously familiar. She had not learned to put a brake on her inclinations, which had, in any case, been rare and always borne toward young creatures of her own sex. She was smitten with the Syracusan. That affection was keen, passionate in a sense, but devoid of amorous disturbance. She had not cherished her companions differently.

She arrived in the bright morning to surprise the young man. She drew him away among the olive groves and the rose bushes, to the bank of the river. He did not have to make any effort to divert her. She had a taste for life and for making life; she drew speech from her companion, facile games and information, from which she wove gaiety. As she was untroubled, he was only troubled himself in the brief minutes when the young woman's charms mingled with repose and silence.

That happened most frequently in a cove in the Volturne where narcissi grew. The water fell silent there, scarcely moved by the nearby waves. The pale flowers inclined their odorous faces. Shade fell like rain; the river extended its voice and its depths; large birds alighted on the promontories; others fluttered furtively from tree to tree, and black fish were visible drifting in the shadowed water. It emitted a savage and menacing impression, which held the young couple motionless.

Then, Dionys saw his young friend more clearly. She grew in him, among the old trees with wrinkled bark, the young narcissi, the pink menyanthes and the fresh mint. He was stirred in gazing at the young woman mysteriously expanding within the slenderness of the child. She opened her mouth slightly, and her lips were moist. The pleats of her stola indicated contours, as long grass curbing in the breeze reveals flowers. And he sensed a muted irritation against Diana Etrusca.

In the evening, all three of them usually sat on the terrace. The master-potter left his children, and his youth returned to his lips. Days of old crowded in his speech like statues in an ancient city. Something vague and feeble accompanied his stories. It was human fate, immortal and fugitive, crushing and pleasant, a very humble odyssey, but as adventurous as that of heroes.

Dionys listened gladly. He liked to go back, with old souls, through inflexible time. He obtained a greater liking therefrom for watching the burly Campanian oxen bringing back carts with large wheels, the laborers walking slowly along the road, the melancholy donkeys and the children in a last frantic run, like the swallows in the firmament.

Sometimes, old Tarao withdrew in order to give orders or carry out supervision. Dionys and Dehva remained alone. And those minutes threw a charming anxiety into the Syracusan's soul.

The sun, like a great round furnace, burned between the mountains. The death of the day seemed to be the death of the world. An immense melancholy mingled with the flowers of the plain.

It was the desperate hour of amour. A kind of frenzy penetrated the young man. He dreamed, in order to escape the cruel vow, of carrying the virgin away to the abode of Shades. And the voice of clay bells, sounding the decline, rendered that anguish more intense.

Scarcely had the sun disappeared, however, than the hour became milder. Night filled life. At the same time as the stars, fireflies were seen to appear. Their hazardous flight traced meanders of light; their fire increased and decreased like lamps in the wind.

Dehva knew the art of catching them in nets. She put them in a large cage covered with a transparent tissue. It was a magical glow prolonged over the garden: a gleam of life palpitating like a heart, numerous, sparse and turbulent, which mingled its intoxication with the immortal perfume spread over that incomparable land. When she ornamented her hair with them, when the little living stars agitated their brightness in that quivering prison, and the face lit up, or was extinguished intermittently, the musician thought that he was seeing the hair of the queen who is perpetuated among the stars.[11]

Dionys made progress in the art of creating ornaments for vases. He found aspired models for the black pottery that seemed metallic, which was obtained by smoking the baked clay for several days in closed chimneys. He was paid a salary. He received it with a profound joy. It was the pledge of his reconciliation with Destiny. The earth no longer seemed cruel, nor the

---

[11] The constellation Coma Berenices.

nights menacing. He held in his hand the ingenious victory over matter. He could dream without his heart being too heavy or his breath oppressed. Regret for the sea and his island was devoid of bitterness.

The labor gave him a homeland again, as did the scintillating little creature agitating around him. She was stronger than the cargo vessels of the blue waves, the palaces of yellow marble, the temples of Poseidon, Aphrodite and Hermes. And in the dawn, or the evening, under the resplendent constellations in which heroes, amorous queens, fabulous voyagers, beasts, monsters and tresses trailed toward the Occident and navigated around the Pole, the Syracusan winnowed the sonorous wheat of the Syrinx, the plaintive song that awakens the immortal arrow in the human heart.

One morning, Dehva took Dionys to the edge of the village. She wanted to procure pins and a flagon of rosewater. An old man sold those objects, along with powders, mirrors, embalmed oils, jewel-cases, fans, bubbles, alabasters and earrings.

Along the little paths, Dehva was full of life; she exhaled joy as the river exhaled its mists. She threw herself against Dionys with reckless laughter. In passages obstructed by bushes and plants she leaned her youthful body, a flower of disturbance, disorder and long tremors, against his.

She knew the people, and saluted them with a clear voice: laborers heading their oxen, spinners on the thresholds of houses, quarrymen detaching travertine, nenfro or white silex from the cliff, swineherds assembling their grunting beasts.

A farm at the exit from the vineyard interrupted their course. It was surrounded by a lattice fence. Two slaves could be seen, aided by a donkey, turning a mill;

geese and chickens, attentive and quarrelsome, were pecking the grains escaped from the funnel. A young woman on the threshold was preparing pulmentum.

Meanwhile, a slave appeared, his hands chained, whom a man with the head of a legionary was a stiff beard, armed with a whip, was pushing in front of him. Children were following in tumult, with cries of joy. The slave, his head bowed, resigned, allowed himself to be tied to a stake in the middle of the courtyard. He had a humble and faded face, worn by age, shifting eyes, his mouth opening in a sort of mute plaint.

The bearded man brought down the tunic and laid the wretch's scarred back bare. Then he raised the whip, and unhurriedly, as if without anger, started striking, counting the blows. The slave opened his toothless mouth wider; he uttered low plaints that made the young woman who was making pulmentum laugh, and the children dance.

Dehva turned away from the spectacle, but without protest, crying *Ave* to the man who was striking.

He interrupted himself in order to reply, with a hearty laugh: "May the Gods bless you, beautiful girl, and the man who is accompanying you." Then he resumed his function, as placid as justice, with the same regular movement as the donkey and the slaves turning the mill, while the tortured man, his skin striped with violet bands, clamored his dolor more loudly.

As Dehva drew Dionys away she said: "Had he run away?"

"No, they would have put him in the fork. He must have neglected his work or kept poor guard."

The cries made them uncomfortable. A little pity slid into their souls, but which they did not distinguish. They walked more rapidly.

On the far side of a field of flax they perceived a building made of volcanic stone, on ashy ground obstructed with scrap iron, mildewed wood, broken vases and shells. The sound of their footsteps caused an old man to emerge. He was sorting out fragments of bronze, enamels and worn out clothes. All the insults of the sun, the wind and inhospitable nights were inscribed on his leathery jaundiced face and his vagabond eyes. His head produced a curly yellow-tinted vegetation, some as bushy as the coat of an old ram, some in mossy patches. A sharp malice curved his mouth, crenellated with teeth the color of clay; his small, ape-like hands, sly and shriveled, were more expressive than a face.

He turned toward the young couple the grimace of a God of gardens ruined by worms, and asked: "What do you want, my beauty? Amber or pearl, carved coral, alabaster in which the soul of flowers resides? A silvery mirror or a stone that glows in the dark? Anything you desire, I'll be able to sell you…and if it's necessary to bring it from the ends of the earth, it will come at your order."

Thus spoke the old prowler, expert in hyperbolic phrases, picked up along all the roads of Etruria, Latium and Campania. And he said as much to sell a sextant of embalmed oil as for a magnificent pearl.

"I want pins and rose-water," said Dehva.

"What kind of pins, virgin similar to a gilded iris? Those that are as shiny as your eyes, and which come from Iberia, those that are inalterable and come from among the vagabond Rajas, or the small and gentle ones that come to us from Artena? And do you want rose-water sealed in alabaster by the Cilicians of the River Cydnus, or that of Campania enclosed in clay?"

Dehva wanted pins from Artena and Campanian rose-water.

Addressing Dionys, however, the old man said: "Surely, young man with bright eyes, you will not leave the brilliant hair of this maiden without essence of Cilicia?"

"You can give us Oriental rose-water," said Dionys, "but don't hope to make me mistake alabaster from Kymé for a vase from the Magic River. I know all the perfumes that the ships transport in the Tyrrhenian Gulf and over the Sicilian seas."

The old man looked at him suspiciously. "The water that I give leaves its soul in the vase forever."

"That is true of all aromatics and all subtle perfumes," Dionys replied. "The soul of Campanian roses is no less immortal than the soul of Asiatic roses. Show us your marvelous liquid..."

The old man started to laugh, with a kind of bitterness, and went into the house without replying. He soon brought back little boxes and vials of clay and alabaster.

Dehva chose her pins and her essence, while the Syracusan examined the alabasters.

"Old man," he said, finally, "these perfumes are not despicable, and their vestment is gracious, but they come from my homeland; they are imitations made in Corinth and the isle of Crete. My ships exported them to Gaul. It's appropriate to prefer good Campanian waters."

"By Hermes!" protested the other. "My knowledge has grown for sixty years and yours is only just born! It isn't me, young man, who confuses Sicilian and Cilician alabasters!"

"Dionys retorted, with a smile: "I would swear, old man, that you do not make that confusion. But it's not illicit that you want me to make it, for the man is unwor-

65

thy of divine odors who does not know how to recognize them. Nevertheless, I'll buy this vial on which Heracles is seen among the Cercopes, a subject that certainly never inspired an artist in Cilicia. Your price?"

"Thirty sesterces," said the other.

Dionys could have beaten him down by a third, but he had spent too long buying in accordance with his whim in the shops of Syracuse. Nonchalantly, he handed over a half-aureus, all that remained of his salary, and paid for the alabaster, the clay vial and the pins. The old man was not scornful of him, as he would have been of a man less expert in rose-waters, but rather discovered therein a sign of aristocracy.

Looking attentively at the young couple, he said: "Don't you want me to tell your fortune? I've learned to read in the gleam of the eyes and the signs of the hand..."

The malice of wanderers appeared in the wrinkles of his eyelids. For having seen so many destinies pass, he was able to read a little of the future that individuals contain within themselves, and he knew that, if circumstances dominate us, our sentiments are also circumstances, more invariable than others.

Curious and spontaneous, Dehva extended her hand at once. The old man, attentive to the frissons of the little hand, spoke in the voice of a haruspex:

"Young woman with long hair, whose ancestors fought on the shores of the lakes of Etruria and in the Ciminian forest, Diana Etrusca presided over your birth, and your mother made a redoubtable vow. Your heart has not yet blossomed. It is like a closed arrowhead flower in the ponds. But Eros is lying in wait for you, and his cruel tenderness. The image that will no longer quit your days has not troubled you yet, but already you cannot forget it. Be careful, young woman! Three routes are before you: that of separation, which is bitter, that of patience, which is salvation, and that of perjury, which is mortal. Flee the reeds, they will be more terrible for you than sharks to sponge-divers.

Dehva shivered, not so much at the speech as the prophetic tone. It was like a little seed falling in spring into the obscure earth. She laughed, however, but with constraint, and she dared not look up at her companion. He was more troubled than she was, for he knew that Eros was within her, full of menace and strength.

He drew the diviner to one side; his muscular handled the speech of the old man like a papyrus covered in writing.

"You lived close to blue seas; you knew the delight of being rich and living without constraint. Poverty overtook you, but it has not left you miserable for long. You bear within you the magic that will always vanquish, if you can escape death. For death is lying in wait for you. A god and a goddess are in league against you. The god is filling you with tender fury; you abandon yourself weakly to constraint. You are summoning yourself the evil that you ought to flee; you cherish it secretly, taking boundless pleasure is evoking that which is more dangerous than Scylla's abyss. And you no longer perceive the implacable goddess and the place of execution."

They went down toward the bank of the river, pensively.

"What did Somnius say to you?" asked the young woman.

He shuddered. A tragic shadow was in his soul. He forced himself to reply

"It's necessary not to believe that old man. He roams the roads, he seizes words at hazard from passers-by and old women. He knows something about everyone, but he knows it poorly."

He spoke thus in order to dissipate his malaise, for, deep down, he feared the diviner's art.

Anxious at first, she rediscovered her youth, the vivid gleam of her joy. She drew her friend toward the Volturne. Children were searching for insects and frogs there; others, among the stones of the bank, were catching fish. Some were bathing in the fresh water or drying themselves in the grass. Dehva picked up a flat stone and tried to make it ricochet. The stone sank.

"If I miss the ricochet three times," she said, "it will be a bad omen."

She threw again, and the stone did not reappear. Dionys went pale. He agreed with himself that it would be the decree of Zeus, and that he would leave the village if Tarao's daughter failed again. He waited, frightened.

Dehva picked up a small, very flat stone, and, tilting her brilliant head, took careful aim.

Dionys murmured in a low voice: "It will be your will, Zeus, and yours, Diana Etrusca; I shall submit to it."

The stone departed. It skipped three times over the current. An extraordinary delight penetrated the Syracusan. He took his companion's arm and drew her into the shade.

"I was going to leave, Dehva, if the presage was unfavorable."

She looked at him, stupefied. "You were thinking of going away...of leaving?"

"But not now, dear hostess. Fate is surer when it is consulted by an innocent soul..."

"She repeated, plaintively: "Leaving..." That word caused all the unknown of her soul to rise within her. Her eyes filled with tears. She threw herself impetuously against the Sicilian and said to him in a penetrating voice: "I don't want that! You shan't quit our home..."

He had not yet felt that beautiful flesh so close, and so vibrant. He was conscious of its warmth, the semi-nudity through the light stola. And the somber voluptuous bush of her hair collapsed upon his breast.

In a low voice, he said: "I swear it."

She uttered a sigh of joy. She put her arms around her friend's neck. It seemed that an imperious soul emerged from her grip, which bound Dionys, attaching an invincible cable to him.

V. The Festival of the Manes

It was the festival of the Manes. Among the old Etruscans it coincided, every twenty years or so, with the festival of the veiled Gods, but the ancient tradition was almost abolished. It was still found in Veila, where the master-potter had revived it, in accordance with veritable texts, but even so, it had been polluted by Phoenician, Persian and Greek practices.

An hour before dusk, the procession assembled in the shade of the Wall of the Ancestors. It marched in two ranks, the men enveloped in a kind of military mantle, the women in a brown, violet or dark blue palla, with the head hidden. All of them carried black clay lamps in the right hand, the flames of which, pale to begin with, brightened with the decline of the sun. The left hand raised the plants of mourning: box, cypress, maidenhair, asphodel and narcissus. At the head of the procession, a choir of maidens sang, in soft voices, a hymn as monotonous as the sound of the waves against the cliff.

Very quietly, gentle and gripping, there was a harmony of reed pipes, lyres and clay bells moved by veiled hammers.

Old Tarao gave the signal to move off. The cortege spread out very slowly over the paths, toward the elegant hills, traced in lines of shadow by the setting sun, vibrant with a sort of violet warmth. At intervals, the young women, the lyres, the reed pipes and the clay bells fell silent.

Then the men chanted in a somber voice, in such unison that only a single voice was audible:

Manes of the profound earth
And the bright abodes,
For whom all obstacles are abolished,
Who traverse hard bronze like a wave,
Be propitious to poor humans,
Your descendants!

And the women said in their turn, with a single voice, which seemed pure and young, as if there were no old women there:

Manes, inhabitants of days past,
You who left on our dwellings
The perfume of your trace and sweetness of your toil,
Come to the aid of the poor women
Who give birth for the times to come!

Then the clay bells sounded in isolation, in belated punctuation, and the harmony resumed its mysterious hum.

They went as far as the cliffs where the ancestors reposed. The necropolis opened in a cliff. At the hazard of inspirations, from era to era, ingenuous artisans had sculpted the natural facades.

The ruinous image of the primitive gods was visible, the vague and metaphysical gods that the abstract thought of the Rasenas had conceived. Then, not at the hazard of time but the hazard of space, came Melkarth with the dwarfish legs and the colossal head, fecund Astarte, the winged Diana of Iran, Phoebus Citharedes, Heracles taking Cerberus back into the shadows, Hades with heavy tresses, holding the key to the funereal gates, and Charon with the hawkish proboscis, armed with the symbolic hammer.

The cortege stopped; the voices and the chords died in the frisson of an astonishing silence,

Then the master-potter raised his lamp and a branch of box toward the simulacra, and all the lamps rose with a single movement. They resembled little souls of light before the red sun, half-buried in the ether.

And the old man prayed.

"O Gods of great Etruria, Gods of a hundred centuries, Veiled Gods, Complicit Gods, Lares, Penates, Genii, and you, Manes raised to immortal power, cast a favorable gaze upon the piety of the people of Veila. Somber Hades, inexorable king of darkness, listen to our prayer; we promise you two virgin ewes at the new moon. Their faces will be turned toward the ditch, their flesh reduced to ashes. Be favorable to us also, Charon; we never forget the obol that is due to you, and you will receive the flesh of the autumnal dove, which you prefer to all others, for it is black and bears the odor of cypress."

The people then divided up and spread out among the tombs. Night fell; the rocks lit up with a hundred uncertain gleams, decreasing as the visitors lost themselves in the galleries.

In the eternal night, the Manes like light. They have maintained the mild need for lamps. Their joy is sure when the crypt, the funerary niche or the ancient pozzo tomb is brightened like an atrium on festival evenings.

And the people of Veila, through the gaps between pilasters, the sepulchral chambers, and the often-vast dwellings, as numerous as the rooms of a consular house, sensed the friction of winged ancestors, the subtle quivering of souls like birds of darkness and vapor.

Dionys followed the master-potter and Dehva, for the Etruscans' guests were also taken among the ancestors.

The young woman, enveloped by her veils, was marching like a melancholy Aeneas. She was submissive to the power of the Manes, she sensed them, alive and sighing very softly. Dionys admired the rhythm of her sadness, in the glimmers that she cast over herself in holding her lamp high.

Tarao stopped. He had reached the abode of his ancestors, those who, for eight generations, had descended into the Necropolis of Veila. It was a low, round, vast chamber supported by a single pillar, hollowed out with niches that contained the remains.

The master-potter spoke quietly to the dead.

"Ancestral Manes, you see your child become an ancestor himself, and deprived of descendants save for this fragile young woman; and you, Manes who followed me on earth for a shorter voyage, here is your father and your husband, and the father of those who engendered you. Watch over this tender plant. She is all that remains of a noble blood that flowed on the shore of Lake Regillus, Lake Vadimon and the Ciminian forest. Give her life and fecund loins. Let a posterity emerge from her like the indefatigable inhabitants of the sea; may she be pure, strong and faithful, for races are condemned who are born from an adulterous womb."

He took Dehva's lamp, put it on a ledge of the pillar, and said: "This is the lamp, dear Manes; you have all loved the light, when alive."

Then he turned to the young couple. "I shall go alone, as is my wish, to the primitive tombs." He went into a narrow corridor, Dionys and Dehva watched him disappear, like a glimmer at the bottom of a shaft,

They were silent. The Syracusan, full of a religious and tender disturbance, considered the cloudy silhouette of the virgin, the long pleats of the palla woven in wool from Canusium.

Eventually, he said: "I am glad, cherished maiden, to have come with you to your ancestors. It seems to me that I am the guest of all your race, and that all of them are welcoming me as one of yours."

She did not reply. A slight frisson shook her shoulders.

Dionys went on: "Do you not want me to do likewise at every festival of the Manes, with Tarao and you?"

Dehva's voice replied, as faint as the light of the cave: "But you know, Dionys, that I am consecrated to Diana Etrusca until my eighteenth year."

"I spoke for ever, Dehva. We shall wait for the termination of your vow."

She trembled more, while he reached out slowly with both hands. Her eyes were hidden. Only her mouth was visible. He placed his lips on that red mouth for a long time; and the lamp flickered with a very soft crackle, as if the Manes were burning their wings in its flame.

Meanwhile, the master-potter had reached the primitive graves, the shaft-tombs. They were situated higher than the others, on a small plateau, linked together by very narrow tunnels, where the passage was very inconvenient. Large vases of red clay were found there, cinerary urns and cabin-urns, amber and jewels contemporary with the ancestral Lucumons.

The old man set down his lamp in the well that was reputed to be the most ancient. He remained bowed down beneath memories that he had not lived himself, but which moved him nevertheless.

Then he said, softly and with resignation:

"Divine, glorious, invincible spirits, you who curbed under your strength the men of Rome and Alba, and the indomitable Sanites, you who repelled the Gauls with red hair who made Tyre and Carthage tremble, be happy in the imperishable world! Alas, your sons have had no fatherland for centuries. Will not a day arrive when they will shine again in the world, if not by means of glory, at least by means of beauty?"

VI. The Veiled Gods

The festival of the Veiled Gods was still celebrated in a few Etruscan districts of Campania. That nocturnal and mysterious custom was scarcely known to Roman authority. It had to coincide with the full moon in the months of May, while the festival of the Manes invariable fell on the kalends.

It commenced in the middle of the night and continued until dawn.

When the gnomons projected the shortest shadow, the master-potter struck his great clay bell seven times.

At the same moment, the voices of men called to one another through space. The first voices departed from the east of the village, and the last from the west, near the edge of the marshes.

They said:

We implore you, Veiled Gods,
Fathers of matter and beings,
Born before the waters and the stars,
Source of all growth and all fecundity...

Those voices fell silent, but a hidden woman sang in the middle of a garden. Then other voices joined in with hers. The choir was swollen thus like a flock of migratory birds gradually gathering for the great voyage. One by one, the voices of men joined in with it, and all of them, invisibly, celebrated the invisible powers.

From the invisible force
Is born light.
From obscure and shapeless powers
Spring the Chariot of the Sun,
Number and figure...
O Gods who floated over the primal sea,
Have pity on the Rasenas.

When the entire village had completed that strophe, the voices resounded one by one, and the last rose solemnly into the silence, sung by old Tarao:

Have pity on the Rasenas.

For half an hour, the space remained motionless. Tarao had gone inside with Dionys. He gave his guest a wolfskin to put on, and covered himself with the skin of a stag. The hairy heads fell over their faces like masks; two holes were cut out therein at the level of the eyes.

"Be careful, Dionys," said the master-potter, "not to remove that mask from your face; you would be punished by three months of servitude, and I could not get you out of it."

Dionys lowered the mask carefully. They went out. From all the houses in the village, fugitive forms emerged, clad in animal skins, with their faces hidden. There were only men and one single woman: a virgin slave fifteen years old, almost naked, her hair scattered, led by an old man. She was pretty, as the rites prescribed. A certain anguish dilated her long Oriental eyes and caused her charming brown shoulders to quiver.

Gazes sparkled toward her through the beasts' muzzles.

Two shepherds brought a black he-goat and a white she-goat. At a sign, Dionys intoned the hymn of the Veiled Gods, which Tarao had taught him.

The troop set forth and marched to the confines of a silvery pine-wood and a field of roses. Two spacious ditches had been hollowed out next to an altar made of one of the stones carved by men who lived in fabulous times.

The procession halted there, Tarao ordered the slave and the goats to be brought forward. Each man brought some small offering: wine, eggs, doves, milk, alica wheat or fruits.

The master-potter cried:

"Gods who were in Chaos when the earth and the planets were floating in eternal night! Precursor Gods born with all the gods, already eternal when Time did not yet exist! You who revealed the Rasenas, sons of men armed with clubs, who lived by the strength of their arms alone...

"Veiled Gods, tutelary, formless, omnipotent and merciful, we give you the virgin slave, the white she-goat and the black he-goat, the doves, the fruits of the earth and of beasts."

The crowd responded with a long cry, prolonged like the passage of an equinoctial wind through the oaks. A man set about cutting the throats of the doves while a priest's assistant lit an odorous fire on the altar, The goats were thrown into the left hand ditch; they were to die there, after having accomplished the sacred act,

Then Tarao had the virgin slave brought before him. She was afraid; her charming shoulders and her small new breasts were heaving forcefully. The fear of death replaced tears in her eyes.

But the master-potter said to her softly: "Your life is not threatened, young woman. It is necessary to flee through that pine-wood. You will be pursued. The first man to catch you by the hair will be your master and will sacrifice you to the Veiled Gods, but not by your death."

She raised her somber head with a smile; her terror fled. A mocking gaiety appeared at the corners of her mouth, for she had confidence in the old man.

"Go," said Tarao, "and remember that the Gods will be discontented if your flight is not rapid enough, or if you do not seek the surest retreat."

He gave the signal. She ran away lightly over the dusty path. Her white form, her loose hair and the sway of her run caused all the men to shiver. She was the enchanted legend of little nymphs fleeing before satyrs and fauns. War and amour followed her agile trace.

She went into the wood, Tarao rapped ten times slowly, and all of them, young and old, launched forward, the former confident in their speed and the latter in cunning or fortune.

Only Dionys, still intoxicated by the scene with Dehva, remained immobile.

"It's necessary to pursue," said the master-potter. "I alone am exempt, with the two assistant priests."

Dionys set off. He penetrated among the great silvery columns. No breeze rose up from the Campanian plains; the silence of the trees was as profound as that of the stars; hamadryads filled their souls. But the running footfalls of men were audible, carried away by frenzy, mystery, and the petty prodigy of the adventure.

Dionys sat down on a branch. He listened to the hunt. It reverberated within him, alloyed with the beating of his heart; and he thought without respite about the lips that had flexed beneath his own with the suppleness of young roses. They were his life and more than his life, they added to his being what spring adds to the joyful earth. They made his soul a fertile field, a palpitating forest.

A furtive noise deflected his dream. He saw something white passing, and recognized the consecrated slave.

Desire, in spite of everything, surged in his flesh. He only needed one bound to seized that floating hair, and the virgin, as mysterious as any beautifully shaped virgin, would know through him the magnificent law. He was too late. The slave had already disappeared; and he was falling back into the moving indolence of reverie when a clamor caused him to spring to his feet.

The slave had come back. A man had sprung forth, agile, who threw himself upon her and seized her by the hair with a triumphant cry.

"The gods have given you to Mantus, beautiful girl. Cease struggling." For, instinctively, the slave was trying to tear herself away from her captor. The words calmed her. She lowered her head, she followed the man, and, summoned from clearing to clearing, everyone returned to the field of roses near the altar.

A great fire roasted the doves, and the priest's assistants, at a sign from the master-potter, began to carve them. They gave a piece of meat to everyone there, except for the slave and her captor, isolated, standing next to the right-hand ditch. And the scene, silent and slow, seemed veritably to be unfolding in the fabulous centuries in which the heroic legend, the history of the world, was still in formation in the depths of the woods, the sinister marshes and the yellow deserts, between Heracles armed with an oak branch and wild beasts armed with claws.

At a sign from the assistant priests, the muzzles were removed from the faces; the master-potter murmured in a profound voice:

"Take away this beautiful slave, Mantus; and remember that her daughters will be consecrated, like her, to the Veiled Gods, if they are born among us and if they are desirable. Although she will be yours forever, it is necessary for you to treat her as if she were free, for her flesh is sacred. She must not know punishments or servile tortures. The Gods would be irritated by that, and you would know misfortune."

He led the couple to the edge of the ditch. And at that moment a sort of melancholy fell upon the watchers:

the vision of the ancestral sacrifice in which marriage and death were confounded in subterranean darkness.

Torches were burning near the Wall of the Ancestors; the Veilans had concluded the repast in which they communicated at great festivals. The flutes, lyres and bells mingled their voices with the songs of drunken men. Licentious couples disappeared along the Volturne.

Slyly, Dionys drew Dehva into a path that led to a marsh. Tall green reeds, parting and closing their blades, soon separated them from everyone else.

Their hearts beat more rapidly with every step they took. They stopped. He pulled her toward him gently, but without embracing her. They did not speak.

The water, cool beneath the nocturnal sky, exhaled a delicate breeze. The distilled perfume of the sunlight emerged from the flowers with the breath of Campania, full of incense and aromas: the odor of Venus, which springs from plants like a tender cry, in which intoxicated joy and a subtle plaint are mingled.

The reeds, inclining in the abundant silvering of the moon, the sound of frogs, sometimes hopping, sometimes appealing with little human voices, the undulating shadows of the foliage, the waves extending over the expanse, and the pallid stars in the bright firmament, increased the languor of the young souls.

Dehva made a slight movement, and the Syracusan, moved by the perfection of her allure, said: "Blessed by the god or goddess who watched over your birth and gave you such beautiful gestures."

She blushed. She looked at Dionys with a tremulous gaze. Eros was within her, like a warrior.

Fear and delight tormented her simultaneously. The instinct to flee mingled with tender surprise; a gentle and unbearable asphyxiation inflated her bosom. She was like a fearful being lost among wild beasts, or a rose quivering at sunrise.

Dionys picked an iris flower and handed it to his friend. Then he murmured: "My heart is glad of your existence, beloved. You render the world more elegant by consenting to live in it. Of all the prodigies that there are among humans, the most beautiful is that you were born in my time and that I have encountered you on my route. By virtue of that, my days are divine and I shall have lived tenfold!"

She did not know how to reply. She had no terms that corresponded to her emotion. She was ill with Dionys. She was full of submission. Her indecisive head tilted slightly in the white stem of her neck, with a languid mouth in which the little mirrors of the teeth reflected the light of the moon like nacre.

The tender frenzy of caresses burned Dionys. He took that charming head in both hands. His kiss could not quit the moist lips from which he drank the soul of his beloved.

Wisps of hair drifted in the breeze; Dehva, paling, had her face upturned and her eyes closed.

The fastening of the stola broke. The cleavage appeared in its divine youth.

The small breasts rose up, soft and proud, with their hesitant areolas. Their present beauty was full of their future beauty. A white shadow separated them, and undulant lines, in infinite nuances, attached them to the neck and the shoulders. Pink, mauve and blue gleams mingled with their dazzling whiteness. Dionys sighed sensuously, but also with a sort of plastic ecstasy. His hand stroked them, like vases created by a prodigious potter.

And the child, under that light hand, reddened less than under the kiss on the lips. She felt respect, the worship of art, and almost dread, in the man.

However, in feeling those warm globes palpitate, desire returned to Dionys. He seized Dehva in a rougher embrace.

Pushing him away, she stammered, plaintively: "Don't forget that I'm consecrated to Diana!"

He moved away. A sacred pity, a supreme tenderness, agitated his being. He did not sense against Dehva any of the warlike and vindictive impulses that a woman's resistance stimulates.

From a moment, in silence, they listened to the distant sound of a flute and human voices. Dehva shivered, and said: "It's necessary to go back, Dionys."

They resumed the route through the reeds, in a green shade, striped with lilac, and found themselves back in the plain. They perceived the violet-tinted crowd near the Wall of the Ancestors; couples were moving away, in the trees, along the banks of the Volturne, for the secret festival of amour.

On the edge of a wood of turpentine trees, a solitary form appeared before Dionys. He recognized the Umbrian woman with the tawny eyes. She darted a strange, ironic, familiar smile at him, which held him astir, while he slowly took his companion home.

VII. The Umbrian Woman

One night, Dionys could not sleep. The sweet and terrible hours passed over his couch. Eros was within him. The god tormented his flesh and his soul, sometimes as suave as the odorant approach of Carthaginian shores, sometimes as wild as the wind of Khamsin.

The Syracusan sighed toward Dehva's beauty. He raised imploring arms in the darkness. He talked to himself.

"Why have I seen the secret form of her breasts? It has given me a burn that will no longer be soothed, but I cannot betray her vows, nor belie an oath made to my host!"

He got up, opened the door and looked out into the night. The moon, red and diminished by a third, rose above the black poplars of the Volturne. It was like a potters' kiln when the wood has lost its flame and only yields a somber light. It populated the solitude, the only living thing in an immobile universe. The perfume of the flowers seemed to be its perfume, and its mystery augmented Dionys' anxiety.

He picked up the Syrinx and walked all the way to the river. The naiads were amusing themselves among the willows. Their vaporous voices mingled with their luminous smiles; and the reeds extended their tips like a legion of swords.

Dionys inhaled the moist air. He gazed for a long time at the sycamores casting their shadows all the way to the horizon. But the star was rising in the blue flesh of the firmament, as pale as the broken mirror of a hetaira. The young man sighed more deeply. Eros rendered the beauty of things too visible. The entire earth seemed penetrated by Dehva.

And the force that had impelled him to the bank of the Volturne drew him all the way to Tarao's garden.

His heart was groaning like a torrent. A mist covered his eyes. He leaned against a turpentine tree, overwhelmed by the excessive tenderness of his desire.

He finally emerged from that swoon. He could not help confiding his trouble to the darkness and to the one who was asleep under the great somber roof outlined amid the serpentine vines.

The flute told the adventure well, melancholy and forever mysterious. A thousand sighing souls rose up. They murmured the splendor of the world, and its anguish, the fearful daughter of desire, and united in the amorous heart of Dionys the amorous hearts of times past; for such is the power of Syrinx.

Dehva was asleep, her slumber devoid of strength. She awoke to the magical peril, of which she was afraid, and which she found cherishable. The extended hand of Dionys never ceased to weigh upon her breast and cause her to respire languorously. She did not know whether she ought to implore Diana to preserve her, or whether she would rather die than not know that disturbance.

She heard Syrinx in a dream. She woke up. The long, light voice enveloped her as the voluptuous hands had before. She knew that she had been told how the origin of gods and men was her own petty origin, and that the plaintive sighs and dying embroideries of the flute were saying everything that inhabited her heart.

It became intolerable for her to remain lying down. She got up and looked out into the airy darkness. Her heart agitated like a grouse in a snare. She could not help opening the door. The light of the little lamp in the hearth of the atrium, and the lares outlined in their niches, gave her courage.

She turned toward the most ancient of the gods, devoured by the ages, which she believed to be the most indulgent and the most tender.

"O god of the hearth," she whispered, "you who protected all my ancestors, I cannot resist the voice of Dionys. Enable my action to be innocent!"

She dared not pray to Diana. She feared that grim goddess, whom she knew to be harsh and unforgiving of offenses. But she also felt that she could not flee the force of the imperious Syrinx.

However, she had picked up her stola and she draped it over her shoulder. She tied the laces of her shoes; slowly, she traversed the atrium and the vestibule. Nothing could be heard but the sighing flute and the slight creak of wooden paneling. It was the hour when Tarao's slumber was heavy. Lying on his good ear, he could scarcely hear, and the slaves would be like logs until dawn.

Dehva lifted the latch. She saw the sapphire and nacre space, the face of Hecate all white beneath the sycamores, and then, at the far end of the garden, Dionys among the Libyan fig trees.

Then she felt faint. Her flesh seemed to be a warm liquid. She advanced toward the Syracusan like the girls who, touched by Persian mages, walk in their sleep.

The voice of the flute died away. Dionys watched the white form approach. Then he ran over the field of clover with a prodigious joy.

"You've come, Dehva? You've come?"

She replied in an ardent voice that was also plaintive: "I wasn't free not to come. You have put into the Syrinx a voice more powerful than that of the gods. I have come as a cloud comes in a storm."

He took her on his knees.

"Oh, little daughter of men, I consent to die for having been loved by you...and it is more than immortality to embrace your divine form!"

She pushed him away gently; their eyes filled with one another. He saw that new bosom rise, and as before, he drew it against his heart. She did not put up any resistance. She merely adjusted her stola at the waist.

Dionys uncovered her shoulders gently. They appeared, swansdown, nacre, or rather made of the flesh of white flowers, pensive nymphs over solitary pools, lilies of the valley hidden in ravines. And their tender and pure lines were lost in the troubled young breasts, admirable reserves of amour and life. Dionys' tremulous hand modeled itself to their form; Dehva felt herself entering into him through the amorous hands as through the sparkling eyes. But when he reached the girdle, he found himself stopped by little trembling hands.

"Have pity on one who loves you! She would die for violating her vow!"

She buckled under his arm, with her breasts palpitating with sensuality, set ablaze by implacable Eros. And he, gazing at her magnificent nudity, was like a ship in a tempest.

But Dehva's supplication filled him with fear. He saw the torture and death distinctly. Grimly, he lowered his head. They both execrated the grim goddess.

"Leave!" she said.

Their faces encountered one another, they took one another by the mouth, with a violent tenderness. He understood that all courage would be annihilated if he did not leave at that very moment. With a great effort, trembling in every limb and uttering a plaint, he fled toward the Volturne.

He walked for a long time, without seeing anything, without hearing anything but his desire, striking him within like a blacksmith's hammer.

He finally stopped at a bend in the river, where exceedingly old trees were leaning over, some burned by lightning and others half-stripped of their branches. On the far bank, a plain could be seen, marshes, and, near the sky, a blue forest. In the far distance, a wolf howled. The water flowed more blackly, more alive. It elongated in its bosom the image of Hecate and the figures of the constellations; she fled grimly with her thousand voices, under the hanging branches, and reappeared like a lake of quicksilver.

Dionys sat down on a promontory surrounded by tall trees, where the grass was as beautiful as if it were maintained by a skillful gardener.

He dreamed about his adventure. It overwhelmed him with a prodigious happiness mingled with a savage impatience. His breast was bursting like a volcano. He plunged his face and bare arms into the grass, in order to find a little coolness and tranquility.

Then he heard a rustle under the trees.

He raised his head, and saw the form of a woman in a long brown palla. Her head was covered by a veil, her feet clad in little red shoes held by numerous laces.

He recognized, in the visage placed in the moonlight, the charming Umbrian woman who had sung the Arquinian dance.

He leapt to his feet and, in a laughing voice, she said: "I followed you, Syracusan. I know what god has chased you from your bed. It's the same one that drew me into the night!"

He remained speechless. That woman alone could contest with the image of Dehva. And Dionys, without thinking about the singularity of the adventure, but drawn by his delectation, put out his arms tenderly. The Umbrian woman threw herself backwards.

"I'm not a she-wolf! And the voice of Amour, whom you call Eros, doesn't invite me to any sudden action. You don't even know why it's you that I followed. I might have preferred one of the young potters with skin of clay and imperious arms."

As that mouth spoke, quivering like the clay bell in Tarao's house, Dionys felt a measure of patience returning. The area was tranquil, the village distant, the woman quite alone beside him. He could wait.

"I'll listen," he said, in a soft and hollow voice, "to anything you want to say to me. Why have you preferred me?"

"Because, being beautiful, and truly beautiful, I venerate beauty—like you and Tarao, alone in this lost village."

She fell silent, gravely, but without a smile ceasing to appear in her magnificent eyes, full of changing fire, and a power that penetrated the Syracusan's flexible soul.

"I'm not jealous," she went on, "and I don't intend to detach you from another amour. But I want your worship!"

Then, slowly, she removed the veil from her head. Her hair shone like a sunset. Then her long brown palla was detached from her shoulder and breast, but retained and closed above her hips. Dionys uttered a great sigh of anguish and ecstasy; for she was as beautiful as Dehva, but quite differently, the shoulder rounder and the arm and the marvelous line that cambered her loins. Her skin was molded from Alpine snow. One might have thought that as much light sprang from it as from the star itself. The admirable globes of her breasts, endowed with force, race and delicacy, seemed beautiful vases full of a youthful, interior flame. Every movement underlined the perfect curve of her neck and the triple crease of sensuality.

He stood there, bewildered, as if before some perfect statue of Cytherea. And he also thought that she resembled, with the veiled lower part of her body, the daughters of the sea who drag men down into the gulf.

"You may also," said the Umbrian woman, "see with your hand whether my form is excellent—and I desire it."

He closed his eyes, and stroked the contour of that resplendent skin; he found no fault in it. That contact was also different from that of Dehva, like a flower as silken, but born on other shores.

Dionys' gaze darkened, the disturbance of the man dominating that of the artist. He seized the Umbrian woman's waist violently, and sought the flavorsome lips. But she did not want that. She stopped him with her folded arms, as wrestlers do.

"Not now," she said, and she pulled away, proudly. "See how my hair clothes me." She undid it; the tresses streamed. The cascades of copper and Arachne's webs hid her torso.

The Umbrian woman appeared in profile, sometimes as in a glorious shadow, sometimes as in a wave, and sometimes as in autumn foliage. Her skin was reminiscent of a bed of sparkling sand, her eyes of torches in a forest. That hair fell over the palla, extending all the way to the red shoes, and quivered like a wild animal or a sycamore in the rain.

Dionys understood more fully that a woman was the representation of all nature, a universal work of art in which the sky, rivers, hills, meadows, forests and animals were reflected in beauty. Before that tawny fleece his lust rose up, roaring. He advanced with prayers.

But the Umbrian woman disconcerted him with her laughter, took her hair in both hands, and threw it back over her right shoulder, like a lion's mane. She appeared beautiful, with a more terrible beauty. Her eyes were magnified. They quivered, like the star Sirius when it rises in a vaporous night. Her mouth opened; between her parted lips of red fire, the teeth shone like little snowy seashells between two coral stones.

"Ah!" he cried, in a supplicant voice. "Have pity on me, Umbrian! To see your beauty makes me suffer!"

In her turn, she said: "You aren't suffering, or, at least, your suffering is preferable to lust. It's desirable that men know that tormenting beauty." She raised her arms toward her head and, with rounded arms, formed the double handle of an admirable amphora. Dionys was surprised by her words. She continued: "I haven't always belonged to old Licinius. The man who bought me when a Roman merchant sold my father and his posterity at auction made statues for emperors. He taught me to adore myself and to conceive that the men whose desire I slaked without proof could not render me a just homage. I am worthy of worship, and I prefer the impotent admiration of old Licinius to the amour of a Campanian brute."

Dionys could find no reply, for he sensed, through the burning of his desire, the justice of those words.

She went on: "You haven't seen all of me. Look: my gestures are as beautiful as my figure and my hair."

She covered herself with the palla again. She mimed things and beings with the sacred rhythm of the art. She was an agile oread, a Diana with deadly arrows, a naiad shivering on the rocks, a sylvan fleeing in the vast silence, a virgin tormented by Aphrodite, a passing cloud, rustling branches, and a Nereid rising and descending with the agitation of the waves. Then, stopping in a hieratic pose, she appeared as the lascivious Cytherean, stimulant of lust.

Then he prostrated himself before her and cried: "Don't cast me into despair! I know your power now. It will be complete if you consent to intercourse!"

She did not reply. She looked at him with languid eyes, and smiled at him with a troubled expression. Her bosom seemed to be panting with desire. He thought that his wish was granted. He seized her with all his force.

She stood up to him and pushed him away by the shoulders, weaker than him but too strong to submit to violence. In any case, violence would have seemed odious to the young man. So much beauty could not be tender without consent. He struggled, however, in order to feel the resistance of that quivering bosom. But the Umbrian woman became angry, and her voice became harsh.

"I don't want to!"

He let her go.

He looked at her, very humbly.

"Don't speak," she said. "Make the Syrinx speak."

He raised the reed flute slowly and related the legend of his heart. He narrated his disturbance, his uncertainty, his vast surprise, everything that the Umbrian woman had thrown of enchantment into the night. He related his intolerable desire, the fury of Eros, the triumph of eternal beauty.

Any when the euphony expired on his lips, when the pathetic plaint vanished, lost in the echoes of the Volturne, he saw the emerald eyes brilliant with tears.

"Your speech is full of force," she said. Then, recovering her laughter, she added: "I also want you to make me hear the song that you often repeat for Tarao's daughter."

But that request revolted Dionys. He replied: "I will make, if you wish, a song for you alone; but I have consecrated that one."

She drew nearer. She darted a dominating and tender gaze at him. "It's Dehva's song that I desire. I'm not jealous; I know that you will love that virgin invincibly; there is room in the heart of a man for two women. I ask for nothing that she cannot claim as well, but I want as much as her."

He felt full of weakness. He said, in a whisper: "Will you at least put an end to my suffering?"

"Not tonight, Dionys. My beauty is not profound enough within you."

"Will you give me a kiss with your mouth?"

"I will not give you a kiss with my mouth." She seemed thoughtful; then she added, in an ironic voice: "But you can have my bare foot.

He played the hymn that he had consecrated to his beloved, resignedly, but nevertheless full of a singular joy for having submitted to the victory of the woman.

The Umbrian woman cried: "Be blessed, son of Sicily! You have given me a very profound pleasure, for I know how infatuated your soul is with the old Etruscan's granddaughter. You have been my slave for a moment, and with the sacrifice that gives the greatest price to that slavery."

Having said that, she sat down on the promontory. She undid the laces of her shoe. Her small bare foot shone on the green grass.

Dionys prostrated himself.

On that foot, high and arched like the prow of a galley, the moon could be glimpsed, so fine was the skin, and the network of veins. The Syracusan placed his lips upon it with a cry of lust. He kissed it frantically on the sole and on the nails of supple onyx.

And toes embalmed with myrrh and incense clenched against his mouth, responding to the kisses, and penetrated Dionys with the unslaked desire for that woman.

PART TWO

I. The Adventure

It was after nightfall on the eve of the kalends of August, The great Kiln of Veila had been lit; the red fire projected a palpitating twilight over the darkness, punctuated by mobile shadows.

The ceremony was still imprinted with mystical solemnity, a memory of prodigious epochs when humans were bewildered by having conquered the subtle and formidable element. The fire was taken from the temple of Diana Etrusca, transported in a lamp from the times of Porsenna and transmitted to an oaken cross to the sound of great harps, which played in unison three notes of a chant as sad as the plaint of wolves in winter.

As soon as the light had sprung forth, the watchers uttered a cry of joy and deliverance: the cry of the ancestor, vanquisher of the monstrous night. But it was necessary that the flame was not extinguished; that was a baneful sign, scarcely compensated by sacrifices, and the furnace remained cold for days. Never would the man who had failed be allowed to transport the divine fire again.

The master-potter was delighted to see the oven full of a vivacious light. He said to Dionys: "No other kiln as well conceived exists in all Campania. The man who constructed it, under the reign of Claudius, merits never seeing his name perish; he knew all the virtues of stone and clay, and the curves that concentrate or moderate the

94

heat. So, vases of different sizes can be cooked in a perfect manner, in accordance with the place assigned to them. And it is an admirable thing to guide the most ferocious element like a submissive horse."

Thus spoke Tarao, indefatigable in marveling at his art. Dionys was not listening. His soul was savage, scattered and diverse. The little shadow of Dehva, reddened by the flame, was mingled with the memory of the terrible Umbrian woman. There was an incessant war within his breast; it was a battlefield, where everything struggled except his will—it was the captive of Ananke, like the hero of old Aeschylus.[12]

In contemplating Dehva, he experienced a sort of unfathomable regret. She seemed to him to be younger, more fragile, and it was as if he had offended her. He did not analyze that melancholy; he could feel it, but not understand it. On reflection, he might rather have rejoiced for his friend, for he had sensed, fearfully, through the sensuality of their last encounter, the homicidal menace of the mortal fury of Diana; he had perceived the field of execution where those who braved the goddess had to perish.

The Umbrian woman appeared like a savior—a messenger of favorable gods turning him away from temptation—and whose presence he ardently implored. Dionys' soul was softer for the granddaughter of the master-potter, but while his roaring desire bounded toward the other, the virgin was closer at hand, more delicately intimate.

---

[12] The reference is to Prometheus in Aeschylus' *Prometheus Bound*; Ananke is a personification of the Necessity to which even the gods are subject.

Anxiety was gnawing at him. Since the night by the Volturne—two days ago—he had sought the Umbrian woman, prowling at dusk or by night around the Villa Licinius, but he had not been able to perceive the flexible silhouette.

Meanwhile, Tarao continued his discourse, his gestures echoed in the distance by this shadow, elongated on the square in the dancing light.

"It isn't the fire," he said, "that is submissive to man, but rather man who has consented to nourish the fire. In savage lands where flame is little used, the woods light up of their own accord, and the plains are consumed. See, on the contrary, that in civilized lands where forests are burned every season, the conflagration hardly ever spreads. Who can count what flame demands in a single city like Rome? I contend, therefore, that conflagration is warded off by the custom of lighting numerous fires, and if it bursts forth among us, it is, above all, in the years when man has been most miserly with the flame."

A man approached Dionys and said to him, in a low voice: "Let us move away into that shadow; I have a message for you."

Dionys recognized the old wanderer who had sold him the rose-water and given an oracle. He followed him to the rear of the kiln, where the darkness fell in dense masses, in a rain of ash and bitumen. From that black island the flame seemed more vehement; the holm-oaks, the olive trees and the vines animated their illuminate foliage.

The old man spoke in a mysterious voice.

"I have been charged with a message for you, young man. But know first that old Somnius, if he is a skillful merchant, as is appropriate when one practices the art of Hermes, is faithful to his word and never betrays a secret. May the somber Hades summon him this very moment if that is not the truth. The one who sent me to you knows that no choice could be preferable. That is Flavia, the Umbrian woman with the lion's mane. She consents to see you and has sent me to lead you. The road by which we shall go is not exempt from perils..."

The old man suspended his speech, and then resumed in a sibylline mode: "It is nevertheless les perilous than the wrath of Diana Etrusca."

Dionys only heard the final words vaguely. A quiver of adventure and desire was agitating his entire body. He turned toward the shadow and the stars, and sniffed the air like Diomedes and Ulysses on the evening when they took possession of the horses of Rhesus.

In a low voice he replied: "I'll follow you, Somnius, even if it's necessary to cross a marsh full of hydras."

"I'll wait for you," said the other, "within half an hour, behind Raso's field, in which there is a figure of Saturn."

He disappeared over the pale ground, among the holm-oaks.

The kiln had just been closed. The starry darkness fell over Veila again. The indefatigable cicadas, crickets and frogs spoke across the plain and the waters.

Dionys went back down with Tarao and Dehva to their dwelling. The old man said: "Everything done well gives happiness. There is a veritable joy in the man who has woven three strands of osier properly. That is a profound law, Dionys, that must go back to the origins of art. I've observed it even in beasts and the birds of the woods. And I feel that my soul is content because the kiln has been lit irreproachably, from the moment that the lamp touched the oaken cross..."

Dionys listened emotionally. His soul had never been more faithful to the grand old man and Dehva. He felt indefinably culpable toward the two of them, although his reason dictated to him, for the security of his hosts, that he should go to the Umbrian woman.

He did not go into the house. Neither Tarao nor Dehva was astonished by that, for he was subject to caprices. He watched the silhouettes of his friends disappear under the large awning; he responded in a troubled voice when they shouted the evening salutation at him.

Dionys marched rapidly through the vines. The leaves struck him gently in the face; a thousand invisible little creatures fled in the silvery darkness. In accordance with the distance, ponds reflected the stars of the zenith or those of the horizon. The breeze rose up in small gusts, like a swarm of insects, and immediately died down. There was an anxiety in the depths of the firmament; here and there, a constellation was veiled, and then reappeared, moist and more scintillating. Nervous dogs called to one another across distances.

The Syracusan submitted to the frisson of the troubled night, but he did not perceive its details: the image of the Umbrian woman was shining within him more brightly than the star of Osiris in the sky. He slid behind the farms, crossing streams. He finally reached Raso's orchard, near the figure of Saturn. The gray silhouette of Somnius advanced toward him.

"Is that you, Syracusan?"

"It's me."

"Are you ready to follow me?"

"I'm ready."

The old man did not add another word. He set forth, at a brisk, agile pace, which faltered at times. They emerged from the village and came to the cliffs where the tombs were. There, Somnius paused to catch his breath, and said: "Let's breathe before climbing those cliffs, young man, for it's necessary to climb them; they lead to the brilliant fleece."

He sniggered. "I like to look into the past," he continued, "because my days were dearly bought. Everything would have seemed insipid and sad to me, if it did not carry risks. I lost three fortunes, acquired with great effort, but I don't regret them. I also loved, young man with the keen eyes, the adventure that is offered to you. It's agreeable to me to participate in it. It makes me remember joyous nights when we deceived the surveillance of the agents of Rome, and cruises when our boat slipped between the triremes of pirates. So, you can count on my faith; those who have run great perils have learned the virtue of oaths. Know that it's necessary for us to enter the gardens of Licinius; they are guarded by Thessalian mastiffs, three of which are sufficient to kill a lion. They've even been trained not to give voice, and to devour in silence anyone who crosses the enclosure."

He sniggered again. Dionys looked at the vague face in the shadow; he did not experience any fear, only annoyance that obstacles might prevent him from meeting the Umbrian woman.

"That's a danger that we can counter," said the old man. "Flavia knows how to take measures. But something unexpected might occur in these well-guarded gardens; that's the peril we're running. You can still avoid it."

"And what happiness would I merit," replied Dionys, "if I recoiled before that which an old man braves?"

"You wouldn't merit any, above all what a woman more beautiful than Cleopatra is offering you," said the prowler, with a hint of bitterness. "At your age I'd gladly have burned a city and endured torture for her. Any man who can't show the fig to death, is only worth slavery. But let's resume our course; I've got my breath back."

They took a little goat-path in the cliff. They marched between two walls of stone, which the firmament only dominated with a narrow strip of spangled dark blue. They turned into a kind of great triangular well that was the crest of the route, and went downhill again.

Soon, they reached the edge of Licinius' gardens. Those gardens were vast; they poured the odor of suave plants, amorously assembled, over all of their surroundings.

Somnius circled the enclosing wall for some time, feeling the hanging branches. In the end, he stopped. He lifted up two dark garments that were hanging next to a postern; they were hooded cloaks, left there by a complicit hand.

Somnius whispered: "Thus precautions turn against those who take them. Licinius has trained his mastiffs not to attack those who wear these cloaks, impregnated with a special odor, known to him alone, scarcely perceptible to human nostrils. His foresight will serve us to penetrate into the gardens. Follow me; walk quietly—in addition to the dogs, two guardian slaves are on watch, in the entrance and on the peristyle."

"How will we deceive their vigilance and penetrate into the dwelling?"

"It's not the dwelling that we're going to penetrate."

He had opened the postern silently, with the aid of mysterious implements. He went into the gardens. Dionys followed him without hesitation.

Three massive forms loomed up before them.

"The mastiffs!" said Somnius. "Walk without flinching; the dogs mistrust men who hesitate, with reason."

The formidable beasts had come forward. They sniffed in an anxious fashion; their huge heads touched the two men. They seemed surprised, uncertain. The largest uttered a dull growl; then, pushed back by the firm stride of the two men, it allowed itself to be bypassed. But they followed, ready to pounce.

Dionys, with a prickling in his ankles and his back, held at the ready a knife forged in Agrigento, which could pierce a bronze plate.

They advanced in the shadow of bushes and trees at a brisk, furtive pace that could not be heard, for a thousand voices filled the darkness, all the little naiads of the springs, fountains and streams hidden under the branches and the grass.

They were approaching the large while dwelling, which appeared behind a grove of pines and plane trees, when Somnius murmured: "Stop!"

They were near the edge of a lawn. The light of the stars drew a slight scintillation from the lustrous plats and whitened a small stream. They saw a dark silhouette advancing slowly.

"One of the watchmen," murmured Somnius. "That's unforeseen, young man. One movement of the dogs, and we're denounced."

He had seized Dionys' arm; his clenched fingers marked the peril. Everything, in fact, depended on the attitude of the animals. If they continued to follow tranquilly, the watchman might not perceive anything. The shadow of the trees rendered the two invaders invisible; the rumor of the waters covered the sound of their footsteps.

"We have scarcely a stade to go" said Somnius. "Let's go. It's immobility that is most likely to trouble the mastiffs."

The digs were agitated. The presence of the slave watchman reawoke their vigilance and they stopped, uncertain. One of them made a decision and bounded across the lawn with a dull growl.

"What's up, Leo?" asked the slave.

The enormous beast pawed the ground, and leapt. The man divined a danger, but did not decide to take immediate action.

"Quickly," said Somnius. "The slave's hesitating. He knows that the dogs are inaccessible to fear—at least to that which results from the presence of men or beasts. He fears something mysterious, more terrible."

At that moment the watchman uttered a guttural cry, which echoed in the distance.

"The alarm call," said Somnius. "Faster!"

A rumor went up in the distance from the white dwelling visible through the pines. They sensed the awakening of people who would soon become visible, by the light of torches flickering among the colonnades, over the grass and over the waters. Somnius and Dionys saw forms stirring under the peristyle.

"We've arrived," said the old wanderer. "And the dogs, attracted by the noise, are no longer following us."

As he spoke, a whistle rang out; the dogs launched forward, picking up the abandoned trail with great bounds. Already, the fugitives had reached a small isolated construction. With a groping hand, Somnius found the door and introduced a key. The lock resisted. The dogs appeared, fifty paces away. Throwing open the door, however, and shoving Dionys through the gaping opening, the old man began laughing sardonically.

"Only blind Destiny knows whether we're saved or doomed."

The door closed again, they waited. In spite of the darkness, Dionys vaguely perceived furniture and pale walls, and a very soft perfume, as if arrived from a distant coast, mingled a voluptuous disturbance with the sentiment of peril.

Outside, the dogs had just stopped. They were growling.

"By Neptune!" said the old merchant. "I fear, young man, that the balance is not leaning in our favor."

Voices were heard approaching. Dionys, who had received lessons from stoics and fatalistic mariners, replied: "We shall obey the decree, Somnius. I do not see that we can aid ourselves further, except with our weapons."

As he spoke, he heard a rustle of fabric. The young man sensed a head close to his own that was spreading, more forcefully, the perfume that had stirred him. A soft voice murmured: "Don't move!"

He recognized the voice of the Umbrian woman. He tried to advance his hands, but a bare arm, moved him aside. The door opened swiftly and closed again.

"Fate has spoken," said the old man. "Have no fear any longer. That young woman is fecund in resources; her mind is as prompt as it is sure. She will save us."

The dogs were no longer growling. The Umbrian woman spoke to them in a low voice and drew them away with her, by winding paths, toward the building that the slaves had quit in order to run across the gardens. She reached the peristyle, and from then on took no further care to hide, for it was natural that she had would have arrived there, attracted by the noise. She began to speak to the mastiffs, in a singing voice that was audible in the distance.

"Leo, Niger, Robur, what's the matter?"

The men, dispersed, no longer knowing what direction to take, turned round at those words and, seeing the dogs running between the columns, they renounced their pursuit.

"What's happening?" the young woman demanded.

The oldest of the slaves replied: "The dogs seemed disturbed, Flavia. We thought that we ought to visit the gardens."

"The dogs fear no one," she retorted. "They would devour anyone who invaded this dwelling, or would perish. What danger can you fear, Lucius?"

"I don't know," the slave replied. "A man might have hidden."

"You've done well," replied the Umbrian woman, "but it's surely nothing. Dogs have their caprices, like men. You can see that they're tranquil now. Put out those torches and disperse in silence; it's necessary not to wake the master."

They were accustomed to obey her as promptly as Licinius himself, even though she was a slave. The old man intended that she be respected. They obeyed.

She remained alone with the mastiffs and the two watchmen.

II. Sensuality

Half an hour had passed. Dionys was waiting, his
nerves increasingly taut. He no longer had the patience
to listen to his companion or reply to him. The waiting
emptied his soul; and the adventure ended up seeming so
distant and imprecise that he scarcely desired it.

A slight sound made him shudder; almost at the
same time, a very soft hand grasped his, while someone
murmured: "Come!"

His being returned, like a firmament of clouds when
the wind rises. He no longer had any memory of anxiety
or waiting. The woman took him away in a prodigy of
joy, scintillating hope and voluptuous agitation.

They went through a narrow corridor; a door closed
behind them, and, lifting a thick veil that hid a niche, the
Umbrian woman uncovered a silver lamp, already lit.
They were in a rather small room, with walls decorated
with dark blue and emerald enamels, furnished with
small shelf-units of Mauritanian ivory, tables with lions'
and bulls' feet, a silver perfume-burner that spread a
suave smoke, bucchero nero vases with rhythmic contours, and seats with Syrian cushions.

The young woman had let go of Dionys' hand. She
showed him a chair, saying: "Don't move…let me listen
to the night."

Leaning over, she cocked an ear. Her white garment
fell in marble pleats, lightly twisted around her.

She was anxious, and almost terrible in the gleam in
her eyes, the color of which changed with every movement: green in profile and violet-gray in full face. Her
hair, partly unfastened, either by the haste or deliberately, was strewn with tiny rosebuds. Something cruel and
menacing lifted the shiny corners of her mouth and di-

lated her nostrils, either because she was proudly braving peril or because she felt the species of bitter sensation that often accompanies beauty, which is like a revenge against the Ephemeral, against old age and death.

When she had listened for a minute, she said: "All is tranquil."

And she came to sit down on the ground, her head posed on the young man's knee. He saw her entire, in an attitude marvelously adapted to exasperate desire. He tried to lean forward, place a kiss on her hair and seize the woman.

"No!" she said. "First I want to thank you and apologize to you. For if it suited me that you believed that you were in peril, I had anticipated everything, in order that that peril should not be the reality. Hazard defeated my prudence; you nearly paid dearly for your enterprise. I feel a very keen regret."

"But I do not!" he exclaimed, vehemently.

She looked at him smiling, and began slowly to undo a part of her hair. An ironic provocation illuminated her eyes.

"It's appropriate that you have no regret," she said, "and that you don't regret having run a few of the risks that two peoples once consented to run for a woman. I would have no pleasure, Dionys, in receiving a man who would not be ready to go to war to conquer me. So I wanted to know that you would not recoil. It was a necessary proof, without which the adventure would have been insipid and devoid of beauty. But I trembled for you myself, and that was not useful."

She spread her hair over the Syracusan's knees, and stroked it delicately. Reflections of copper scintillated there on a backcloth of tawny silk. He plunged his hands into it with a sigh; he seemed to sense it palpitating, and his desire was exalted like a warrior beast. The Umbrian woman still contained him with her smile.

Then, seeing that he was becoming impatient, she said: "Take off that long cloak, I beg you...I'm stifling, seeing it over your shoulders."

He took off the cloak, while she put up her hair again. Her marvelous, round, shiny neck, taut, with two childlike pleats, a nape both delicate and fleshy, held the Syracusan's attention. It sprang from the stola with a kind of amorous boldness; it seemed a complete being, limited by the roots of the hair and the jawbone. Dionys could not recall having seen a contour of flesh orna-mented to that degree with the gifts of Aphrodite. He conceived more pleasure in plunging his lips thereon than in possessing a beautiful courtesan.

And he thought that he would find the night fortu-nate if the young woman simply realized that wish. He said, passionately: "There is only one Hellenic statue, Umbrian of which the neck is resplendent with that beauty and that grace..."

She turned toward him; with a singular softness, she said: "I am not unaware of it, Dionys. I honor therein the mysterious work of a god; I experience, on contemplat-ing it in my mirror, a frisson that enables me to under-stand the desire of men."

He moved closer, his eyes humble and supplicant, for he understood that he would obtain nothing except by prayer. He said: "Let me place my lips upon it, and tonight will be blessed!"

He was very close to her. She recoiled with a shiv-er.

"Be careful to do nothing by surprise; you would cause me chagrin and would prevent me from loving you. And I desire to love you. But that is only possible if you respect my body as a holy work. Violence horrifies and disgusts me. Those who are veritably able to discern beauty are not capable of it, when one has taken care to warn them. There is little calculation in my resistance, or, at least, the calculation is only the effect of strong sentiments. It is necessary for me to conquer. I feel the necessity of that for myself, and for the man to whom it would please me to yield. It is a common interest. Dionys. It would be as fatal to you as to me to misunderstand it."

"I would not misunderstand it," he said, "if your amour were to be the prize of my obedience."

She placed her head on his shoulder; he saw, obliquely, the emerald eyes and the crimson lip, full of the same cruel expression as before.

"But I have no idea whether I will love you," she said. "I only have a desire to love you, because it appears that you can recognize the value of my body. You know, and you shall know better, that to possess me is to possess all women. Beauty is a people. It represents a thousand extraordinary things, the entire mysterious prodigy of life. Those who are astonished that Mark Antony preferred Cleopatra to the Empire have not thought that the Empire is the insipid repetition of ill-made creatures. One woman alone in whom nature has succeeded is worth a myriad. What would she be worth if nature had succeeded *perfectly*? She might well be more that everything human that exists, beyond peer...."

She fell silent. He remained pensive. Those words corresponded to the depths of his nature, imbued with the religion of the Beautiful. He enveloped the young woman with a long admiring gaze, while she continued.

"I would be a vain and poor thing, Dionys, if I surrendered myself without resistance. Instead of a profound adventure, you would only have a miserable game. It is appropriate that beauty be dear, in order better to exalt the soul of men, and is it not, in any case, to insult the gods to grant without proof that which ought to cost so much difficulty?"

She held herself as grave and proud as a Pallas Athene with the grace of Cypris. No perversity shone any longer in her luminous irises. She was pure, by virtue of the honesty and fervor of her belief. And a bitter distress slid into Dionys' heart, the fear that that woman was not made for amour.

In a hollow voice he said: "Do you not fear, Flavia, being too similar to a work of art sculpted in stone? It is also necessary that beauty be emotional, or it would be in vein that it was made of palpitating flesh. No divinity could have determined that those who were to trouble the souls of men would be untroubled themselves. They would lack the supreme grace that is in Life."

"Ah!" she cried, vehemently. "I don't want to be a statue, and I have no fear of that. This flesh is not insensible; it aspires to charming intoxication. I am full of secret desires, Syracusan, but they have not been able to blossom. You would not reproach the flower of Libya for being unable to grow in the indigent light of the Bretons, nor the bird of tempests for being unable to find pleasure on calm shores. Do not reproach me for being insensible to the love of brutes, nor for wanting to be the prize of long effort; I shall be more ardent for having been more skillfully elected."

He wanted to reply, but she put her hand over his mouth and the softness of that small palm recalled that of the silvery foot on the grass of the Volturne.

"Don't reply," she said. "I have chosen you. You please me. I know that we practice the same worship.

But you are still my enemy; that is the law. Try to vanquish me by submission, as you would strive to vanquish the Anadyomene if she sprang from the foam for you."

She picked up a silver vase and an electrum cup and held them out with an almost humble movement. He placed his mouth avidly on the place that she had touched.

"It's the wine of my homeland," she said. "It is harsh, and not durable. I wanted you to taste it, as a sign of hospitality. Would you like fruits now, meat, Falernian, or the sweet liquor of Syracuse?"

She served the things as she named them, on a lemon-wood table encrusted with enamels and tortoiseshell; but his stomach was constricted. He watched her do it, and every gesture created a memory.

"You're not eating?" she said.

"It's sufficient for me to see you to be sated."

She nibbled a little alica, a yellow fig, and took a sip of Syracusan wine. While eating, she had an air of naïve, mischievous, cheerful pleasure. Her cheeks seemed more rounded.

Then, a melancholy expression passed over her face. She leaned toward Dionys, her eyes plunging into his. The child had disappeared; a somber queen remained, beneath the abundant hair whose height matched that of the entire face. He sensed that he was under an obscure and redoubtable yoke.

She stopped eating, and spoke in a clear voice that was hollowed out at intervals.

"My beauty has not been helpful to me. More often than not, I have carried it like a heavy burden or a thorny flower. It seems that I owe ransom for it to some invisible power. Apart from Cneius, who taught me to know it and gave me the joy of it, I have been the captive of

110

jealous brutes. My masters have had a taste for my body but no respect; they kept me far from other men. Three times I was sold; three times I fell into misfortune. Free, I could have made myself rich, for it is scarcely to be hoped to see the beauty recognized by men of Rome, Athens and Phoecia without it being surrounded by lust…and old Licinius is, all things considered, the best of those who have possessed me."

She detached her eyes from those of the young man; a magnificent shadow passed over her face.

"Thus, my fate was to have but one hour of light, and my beauty was like a lost treasure. I would not like to die without having loved."

Dionys remained motionless, bathed in a strange melancholy, which seemed inexplicable to him. The brief plaint of that woman evoked all the fugitive history of humankind. The Sicilian relived his exodus, the sea, the resounding cities, the harsh roads: all the décor of Destiny, the space in which the tottering generations lived and died. There was also the impression of a sacrilege that such a woman has been a slave, and he remembered the words of Tarao on the evening of his arrival: "It's something contrary to divine laws. Beauty is offended by it. Of all offenses, I know of none more sacrilegious."

The Umbrian woman saw his sadness; she was touched by it.

"I like your silence better than your speech," she said. "It's pleasant for me to be lamented. It's something that I shall not forget."

She put her hands on the young man's neck; then extending her nape, she said "You can now place your mouth upon it; but then you'll leave…"

He plunged his face into the embalmed neck. The admirable flesh was fresh; it had a kind of silky ripple of frissons and slight movements. For an instant, the bosom swelled like that of a dove. The Umbrian woman tilted her head back with a sigh; bewildered, Dionys seized her by the waist. She pushed him away, imperious and gentle, threw his cloak over his shoulder and drew him into the next room.

"Go!" she said. "You'll come back."

He found himself in the darkness of the gardens, with old Somnius. He carried away the kiss as Endymion, in the forests of Latmos, bore away the dissolving kiss of the nocturnal queen.

Dionys saw the Umbrian woman again several times, but those meetings were full of uncertainty. The young woman did not surrender herself any more than on the first evening. She escaped all prevision, her tenderness was as capricious as her melancholy; he never knew whether her smile was ironic or tender.

Armed with all the powers of a woman, all the disconcerting gestures, all the contradictory coquetries and all the instinctive ruses, she was not one being but a multitude. Dionys despaired of seizing her, like the leader of an army in revolt.

His soul was heavy; he maintained silence; he no longer took pleasure in his art. Dehva was his sole consolation, but he was fearful of her presence, and strove not to encounter her alone. When the work was concluded he remained alone with old Tarao, or fled along the Volturne all the way to the gardens of Licinius.

He gazed distractedly at things and people living in the approaching autumn. Delicate evenings descended over Campania. The cultivators and the herdsmen quitting the fields and the pastures, the bewildered children in the orchards and farmyards, the drowsy flowers, the great blue, amethyst and coppery satin sky and the shadows of trees gradually fading into the shadow of dusk made him think of Achilles' beautiful shield, on which the god of forges had depicted the tilled earth, fecund and rich, men turning teams of oxen, crops reaped with scythes, gilded vines, silver trellises flexing under black and blue clusters. And when night fell, he thought that Vulcan had also represented, on that glittering armor, the stars, the round moon, the vaporous Pleiades, the strength of Orion, and the cart rolling northwards in an immutable stadium, which never bathed in the indefatigable ocean.

Then, in the crystalline night, he made speeches, for he understood his thought better when he put it into words.

He said: "What do you want of me, Aesa? Why have you put into my heart a double amour full of torments? For the redoubtable vow separates me from one, and the other toys with my desire. It seems that you want to reduce me to despair with the very adventure that ought to be the happiest for a son of men. Why has my heart conceived such a violent agitation therein? You are taking pleasure in making me taste death in life, and horror in beauty..."

Sometimes, too, he blew softly into the Syrinx, and drew laments therefrom. Then his soul sighed, following the magic of sounds. He perceived, obscurely, the profound harmony that links rhythm to joy and suffering. And the kind of scattered soul that art extracts from beautiful beings, as a plant draws its flower from the earth and the daylight.

One evening, when he was relating the melancholy of his destiny to himself, sitting on the stump of a willow near a pool in which the stars were asleep, he saw the master-potter in front of him, who was listening to him.

"My son," said the old man, "you have never made anything heard so sweet. A new life is in the breath of that flute, a voice that I have not heard elsewhere. I followed you in order that we might talk about your trouble, but perhaps it is better that you do not give vent to a suffering from which you draw such music... Only assure me that your existence and that of Dehva—they are now almost equally dear to me—are not in any peril."

Dionys, rendered more tender by chagrin, sensed that he loved the old man veritably; he exclaimed, in a halting voice: "I would commit all crimes, my father, rather than risk Dehva's life."

Reassured, Tarao wanted to hear the Syrinx again. He sat down in the shadow and said: "Doubtless I will not embarrass your confidence, since it is wordless..."

And the old man listened.

Dionys repeated his plaint to Fatality.

After that, the Sicilian sought out the master-potter when his trouble was propitious to his art. It was a consolation, all the more so as Tarao took pleasure in its beauty above all, and let him understand that a dolor that bore such fruits ought not to seem too dear to him.

Meanwhile, Dehva became anxious. She sensed a strange presence in her companion's cares. And, full of the finesse of amorous young women, she searched the face and attitude of her lover for the signs of that hostile force. She had a marvelous instinct for divining the ungraspable, and although no image fixed her anxiety, she was never mistaken regarding the traces of the unknown adventure. In the mornings, when Dionys still had the atmosphere of the Umbrian woman about him, the young woman was wild, capricious and almost hostile. She turned away, her laugher was shrill, her eyes full of a strange gleam; she approached Dionys with a cold visage and did not accept his caresses. Afterwards, she became somber, full of rancor; she isolated herself in her room or in a corner of the gardens, and, silently, a sadness tightened her beautiful mouth, the presentiment of experience that casts a shadow over young beings.

When the trace was effaced, she returned to Dionys with a brighter visage, her smiles rejuvenated. Life candid and full, faith, strength and hope brought her back to tenderness. She hastened to the Sicilian, she used all her weapons of grace; she enlaced him with her youthful beauty, like a net of amour.

As he felt more culpable, she entered more profoundly into his future.

One morning, when they were alone, she took his hand, and drew him into the garden among the tall shady laurels. Something wild and wayward was within her, her eyes were full of disorder and provocation. She was wearing no other garment than a linen tunic that followed the contour of her hip.

"What's the matter, Dehva?" he said, disquieted by the child's wild silence.

She raised a resolute forehead, and darted her amour from the depths of her somber pupils. Then, raising her arms, she crossed them over the young man's nape. Her red lips pressed angrily upon Dionys' mouth.

He resisted at first; she held on to him with all her strength, resolute in trying her power; she leaned her small, elastic breasts, semi-naked, against her lover. Then he weakened. He remained as if buried by her kiss.

Attentively, she listened to the man's heart beating. When she was fully assured of his desire, she suddenly pulled away and fled, without having broken the silence.

All day long she was tranquil and cheerful, but the following day, she recognized the enemy presence again. Dionys had been with the Umbrian woman the night before. Anxiety took hold of her again. She no longer limited herself to scrutinizing her lover. She began to watch what he did. An energy rose up within her, the desire to protect her happiness and to employ all her strength in doing so.

The Syracusan went to the gardens of Licinius twice a week. He penetrated into them without fear. The dogs had become his friends; they welcomed him with silent caresses, as they would once have devoured him in silence. He no longer had anything to fear but the vigilance of the slave watchmen.

Often, the Umbrian woman came to meet him, even outside the enclosure, and guided him to shelter herself.

Dehva knew about those excursions. She got up, quivering, when she heard the sonorous house creaking or the sound of the door grating. She got up and watched the young man departure, furtively; she watched him disappear along the white road. She believed every time that she was determined to follow him, but then she recoiled, seized by an invincible disturbance. Often, too, she thought of calling out to him, of retaining him, but a secret pride, a singular repulsion, prevented her from doing so.

One night, however, she decided. The sky was vaporous, the light of the stars more uncertain. She could see Dionys' silhouette at fifty paces, however. She had difficulty following him, inasmuch as she had to muffle the sound of her footfalls. As long as he was on the white path, she did not alert his attention. Supple and adroit, she did not make a single stone shift. Thoughtful, impatient to reach his goal, already accustomed to traveling the route without any mishap, he did not turn his head.

But in the narrow paths, the rustle of branches attracted his attention. He stopped and listened. She had stopped at the same instant, shivering. He believed that he had been mistaken, and set forth again.

The path had broadened; Dehva was advancing more easily when she tripped over a root. This time, Dionys had no doubt that he was being followed. He drew his knife and retraced his steps. Dehva made no attempt to hide or to flee. She awaited Destiny, immobile.

When he was close he perceived the pale glimmer of her stola.

"Is that you, Dehva?" he said, in a low voice, putting away his weapon.

She began trembling, so much that she did not have the strength to reply. Her constricted heart, full of sinister trouble, seemed to climb into her throat.

"Is that you?" he repeated, and his hand touched her quivering shoulder.

The soul of the virgin burst; she uttered a low and plaintive cry, while tears began to run down her face.

He held her against him; he was full of an unfathomable pity. The shaking of that beloved young body, the warm tears that his lips encountered, the small sound of sobbing, caused an upheaval of tenderness and also of sly sensuality, which rose up urgently at the contact of feminine dolor.

He remained full of anguish between the amour to which he had consecrated his life and the scintillating

117

slave of Licinius. And, thinking that one was sure and the other fleeting, he was ready to yield to his friend's pain, to renounce the garden of temptation.

In a low voice, he spoke, inconsequential, soft and infantile words. She perceived his weakness.

"Stay!" she whispered in his ear.

He did not reply, intoxicated by the slight breath that brushed him. Then, gripping him with all the energy of her little arms, she went on: "Stay, Dionys. It's as if I were about to die."

He turned his head away. He no longer had any strength. He abandoned himself to a kind of gentle vertigo.

Meanwhile, a glimmer of light increased on the black horizon and rose toward the stars. The hills to the west became visible, outlined in silhouette. Suddenly, a horned moon, red and deformed appeared amid the mists.[13]

"You see!" Dionys cried. "Diana does not wish it. She has appeared, bloody, at the moment of response. It's necessary to flee, Dehva, before the homicidal goddess..."

And he tore himself away from her.

III. The Sacred Joy

Flavia was combing her hair. Her small hands had withdrawn the pins and undone the hair. The tresses fell over her semi-naked shoulders; Dionys perceived the tawny hair under the armpits, the breasts pressed against

---

[13] It is a quirk of Rosny's work that the moon often rises in the west therein.

one another, the beautiful cambered loins beneath the transparent tunic.

When the hair was spread out, Flavia untangled it with an agile hand. The comb made a slight hiss, which mingled with the frisson of the cloth and the slight sound of her joints. Her mouth was smiling obliquely, but her eyes were grave and attentive.

Dionys was intoxicated by the spectacle, with a mixture of hope and discouragement.

"You can kiss me," she said, finally, "but quickly."

With one bound, he was beside her. She abandoned her mouth momentarily, passive and closing her eyes.

"Your lips are good," she said. "They're made for kissing..."

He returned to sit down. She put up her hair again; she moistened her face with water mixed with bran and iris. Then she perfumed herself and polished her finger-nails with a pink powder. Then she passed an infusion of mint over her teeth, as shiny as silver and as translucent as the enamel of seashells.

Dionys did not budge, He contemplated all the young woman's movements; it was an accomplished game, a mimic masterpiece of living beauty. He loved those cares as a consecration of the royalties of the flesh, like savant and magical rites.

Flavia interrupted herself and drew nearer to him. He did not budge.

"You're tranquil," she said, with a hint of mockery. "Has your amour become torpid?"

"It's resigned, Flavia. You've taught it patience, and the art of suffering without a quiver."

"And you have no rancor?"

"Sometimes. But that rancor isn't profound. It will only become so if you keep me any longer in suspense.

You're my enemy, but not irreconcilable. Everything is ready within me to love you gently—for I recognize that your will is just, and that it's necessary to know how to suffer for your beauty."

"But you're not happy, Dionys?"

"I'm miserable. I have never been so miserable. I thought I recognized misfortune when I reposed my limbs on the hard ground and lamented my hunger, but then I was full of hope, because a stroke of luck could put an end to my indigence and I sensed youth, strength and long days seething within me. Today, I'm gripped by an obscure fatality. I no longer have an age. I'm at the limits of life. If my adventure is fatal—it doesn't matter whether I am twenty-five years old or thirty—it will have marked me with an ineffaceable seal. I will have lost that which will never return, and which is worth several human existences."

She was grave and charming, her elbow on her knee, her pupils dilated to the point that the iris only appeared as an amethyst ring constellated with tiny topazes. Only those irises and pupils were moving in her face; the Umbrian woman only changed at intervals, slowly, the crease of the hole.

"You can't lose everything, however, for the old potter's granddaughter will remain to you. "

"She's forbidden to me for a further twelve months, Umbrian. It's too great a torture. And when it's no longer thus..."

He stopped, his face turned to the ground, somber.

"I want you to say everything," she murmured.

"Well," he went on, in a languorous tone, "I can no longer imagine life without both of you. With only one, everything is incomplete, the world empty. I need you and Dehva to fill it. But also, what human, what demigod could encounter, in a solitary village, two such marvelous figures to complete one another? Because you are both more beautiful for existing together; and that is why, in losing one, I would lose what could never be again...*what could never be again.*"

"I couldn't be sufficient for you, then?"

"You would have been, once."

She struck a cold attitude: "And if I wanted to be, alone?"

He went pale, and did not say a word. An immense sadness contracted his mouth, in which there was fear and disgust.

She repeated, obscurely and cruelly: "If I wanted that?"

"How do I know?" he groaned. "If I said yes and that I would sacrifice the other to you, would I have changed my soul? The despair would remain, and the horror of being alive. Neither your will nor mine can do it, any more that a ship precipitated into a whirlpool." As if in a dream, he added: "Oh, I ought never to have been born!"

Flavia shivered. She got up and placed both hands on Dionys. She was palpitating, full of the desire of amour. There was in her desire the pity of having vanquished, so dear to a woman's heart, the joy of finishing a profound dolor with a caress, and the unknown agitation, the presence of the capricious god who defeats pride in the quivering humility of donation.

He swooned under the adorable weight of that flesh, but, accustomed to the disappointment of caresses, he did not divine that the moment had come. Then she called to him with a profound voice.

"Dionys!"

She weighed upon him more heavily, her eyes full of a languorous flame.

"You have vanquished."

He raised his head like a legionary at the noise of the battle, and, seizing the woman, with a cry of triumph and servitude, he annihilated himself via her in sacred joy.

IV. The Clearing

There were two festivals of the Olive groves in the Etruscan villages of Campania. One was consecrated to Mnerfa, the Athene creative of the tree, the other to the Etruscan Ceres, who was frequently confounded with a primitive Rhea and even with a formless goddess of Chaos, most often figured by a tree trunk in which the confused pleats of a veil or mantle were perceptible. The festival of Mnerfa fell at the ides of September. She was pure and bright, particularly celebrated by children and adolescents of both sexes.

At dawn, clad in white, little boys and girls ran, in groups of seven, singing, from dwelling to dwelling. They agitated branches ornamented with olives, singing a simple hymn to Mnerfa. A woman came out, sprinkled the little singers gently with water perfumed with roses, and distributed honey-cakes and ripe fruits.

Those infantile visits lasted until a third of the way through the day; then the maidens and adolescents assembled next to a sacred wood where a priest awaited them, or, at least, an old man who fulfilled that office. A bull and rams were sacrificed in a clearing, on a primitive altar, in the shaded of an ancient olive tree. Then cockerels and owls were paraded, birds dedicated to the goddess with the glaucous eyes, and a banquet was prolonged into the night, from which license was banished.

In Veila, the festival of Mnerfa was primarily led by the maidens. All day long they were the mistresses of the village. They exercised an absolute royalty, tempered by ancient regulations. They gathered in long processions that spread out in the boscage of the Volturne, and celebrated, two by two, chaste betrothals, in which they crowned one another with flamboyant roses, olive branches and feathers from cockerels and owls. They were permitted to kiss one another on the mouth.

They regulated the order of the banquet, the decoration of dwellings and crossroads, but did not do the work themselves; the women and the men received their orders and carried them out without a murmur. Even the ancestors obeyed them.

One among them was the queen. She was clad in a glaucous tunic, a corselet and cothurnes. She held a little shield with a head in the center, which might have been a Gorgon or some old Etruscan deity of Fear. A transparent linen veil floated over her neck and could be lifted over her face. She was taken to the sacrificial wood on a cart pulled by rams. A domesticated snake accompanied her and a crow that knew how to pronounce the name of the goddess. In a golden ladle she received a few drops of sacred blood, which she had to knead with flour and olive oil for the symbolic cake of the banquet.

After dusk she retired, alone, to the depths of the sacred wood. She could be accompanied by a young man as far as forty-nine paces from the altar. There, in solitude, she sang a hymn to Mnerfa and requested her protection for the village.

This year, Dehva was the queen. She was pale and sad, but so beautiful that the most boorish were moved by her presence. She paraded her trouble all day along the river, the marshes and the rose bushes, and submitted meekly to her glory of a day. As she was solitary, surrounded but devoid of company, she was able to keep silence. She indicated the hymns, but only sang the first verses. Her frail majesty was more charming for her silence and the melancholy of her smile.

She could not approach Dionys or speak to him. She sought to perceive him, to follow his actions and the expression of his face. An indiscernible, confused jealousy, all the more frightful, ravaged her. She was like a traveler gone astray in a sinister night, pressed all around by hungry wild beasts, a hundred wild beasts whose nature is unknown.

She no longer feared the gods, nor the terrible goddess who watched over her. Her soul was defenseless, even against death.

However, a sort of tranquility came to her toward the end of the day. The hour was about to come for which she had been waiting since dawn, when it would be necessary to sing the solitary hymn in the sacred wood. She would be alone with Dionys.

And it seemed to her that she would extract the sad confidence from her lover. She was not thinking of unhappiness or happiness, but solely tortured by the frightful need to know that had devoured jealous souls for a hundred centuries.

The hour for her departure sounded. She had designated Dionys. And the young man accompanied her among the age-old olive trees. It was one of the ecstatic evenings in which Campania is prodigal, when one no longer feels any other need that to love and to grow. The water is in flower like the earth. The stars project pale wakes over the lake of the sky. It seems that one can see the constellations drifting. The aromal souls of flowers enchant the expanse.

Dehva walked silently beside the Syracusan. The presence of the young man filled her with a sudden bliss, so forceful and so delightful that she annihilated all anterior will within it. She leaned on him, and breathed him in with the odor of darkness.

They approached in that fashion the clearing where the altar of Mnerfa was.

It was surrounded by immense olive trees, the least of which was believed to be two centuries old. They marched enlaced, accompanied by the rumor of cicadas. Their amorous lips encountered one another languorously. Dehva, intoxicated, scarcely perceived the foreign presence any longer.

They reached the limit that Dionys could not surpass without incurring the wrath of the goddess. Then, a slight frisson agitated the young woman, the black suspicion returned and gripped her heart.

In a low voice, she moaned: "I'm suffering from a shadow Dionys—can you not take it away?"

"There is no shadow that can separate me from you," he replied.

She sighed, she could not find anything to say in reply, and, detaching herself, she passed under the shady branches alone. The great clearing opened before her. Ashy reflections trailed over the grass and the flowers there, which permitted her to distinguish, in the center, an olive tree a thousand years old, which neither lightning not hurricanes had been able to fell.

Dehva advanced at a fearful pace all the way to the altar of volcanic stone. Her heart was pounding violently.

She sang in a silvery voice, very feeble at first, which gradually grew louder. She celebrated the intelligent strength of the goddess, victorious over blind Mars, vast Enceladus and the sovereign of the sapphirine sea. She declared her mildness to humans, formed by Prometheus, for the heroes Perseus, Bellerophon and Heracles, for Orestes prey to the Eumenides, and for the fecund birth of the olive tree. She implored it for others, and then, in a whisper, for herself, for her feeble tottering soul and her desire, more ardent than the desire to live.

And she spoke to Mnerfa in a confidential tone, as to a celestial mother, as helpful as Diana was harsh, and who, perhaps, might oppose the anger of the inexorable goddess.

She had stayed longer than she had thought. The passage of a nocturnal bird reminded her of the hour. She returned to Dionys. She went very quietly; a breeze had risen in the trees, which stifled the slight sound of her footsteps.

Suddenly, she stopped, and began to tremble. A few paces away, she had just perceived two enlaced silhouettes. In the gray light, she saw them clearly. She distinguished the movement of their heads. And, recognizing Dionys, she uttered a cry. A great chill passed over her heart.

And she fell to the ground, in a faint.

At the sound, Dionys and Flavia stood up. And the young man recognized, in the starry shadow, the form of Dehva, extended. He uttered an exclamation of anguish. The Umbrian woman, who heart was not hard, was moved. She pushed Dionys, saying: "Go!" And she disappeared into the wood.

The Syracusan was stunned for a moment, and then advanced toward his friend. He knelt down beside her.

Sentiments as vast as the ocean and as soft as evening twilight were agitating in his soul. And his entire adventure, so charming, so bright and so fresh, was represented before his memory like Argos to the dying hero. He saw himself again in the bitter day of misery, when hunger and fatigue were both tormenting his poor body. He heard his plaintive Syrinx proudly singing the indestructible force of Art, and then the pretty silvery voice calling him to the bank of the Volturne. And all the days and all the delightful evenings spent with the old Master and his daughter rose up like a swarm of bees and doves.

It was bitter for him to see unconscious, for love of him, the one from whom all his happiness had come, even his ardent victory over the Umbrian woman. Eros filed him with a tenderness more dangerous than the fury of a wild beast. And with a great sigh he hugged Dehva to his breast and covered her with kisses.

She woke up.

She saw that she was in the Syracusan's arms. Joy and dolor filed her with tears. Her bright arms and her mouth attached themselves to her lover with a savage violence.

She sobbed: "I want to die, Dionys. I prefer the fury of Diana Etrusca and the inexorable Aidonea to the fear of losing you. I love you more than anything on earth and all the gods... Don't push me away... Don't cast your poor little one into despair; everything of her is yours... Your presence has become her life... I love you, Dionys."

He was increasingly moved by that voice, so plaintive and so pretty, with which sobs mingled, the sound of waves upon a rock. She knew that he was even more troubled than on the evening when he had fled toward the river. And from the depths of her little soul, an implacable will rose. She braved Diana and all the menacing mystery of the world and glacial death. She cast her destiny as a plant casts its seed; she precipitated herself toward intercourse like an ambitious soldier into battle.

Astonished, Dionys, submitted to that superior force. And in the grim silence of the wood, beneath the stars of the Swan and the Eagle, they espoused one another in an ardent and convulsive panic.

It was nearly an hour since Dehva had set off for the altar of the goddess. That time exceeded previsions by half. The elders were becoming anxious and suspicious; a subtle fear slid into the heard of old Tarao, but he did not let anything appear. It was him who, reassuring minds, prevented anyone from setting out in search of her; for he feared a peril a hundred times more terrible than wolves or prowlers. His blood was icy, his breast breathless, when the deadly image appeared before him, and he found no repose except in the oath sworn by Dionys.

When the red star of the oxherd was near to the horizon, Aulei, the priest of Diana Etrusca said, authoritatively: "It is not appropriate for us to wait any longer. Let us designate ten men to go in search of the maiden."

"Dehva is pious," the master-potter interjected. "It is not good to interrupt the prayer to Mnerfa; that goddess is just, but she avenges herself cruelly. Let us refrain from offending her."

"We shall not surpass the sacred boundary," said a young potter with muscular arms. "And we shall find the Syracusan to inform us."

Tarao did not continue a dangerous opposition. He only asked, and obtained, to be among the twelve.

Along the route he talked in a loud voice, marching at a slow pace and making tree branches crack as he passed. But the young potter had slipped ahead, as light and furtive as a wildcat. He had keen ears and piercing eyes, and a heart full of hatred against the foreigner, for he coveted the master-potter's granddaughter and was in despair at not attracting her gaze.

A savage instinct led him to take a different path from his companions. He came to the place where Dehva had quit and rediscovered Dionys. And suddenly, he saw that which horrified him, but which he had nevertheless desired. Then he uttered a great clamor.

And the envoys of Veila saw the shame of the holy virgin and the crime of the foreigner.

Old Tarao had not had the courage to go back to his dwelling. He dragged his weary body over the plain. He felt, for the first time in eighty winters, that life had become intolerable to him. He had known all human dolors. His generation had died around him. He had seen the eyes of his sons, daughters and grandchildren glaze. His heart had cried out in distress, his flesh had writhed in despair, but he had always recognized the Beauty in the Misery. And that terrible world had continued to seduce him. He had not wearied of the form of things, of fabulous tales, of the profound art of those who constructed temples, carved gods in marble or assembled all the confused voices of the forest, the ocean and the sighing night in the harmony of lyres, flutes and winged words. And even after the great groans of suffering, he had not been able to help telling himself that a magical splendor sprang from sad souls and dolorous flesh.

But today, he recognized that only those saw reality clearly, one of whom wept and the other laughed at the spectacle to things.

He came, in the ashen night, to the Temple of Diana Etrusca.

That Temple dominated a hill, in an enclosure of lemon trees and oaks. It was built in basalt, square in form, with a double portico, with a harsh and dilapidated, tenebrous appearance. One might have thought it a thousand years old. The fire was continuously maintained on the altar, sometimes by consecrated virgins, sometimes by the priest and his assistants; the rites recalled those of the Roman Vesta, which probably had the same origin.

But the Diana of the vanquished Rasenas, more rustic, was not served by a college of noble virgins, and its regulations had scant refinement. If the fire went out, a fine was sufficient to punish the guilty parties. Virginity could not be demanded after the age of eighteen. But the Etruscan goddess was implacable with regard the violation of the vow, which had to be expiated by the death of the guilty and their accomplices.

The procedure was simple. An intimate visit of the matrons decided the fate of the young woman. The priest immediately pronounced the sentence.

For the accomplice there were only three means of accusation: *flagrante delicto* observed by two or more witnesses, personal confession and designation by the guilty party. One of those three cases determined an unforgivable condemnation; if not, the accused escaped without return.

There could be no hesitation over the fate of Dehva and Dionys.

Tarao, lost under the lemon trees, contemplated the temple of implacable Diana, and a grim hatred rose in his poor heart. He had cherished that temple for its age, because, because it had the form in which people built in the time of the Lucumons and because venerable rites were observed there. He loved, on days of rest to indulge his reveries there and his prayers for the renaissance of the Rasenas. In the great red moons he addressed, confusedly, a prayer to the Life that guided the skiff through the Ether. His beliefs were veiled, numerous, full of contradictions, but nevertheless, he recognized the presence of a Power and a Will.

That night, he rose up against that Power, and he said: "You ought not to take that daughter from the race that adores you, for she is of the purest and most ancient of our blood. That blood flowed not only for our cities, our hearths and our customs, but for you, a thousand times. And she is the last one who can transmit it to the vast Future.

In the distance, were dogs howling. The stars seemed to be illuminated in an immense cavern. And the old man saw the light that preceded the half-moon spreading slowly toward the zenith. He awaited the advent of the star. He watched it surge forth, still indented, like one of the red ships of Odysseus.

He clamored in his despair: "I cry toward your justice, navigator of darkness, somber and violent queen, terror of forests and mountains. I adjure you not to sacrifice my race. It has merited your being favorable to it! You appeared once to save one of my ancestors on Lake Regillus; you cannot deny it today without meriting execration. And my clamor will rise up against you from the depths of the profound earth!"

He spoke, and he wept. He had the vision of his charming child awaiting death, He cursed deadly hospitality.

"Why did you come, stranger with the beautiful tones? Your magical art was accursed and your smile poisoned. You ought to have been swallowed in the Sicilian sea, since you were unable to be propitious either to others or to yourself. And I should have mistrusted you like the gulf of Charybdis, for those whose parents have died in misfortune are baneful."

The moon rose, decreasing as it did so, over the dark blue waters of the firmament. It was rising through a gap between tall trees, the crowns of which were outlined jaggedly like a black and savage coast. The little wrinkles of a spring divided its image; and the silent beauty of the hour still astonished the old man accustomed to admiration. He remembered the delightful Syrinx singing in the depths of his garden. He no longer found any hatred against the foreigner; rather, he felt sorry for him, a victim of fatality more powerful than the force of oaths. It was against the argentine star and the obscure energies that his rancor and his plaint rose up.

"Jealous goddess, whose makes the abysms of the sea and the blood of women raise, protectress of wolves and she-bears, with the inflexible arrow, Diana, Artemis, Phoebe, who killed the great Orion but saved pale Iphigenia.... Silver Selene, Eurynome, mysterious light of Lake Stymphale, weaver of nights with the golden distaff, I implore you for my old age without descendancy!"

Thus he assembled, at hazard, the names of the goddess, and it seemed that she ought to have heard him better; but the star, rising above the highest treetops, cast a glacial light. The old man despaired. He resumed marching through the clear and profound night.

He wandered for a long time, at the hazard of chagrin, talking to the grass, the trees and the water. For his dolor, like his joy, was full of words.

Instinct brought him to the door of the priest Aulei. It was there that the two captives were detained.

Tarao looked fearfully at the blue door, guarded by an earthenware dog. Then he remembered that the priest was the most assiduous of his guests. He saw again the luminous banquets in which Aulei showed so much pleasure in savoring the culinary art; and a faint hope rose in his heart.

He knocked and shouted his name through the door.

But Aulei, fearful of the old man's discourse, did not open it.

Only a faint and plaintive voice replied, and the master-potter fled toward the river.

His thought had departed. A funereal lassitude covered him like the earth of a tomb. He gazed for a long time at the flowing water full of stars, and memories passed by, as confused as the silvery bodies of fish in the abyss or the delicate flight of insects.

In the morning, dolor woke him up. He no longer had the strength to feel it in his heart and his entrails. He uttered a final plaint, and confided his body to the river.

V. The Execution

It was evening, by the light of torches, before the Temple of Diana Etrusca. Dehva and Dionys, covered in black veils, charged with bonds, were crouched before the peristyle.

The people of Veila, including the little children, had assembled around them to charge them with opprobrium. Their faces were uncovered.

They contemplated them, in the beginning, with a kind of surprise. Many felt pity for the maiden, issue of the Lucumons. The elegance of her face was brightened even further in the barbarous light of resin torches. She moved the woman, peaceful adolescents and men who had not suffered from seeing her beautiful. But only the women felt pity for Dionys. Even those who believed, once, that they did not see him with displeasure, sensed a leaven of hatred and that it was good to put a foreigner to death. A thousand furious things, coming from ancestral depths, a thousand souls within them as in the black earth, rose up with amorous jealousy. They were animated by the insult and the outrage, without any need to look at one another or to look at the pale Syracusan.

A deformed adolescent, thin with twisted legs, approached first, who said: "He merits death twice over, who insults both the goddess and hospitality!"

More impatient, the young potter with the bronzed arms shouted: "Death to the Sicilian dog!"

That speech unleashed the clamors of the crowd. Like a waves pursuing waves, the same word ran from mouth to mouth, colliding with the Peristyle and the Sacred Wood: "Death! Death!"

Gradually, the sanguinary thirst rose up as in the soul of a hunter when the dogs howl at the sight of a wild boar or a stag.

The young potter approached Dionys. He spat in his face. And with great cries, animated by the example, the others rushed forward. But the priest of Diana and his assistants had advanced.

"This man belongs to the goddess," said Aulei, "and his execution must not be the game of the multitude. You will give a white kid, young man, for having misunderstood the law."

Dionys maintained an impassive face, like the Sarmate chiefs sacrificed on the eve of a battle. He searched in his soul for the teaching of a Stoic sophist, an old blind man who recited maxims on the harbor wall of Syracuse, but he could not defend himself against the terror of dying; for he, among all men, had experienced the magnificence of life.

It was hard to quit the light country where the Umbrian woman and the brilliant potter's daughter had flourished. The idea that it is excellent to die young, in order not to know burdensome old age, did not bring him any consolation.

Full of fear, he turned toward Dehva. His sole consolation was not to perish without her. He did not recognize himself as culpable; he knew that he had not acted voluntarily, but solely by virtue of the force of the virgin. She alone had led him to futile death. He accused her bitterly, and yet he loved her still. In his anguish, he saw again the delightful garden, the divine flowers, the plains of roses in which his friend had scintillated. It was there that he would have possessed her, without chagrin and without anxiety, if she had been able to wait.

Dehva had no dread. She did not form any gripping image of death. She would have been joyful if Dionys had shown joy, but she saw her lover's despair with despair, and she began to weep when he turned his pale face toward her. She sighed confused and supplicant words. All of her simple little soul was agitated by the distress of beloved eyes, indifferent to the movement and insults of the crowd. But for her too, it would have been unbearable to die without her accomplice.

The blade of Phoebe rose into the firmament. The star rose, almost a streak, among the black branches. It seemed tragic through the smoke of the torches. There was a tremor, which extinguished the clamors one by one, and became silence. An odor of incense rose up.

Aulei straightened his corpulent torso and sang:

"O Diana Etrusca, who reigns powerfully over the Abyss and the Darkness, we fear your image and your long arrows of darkness. Those who have offended you must die before your face, and their crime will not return against your servants."

The executioner advanced with the sacrificial knife; the assistants bound the limbs of the condemned more tightly. Then Aulei said: "You may make a prayer. If it is not excessive or contrary to the gods, we will grant it."

Dionys replied: "Cursed be you and all your generations, and your infamous goddess!"

Dehva repeated those words.

Then the priest said to the sacrificer: "Do what must be done."

The other ripped Dionys' veil.

Aulei cried: "Let the sex that has braved the goddess be cut off!"

The executioner bent down. The Syracusan uttered a frightful plaint and his thighs we seen to be full of red blood.

"Let the mouth that has murmured sacrilegious words be cleaved."

The executioner sliced the mouth.

"Let the eyes that have coveted the sacred virgin be deprived of light."

And the executioner punctured the eyes.

Dionys uttered another great lugubrious cry. His breast heaved; a convulsion shook his shoulders, but he created within himself a resignation as vast as the void.

He heard Dehva weeping, and saying to him: "Forgive me Dionys. I know my crime!"

He replied: "It was fated. Have a little patience. This will finish forever."

The multitude, with sighs and murmurs, were satisfied by the torture. Each individual had become a crowd, in which the barbaric fury of beasts and men agitated. Now they desired to see the daughter of their Lucumons attained in her turn by the sacrificer's knife.

A respiration of joy went up when Aulei resumed speaking.

"Let this one be subjected to the punishment in her turn."

The executioner tore the young woman's veil.

"Let the impure belly be opened."

The red knife lowered. Dehva uttered a soft and feeble plaint.

She was suffering in her flesh, but without fear. She did not cry out when her mouth was sliced and her eyes punctured. She was not unhappy for her own pain: she was dying in Dionys as she had lived in him. And she said again with her bloody mouth: "I know my crime toward you, Dionys."

Meanwhile, the executioner opened the arteries of the wrist, and the priest Aulei prayed for the last time.

"You are avenged, profound Goddess; thus perish and will perish all those who offend you. Protect this people who protect your holy rules; may our wheat be blessed, and the beasts of our pastures, the vines that grow on our hills, and the generation that will be born of ours."

With a gesture, he dissipated the crowd. And until morning, the hill remained forbidden.

When they sensed that they were alone in their agony, Dehva said softly: "I have been fatal to you, and you cannot forgive me."

Somber and fraternal, he said: "There is no rancor in the profound earth..."

Lassitude prevented him from saying any more. Their blood, drop by drop, carried away their life.

They departed toward a dream ever more obscure, which dissipated their thought and their suffering. And they had no longer felt alive for a long time when their hearts stopped, almost at the same time.

SETNE'S WOMEN

PART ONE

I

Setne's palanquin stopped in front of a pylon reddened by the sunset. It was the month of May, near
Thebes; the waters of the Nile was flowing at a low level; the land of Egypt, hard, dry and miserable, was waiting for the flood. Setne rapped twice. A Kushite slave
led him though profound and admirably cool gardens;
the fountains, the odorous flesh of flowers, the rustle of
foliage, the elegance of the wading and swimming birds
among the lotuses on the blue ponds, and the long avenues of sycamores, invited abundant sensualities and
disdainful idleness. The young man perceived granaries,
warehouses and stables, with immense provisions of barley, fruits, beans, onions, dates, olives and oil, for Egypt
was living in the tradition of wealth and nature, the mere
sight of which reassures souls.

Going past the portico and the pylons where the
guards stood, Setne saw the interior courtyards. The cen-
tral one contained the family habitation; it was the least
luxurious. The young chief of the phalanx entered the

third, where the reception apartments were. He heard clear adolescent voices and a harmony of musical instruments.

Through the open door, the great sun was visible, setting over a sea of copper.

"Salutations to you, Setne, son of Raneferka, your presence honors this house," said a young man, the son of the master of the house, as he introduced the leader of the phalanx into an enameled chamber.

A slave filled a syenite vase with pure water and began washing Setne's feet, while he contemplated a red hind fleeing between two sycamores. painted on the wall in a simple style.

When he was purified, Setne went into a spacious room where lamps were already burning for the evening. He went to salute the host and hostess, sitting on high seats encrusted with ebony. Everywhere, there were ingenious tables, ornamented with enamels, curtains woven in Nineveh or Thebes, familiar statuettes, small forms sparkling with color or gilt, and on the ceiling, light and lively lines whose rhythm was as soft as the song of a flute.

After a pause, the chorus and the harmony resumed at the back of the room. The invited guests were gathered around little tables, the men with thick, square ceremonial beards, the women wearing vast wigs strewn with pearls. Young naked slaves were offering wine, cervoise and fresh fruits like fountains. One of them approached Setne and wove gladioli into his hair. A girdle of byssus cloth brightened her loins. She wore no other garment except for long blue-tinted tresses thrown to one side like a mare's mane. Fate had ornamented her for the beds of princes and priests, perfecting her limbs, her small arched feet and her pert bosom, giving her long eyes the menacing softness that dissolves the will of men. She did not seem to have served for amour as yet. Setne shivered with pleasure while she put flowers in his hair. Dreams rose up tumultuously at the friction of the young breasts against his shoulder and her agile fingers, fixing the gladioli.

When she had finished, her eyes could not avoid those of the young man; there was a kind of exchange of youth, energy and beauty. In a voice that could not surpass the hearing of the slave among the singing and the harmony of the music, he said: "Tell me your name and your country?"

"I am Gaila, daughter of Rub," she said. "I was born in the tribe of the Bene-Asher, on the far side of the Red Gulf."

She had a singular voice, a voice that was simultaneously clear and hollow, caressant, anxious and sensual, which harmonized with her gaze. With a shiver, fearful of annoying her, even though she was merely a servile object, he said: "You're a virgin, are you not?"

She replied with simplicity: "I've served many men."

He felt discontented; he was one of those men, rare in those days, who preferred virgin girls to those who had been prepared for amour. However, his ill humor disappeared before the slave's troubling smile. He went on, softly: "May your fate, daughter of the Gulf, be as pleasant as your luminous youth."

"May Aoth heap you with wisdom and renown, Lord, and Païr shield you from ambushes."

He listened to the strange names,[14] which did not displease him. Already, the slave was moving away to ornament a new guest. The sad young chief strove to listen to the harmony of harps, flutes, citharas and a song celebrating wine.

> *Red as somber fire*
> *Wine is the blood of Osiris*
> *The strength of the body and the mysterious movement of the soul.*
> *Voyager of the earth,*
> *Drink the impetuous liquor,*
> *Rejoice in your works.*

Following the advice of the singer, Setne emptied his cup; happy images floated around him.

What is the spirit of courage that dwells in wine? he wondered.

The song was interrupted, and the master of the house proclaimed: "Dear guests, sent by the gods to fill my dwelling with a joy more brilliant than the acacias and the nelumbos, some like to respire in the gardens before the meal, others prefer tranquil games; let everyone follow the desire of his heart!"

Setne preferred the gardens, by inclination and in the hope of finding the slave from the Gulf there, for she had disappeared.

A violet veil was thickening over the tall trees, the pale paths and the fish-ponds. Resin torches were lit, while adolescents sang in a bush to the vivid languor of the nascent stars. The slight turbulence of the wine made

---

[14] Rosny appears to have invented both names, presumably the gods of the fictitious Bene-Asher.

life strange and magnificent for Setne. Amid the pretty bodies of the slaves bearing torches, he searched for young Gaila.

A man he did not know spoke to him.

"By Apis, the freshness is good that falls from the stars of Nut!"

They were on the edge of a pool, where ibises and geese were awake in the torchlight, and large vaporous fish drifted under the diaphanous water. Babylonian trees bathed their elegant and plaintive tresses. The odor of balms, precious woods and flowers that loved darkness accompanied the youthful singing voices ardently.

"In truth," Setne replied. "Ankhi, our host, is expert in feasts. His wine is warm in the heart, his slaves as beautiful as the star of Osiris."

"But above all, he has harmonies of musical instruments that are incomparable from the cataracts to the sea, and singers who could sing before the Pharaoh."

Setne saw then that the stranger was wearing the ornaments of a priest. His false beard was a cubit long, and his face had the disquieting immobility that the habitude of sanctuaries gives.

"Yes, the music is beautiful," said Setne, who was savoring it without really listening to it.

"It's the speech of the world," replied the priest. "It dwells in all the soil and all science. The young woman who is singing to us is a feeble, though very beautiful, part of it. If our hearing were delicate enough, we would hear the rocks and the grass singing."

Setne listened without astonishment, accustomed to the company of priests and their singular discourse.

"That must be true," he said, gravely. But he was still searching for the daughter of the Gulf.

The priest continued: "Be assured that no flower opens without a mysterious song, and that young women are more beautiful who were conceived after a harmony like the one we are hearing now."

Setne, motionless and searching the garden with his gaze, seemed attentive to those words.

"Although you wear the costume of a warrior," said the priest, "you seem to listen with pleasure to a good scribe..."

"She who engendered me was the daughter of a priest," Setne replied.

The other, under the agreeable fire of the wine, rejoiced in those words. "I am Knoum, son of Seba," he declared. "My family have served Ammon for six generations."

Young men came to interrupt them. There was a companion of Setne among them, the leader of a phalanx, with thick lips and burnt eyes, who exclaimed: "Come on! Ankhi is permitting us to hunt the beautiful slaves all the way to the bottom of the garden!"

Setne recognized, by virtue of a feverish chagrin, that he was jealous of Gaila. An ardor like the one that bore him to battles inflamed his temples.

"I'll go with you!" he said, in a harsh voice.

"What!" said the priest, who, being full of discourse, had been counting on the young man to listen to him. "Are you like these others, then?"

Setne had already launched forth, like a young horse among onagers. The priest sighed; he served his speech to the herons.

The young men reached the tall turpentine trees, where the moon, scarcely nascent, slid a milky shadow into the darkness. Without having made any agreement, the fell silent. The impalpable presence of the young slaves gave a voluptuous anguish to the mystery. Suddenly, there was a fleeting frisson, and something white glistened.

"There they are!"

They all ran, sensual and furious, their faces colliding with branches. The moon showed itself amid the columns, vast, bloody and as grim as a Ninevite furnace ignited for a sacrifice. The agile slaves ran toward it; one might have thought that they wanted to hurl themselves into it; but the young men were faster. Setne was the first to reach the fugitives.

They stopped then, fearfully, surrounded. In the ruddy light, their bright procession was the emblem of terrestrial pleasures; their pale veils, descending from one shoulder and only covering a corner of the body, complicated desire. Lust, the hateful spur of amour, breathed in the male breasts.

"Your choice!" said the young men to Setne.

Setne observed the women's faces. Not recognizing the daughter of the Gulf, he remained indecisive. For, simultaneously, vibrant youth sang within him, and, like a mist, the memory of Gaila tarnished his pleasure. The shady sky, the soft earth, the song of the cicadas and the perfume of acacias seemed to fuse within his being and counsel him to sensuality. His thought collided like the confluence of rivers, sands in the wind and ferocious wasps; his desire roared like a lion hidden behind the dunes…again he saw the slave lowering her beautiful sacred eyes toward him.

However, the fear of only pursuing Gaila ravaged his mind. It was in dread of mockery that he said to the nearest of the women: "Follow me."

At first he walked in silence. Then he stopped to examine his captive. She was a Syrian girl with the eyes of a heifer, almost pretty, heavy, with a stupid expression. Se displeased him.

"Have no other slaves been delivered to the men than those who accompanied you?" he asked.

"I don't know, Lord. I think there was one who escaped. She ran faster than us. She's a daughter of the Gulf named Gaila."

They had resumed walking. Between the colonnettes, the glimmer of torches sprang forth, mingling with the moon's rays over the fish-ponds.

"She's not here," said the slave.

He moved her aside gently, and started running toward the turpentine trees. A pale form fled before him. He heard the patter of light feet on the ground. Several times he almost seized a byssus-cloth girdle. Silvery laughter burst firth; he only saw hanging branches or undergrowth. He finally sat down, weary and chagrined, at the end of a pathway, in front of the plain of Thebes.

Then the laughter rang out close by. Raising his eyes he saw Gaila, who was standing next to him. Turned toward the Orient, she had the whiteness of an alabaster Isis; her hair cast a sparkling shadow. He was filled with a tender desire. He tried to draw the slave toward him.

"You didn't catch me," she said. "I came. You don't have any right."

She had leapt back. Already, she was out of range.

"I don't have any right!" he shouted. "Come back."

She came back, and smiled at him. He contemplated her with a sort of dread. He respired her hair, as odorous as the confines of the desert where the first grains advertise the divine pastures.

Then a quiver of jealousy ran through him. "Why don't you want to be mine," he asked, "when you've known so many men?"

"It's my right not to be yours. If you had caught me, I wouldn't have put up any resistance. No one has had me yet with my own consent."

He threw his arms round her abruptly. "And if I wanted you now?"

She laughed, but her laughter was no longer silvery; it was troubled, mysterious and grim.

"What could I do? I'd yield to force once again."

"But that would annoy you?"

"Why should such an expected thing annoy me? I'm not free. So what does it matter?"

He tightened his grip, inflamed by the temptation of the rape. Then, astonished, he dropped his arms. A violent intoxication was throbbing in his flesh. Dominated by Gaila's eyes, he hesitated.

"Ah!" she exclaimed. "The signs didn't lie to me. Our lives are linked. I knew it the moment I had woven the flowers into your hair; the amulet you wear on your breast is the image of my father; the lines of your face are favorable. Your projects will be accomplished and you will be a great war leader."

He shivered. A superstitious credulity invaded his soul. He remembered that the women of the Red Gulf, Egyptian or Arab, have the gift of prophecy.

She saw that she could take a risk. "I'm to be sold in eight days' time," she said, vehemently. "Buy me. I'll render difficult things easy for you. The man who wants to master life needs a woman. She can slip in everywhere, where he would be noticed. A woman is invisible; she can hide like a little insect. I'll also be a concubine devoid of jealousy, for I've been violated by so many men that I can love my master like a mother and be a source of pleasure to him without envying him the joy he takes in other loins..."

He listened, fascinated by an obscure force.

"If I'm no use to you," she said, "you can sell me again; I'm beautiful; I'll become even more beautiful. In any case, you won't sell me again, because I know secrets that are worth twenty times my price. You're the first man that I've wanted for a master; you'll also be the first that I'll serve, not only with my body and my labor, but with my soul. Fate has spoken."

He believed her, either because he was prepared by subtle instincts or because he was driven by the violent desire that he had for her. And that was a great thing in his life. Everything was transformed. His destiny was taking a strange route, of which he had a presentiment henceforth.

"I'll buy you," he said.

He was a man of his word, as much by virtue of innate honor as because he had a need to believe the word of others.

"You won't repent of it," she retorted, lying down at his feet.

The silent softness of the stars filtered between the palms. A heron was perceptible, asleep on one foot, and, sometimes, a fugitive animal, a bird with soft wings, or hairy nocturnal insects; in the distance, the shadow of a pyramid, a pale temple, a papyrus hut and date palms were outlined on the olive plain.

Suddenly, she said: "It's also necessary to ransom my brother, who is a child. I saved him from my family's disaster and I've succeeded in keeping him through my servitude. The stars are in his favor; his presence brings good fortune."

148

The Egyptian made a sign of assent. It was a trivial matter for him to pay the additional price of a small boy; but he wanted to know more about Gaila's origin.

"Who were your people and how did they perish?"

She darted a profound gaze ahead of her.

"My father descended from countless chiefs who all had command of the tribe of Bene-Asher. Our pastures extended from the Orient to the Occident. A river traversed them. There was a plenitude of livestock, forage and grain. We possessed gold, silver, necklaces, pendant earrings, dyed and embroidered wools. The men of Daour came with bronze chariots and horses faster than the southerly wind; they came in the evening, guided by traitors from our tribe. My mother was raped thirty times in front of her sons and daughters. Then her belly was opened and her entrails thrown to the jackals. My father's legs were broken with blows of a hammer; his breasts were torn away with pincers; he perished in the furnace, with his descendancy. Since then, the men of Daour have kept our herds, our weapons and our pastures, and the Bene-Asher live miserably in the desert. My brother will avenge us."

She spoke in a hollow and ferocious voice. The mildness had fled her splendid visage. All the fury of her race was shining in the magnificent flame of her eyes. Setne considered her silently and rejoiced in sensing that she was full of strength. He took her in his arms and collected from her red lips a wrathful kiss that bound him more tightly, and asked: "Is it still to force that you're yielding?"

"No! My submission will be voluntary."

"Will you not take any pleasure in your master's kisses?"

"I will surely take no pleasure in them now...but what does it matter to my master? He ought not to desire to know...."

He did not reply, confusedly dominated by the slave. Voices rose up in the garden, calling the guests for the banquet.

"Come," he said. "If I can, I will talk to Ankhi about it this evening."

"Those who are able to decide promptly," she replied, "are made for great destinies."

II

He was in the banqueting hall, with numerous lights. The delicate art of enamel, and turquoise, ivory and gold scintillated on the sideboards and the tables. Amicable Egypt was incarnate in the paintings on the walls, the contours of the vases, the structure of the seats, the brilliant meanders of the ceiling, the proud boldness of statues and the soft grace of curtains: abundant riches, soft and delicate, such that the ages scarcely knew any more harmonious.

The fumes of the meats were tempered by the elegant scents of fruits, the vivid soul of wines and the spicy aroma of cervoise.

Around little circular tables the beautiful naked slaves circulated again, except for those that the ardor of the young men had made impure. Next to Ankhi, with a very long square beard, and his wife, in the place of honor, stood a mummy with a made-up face, which was not intended inform the guests of the vanity of things, but merely that it is necessary to make haste to enjoy ephemeral benefits. At intervals, with contained voices, the choir of adolescents sang hymns to happiness or satires devoid of bitterness.

"My friends," cried Ankhi, having emptied his cup, and indicating the mummy, "look at this venerable figure. For seven times ten years, the four natures of my father were confounded therein in the same life. That is why we should all divert ourselves before resembling this dear corpse!"

A scribe replied: "May the benediction of Ammon be upon the magnificent host. I compare him to the plains that the divine Nile has known; the sacred barley grows there, wheat, and the mysterious bean that turns underground, the traveling fig and the lotus, in which the gaze of the gods delights..."

Thus spoke the scribe, among the muffled chords of citharas, and the guests raised their full cups.

Setne had thrown away his flowers, in order that Gaila could linger beside him. She wove herbs over his forehead in which tender asphodels shone. She covered his wig with aromatic powders and oil mixed with the philters of spring. He only wanted to drink wine poured by her, more intoxicated by the contact of the slave than the violet liquor.

He rejoiced in the charm that the foreign woman emitted, a mixed charm, like a hatred transformed into desire; one that defends beautiful races against their conquerors. He noticed for the first time how much more flexible than Egyptian hair the mane of hair was that she threw over her shoulder. He said so to her.

"That come to me from my mother's mother," she said. "She was born on the plateau of Iran, far beyond Nineveh. The women, there, and even the men, have hair like this."

A guest called to the slave: "White girl with sharp eyes, be careful to fill my cup! I am like the pool in the land of Kush into which a river pours without being able to fill. As soon as the river stops, the pool dries up. I languish like a heron amid the sands, a dog amid aromatics, a vine in a cistern!"

The man who spoke, with a face as bright as a baker's oven, showed the vast gulf of his fleshy mouth. Gaila filled his cup; he emptied it in a single draught and then held it out again, to the amazement of the others.

"Praise to you, worthy son of the ancestors, of Shesou-Hor who devoured a ram!" cried Ankhi. "Who honors the wine brings good fortune to the host!"

Meanwhile, the hostess and her women went into the reception rooms. The guests followed them; a slave with a clear voice announced mimes and dancers. A thin, grave man was summoned, clad in a blue tunic. He imitated the voice of an onager, the bark of a dog, the cry of a camel, the roar of a lion, the rasp of a saw, the song of a flute, the fury of cataracts and the plaintive grace of fountains. He counterfeited a merchant and a warrior, a wrestler and an acrobat, a hierogrammat applied to his slender writing, a drunkard lurching along the road, a hunchback, a cripple, a stutterer, and a blind man.

The crowd was dying of laughter, but remained insatiable; the mime's gravity multiplied the laughter.

There was a fearful silence when the actor made voices emerge from the corners of the room—a rare trick, which seemed magical, for which a dispensation from the priests was necessary, and which came from the lands of the Chimera, far beyond Mesopotamia and Iran. Many believed that the mime was making souls speak that had been deflected from their great voyage. The women went pale. It was necessary to create a diversion with the dancers; they depicted the acts of amour, the violent languor that excites the senses of men, and the voluptuous sadness that mingles death with pleasure.

The music, veiled at first like an underground stream, expanded with human sighs. The effluvia of sweat mingled with the perfumes, the youthful voices, the harmony of flutes and lyres, rendering hearts tumultuous and mouths savage. Setne stood up in order to look for the daughter of the Gulf, but she was no longer in the room. He took a few paces and found her beside Ankhi, face to face with the mummy, the enamel eyes of which seemed to be laughing at the fugitive pleasure of the living.

"Permit me, divine host, to praise your feast highly," said the young man. "Its beauty is worthy of your great renown."

"The pleasure of the friend is the recompense of the host," the other replied.

The hostess, already on the threshold of decrepitude, added: "It is sweeter to please those whose youth shines like a newly-forged blade."

Their welcoming smiles encouraged the chief, and, drawn by the bold atmosphere of the dance, he said: "In truth, you have gathered everything pleasant that the nourishing earth and the varied labor of men produces…wines rich in illusions, agile dancing and charming slaves. The one that covered me with flowers and aromatics has spoken to my heart. Hosts similar to the gods, I would give for that girl ten five-year-old oxen fattened on the pastures of Khennai! I would also give two oxen for the infant, her brother."

"Chief with the keen eyes," replied the hostess, "before departing to traffic in the lands beyond the Red Gulf, my brother put Gaila in our care. That was forty days before the solstice, nearly two years ago, when the river was preparing to fertilize the crops. Gaila, like a child, paltry and sad, had a taste for death in her eyes, but her face was gracious and full of promise. My brother confided her to me for two years, after which, if he did not inform me otherwise, I could sell her to whomever offered an equitable price. Ten days separate us from that term; I have not received any message for a long time, but navigators have affirmed that my brother is alive, still trafficking beyond the country of Pah. Undoubtedly, he has forgotten his slave, and I can, if it pleases you, exchange her at the next moon for ten five-year-old oxen."

"Your servant," said Setne, tremulously, "can count on your giving him preference, then?"

The hostess contemplated him complaisantly, being already at the age when one likes to please handsome young men other than by means of the body.

"Even if someone offered me six oxen more, I would keep the slave for you."

"You can count on her," he host added, generously. "Her word is as indestructible as diorite stone. Fortunate is the man whose pleasure depends on her promise. Fortunate are all those upon whom she gazes with a favorable eye. I, her spouse, issue of the same father but a different mother, knew that she was the foremost among women, as skillful at governing domains as embroidering fabrics, as ingenious in creating the prosperity of her husband as the strength of his children, adroit in all trade. Blessed be my father for the day he ordered the diversion of our marriage."

Thus spoke the host with moist eyes, moved by the benevolent soul of wine and cervoise.

The woman replied: "It is not arduous to be a good wife to a man who takes pleasure in living with her. His presence is as agreeable as the date-palm on the hill. When Ankhi has gone to his distant pastures, the least of his servants sighs for his return."

She spoke in a voice surer than that of the old man, with the phrases of a scribe; one divined that she had held the scepter throughout her life.

Setne placed his hand on his heart. "As far as the distant nomes, dear hostess, your reputation has spread among the beneficent people of the ibises."

The dance finished; there were a few excessively drunken men here and there who had fallen sleep against the wall; others went out lightly through the vomitoria. The atmosphere was becoming intolerable, overcharged with rancid odors, the smoke of lamps and the intemperate breath of the guests. The wisest gave the signal to depart, naming their porters to the slaves, thanking the lord and his wife with an elegant phrase.

At the limit of the gardens, as Setne was about to go through the pylon, Setne found the priest of Ammon again, who said to him: "Don't forget that if you come to the temple of Thutmose, you will find hosts glad to see you."

Their routes were different, and the young man found himself alone with his porters. It was insupportable for him to be seated; his forehead was hot, his limbs avid for movement and his heart full of agitation. He got down from the palanquin and walked.

On the flesh of Hathor, filling the world from top to bottom, transpierced by the lunar light, the embroidery of the stars seemed more indecisive, of a timid artistry, as if steeped in blue oil. The sighing plain, split like the hide of a rhinoceros, after the violence of the day, was covered then with a cool magic, a fluid light and silence. The river was perceptible between the languid papyrus and the dead grass, and sometimes a hut made of mud and reeds, the nest of some laborer or artisan, on the horizon, the moving eternity of a pyramid or a temple.

Setne was seized by the force of things. One might have thought that his double, abandoning him at intervals, were bringing back the confidences of the expectant plain, the earth ready for the fecund kiss of the Nile, by which it would soon be penetrated. The young man's mingled Ankhi's gardens, the flight of the slaves toward the red furnace, and the daughter of the Gulf bringing her falling mane back over her shoulder. He was astonished by the hazard of days, his existence and that of others, the expanse of Nut, goddess of the sky, and, in a charming vertigo, he sensed himself ephemeral and immortal: a vapor over the grass, a reflection on the water, but also the universe itself, a bizarre and fragile little world without which all the rest would not exist.

III

In the fourth year of the reign of Thutmose III,[15] in spring, the entire valley of Egypt was under arms, full of

---

[15] The reign of Thutmose III is nowadays reckoned to have extended from 1479-1425 B.C., although those dates include a period of regency when the effective ruler was his mother, Hatsheput the Great. In any case, Rosny must be using a vaguer chronology subsequently refined by further archeological discoveries, and he would have been unaware of many of the details of the king's rein that were discovered during the twentieth century. Rosny renders the name Thoutmes, but I have substituted the now-familiar name, as I have substituted Ahmose for his Ahmes and Hatsheput for his Hatasou.

camps where soldiers were maneuvering. Since Ahmose had attacked the Hyksos, or the Shous,[16] in their immense camp at Avaris, the nations had buckled before the kings of Thebes. Amenhotep subdued the land of Kush; Thutmose went as far as the Euphrates; When Hatsheput put a fleet on the Red Sea to seize odorous Arabia, the beauty and the wealth of the earth flowed into the ten thousand cities of the Nile.

The day after the feast at Ankhi's house, in the plain, Setne was exercising one of the admirable phalanges, armed with the long lances that rendered the Pharaohs invincible at that time. They were equally rapid and persistent; their initial impact overturned everything, and, if attacked by an enemy superior in number, they resisted from the shelter of leather and bronze bucklers imbricated like the scales of a fabulous beasts.

The chief led his troop toward the river three times, at the pace of a charge. Then, diving it in two, he made the halves fight one another. He was full of impetuosity, knew the art of making himself feared without making himself hated, and was skilled in tactics.

Before sending his soldiers back to barracks, he spoke about the imminent war, describing the riches of Asia, and concluded: "Those who know how to fight will avoid death and come back with a booty of gold,

---

[16] The word Hyksos, used to describe the rulers of Egypt prior to their defeat by Ahmose I and the beginning of the eighteenth dynasty, probably means "foreign rulers," but the first-century historian Josephus offered a speculative etymology deriving it from Hekw Shasu, meaning "shepherd kings." Rosny's "Shous" is undoubtedly derived from Shasu; numerous late nineteenth century sources in English allege that the Egyptians called shepherds "shous."

silver and precious cloth. The others will leave their remains to rot far from the Sacred Land, Be patient in your labor!"

Those words pleased the warriors; the boldest cheered. The chief dispersed the phalanx, remaining on the drill field alone.

The waters of the Nile would not turn green before June; all the cisterns were dry; on the lugubrious plain, only cacti and aloes grew; all the grass had disappeared; the palm trees extended their suffering little plumes imploringly. But the works of men remained beautiful in the baking atmosphere Thebes of the hundred pylons displayed its magnificent temples, its avenues of fabulous beasts, its little houses of mud and papyrus. All along the river, death showed itself in its harsh and scintillating glory. Old Egypt, drunk on eternity, had heaped up its mummies, hollowed out necropolises, raised the monstrous roofs of pyramids, amorously cleaving, hollowing, sculpting and flowering the savage and divine stone, the indestructible stone...

Marching along the river, Setne soon reached the child soldiers who were drawing bows. Their application was keen, for it was with arrows that they brought down their meals, perched on the crests of walls, on stakes or in trees. For those whose skill was superior the meager repast was divided in portions, with the result that they launched almost as many shots as the unskillful.

Setne paused near the little archers. They reminded him of his natal nome, the brilliant land where he had guided troops of children into the desert. His glory had extended to neighboring villages, for he succeeded in his enterprises. His father explained to him ambushes in the solitude, the cunning of beasts and the art of camping on cold nights.

The chief saw again the bright morning hours, the grass breathless in the sun, the crepuscular beasts, and the russet predators sleeping on the sand.

He was astonished that his life had been so pleasant. As he was dreaming, he saw one of the children, the smallest, sit down, arrogant and discouraged. He recognized him; it was Thutmose's own son, whom the king had condemned to the severe life of soldiers. For the greater part of the day he exercised with the others, and only resumed royal life at the hour when the shadow of the pyramids was double their height.

Setne approached the prince with a tremulous heart, because he believed in the real divinity of the race that had hunted the Shous. The child's beauty, fixed and severe, the charming ennui of his long eyes, the precious grain of his skin made him the statue of a young, sad god: thus the immortal guests in the slumber of sculptures dreamed.

By virtue of an invincible impulse, the chief spoke the child.

"Why have you abandoned your work, son of the gods?"

The child contemplated the man with a proud gravity. A certain suffering was transparent in his red mouth and the wrinkle of his forehead. The chief's gaze, full of a scintillating mildness, acted on the young soul.

"I can't do it."

"Let me try your bow."

The royal child handed over his weapon. The chief extended it, evaluated its resistance, and said: "You have to aim a hand's breadth above the sachet..."

The child took the bow, took aim, and hit the target. Then his face cleared and a smile appeared in his somber eyes. "With you," he said, "I'd become skillful." He added, with grace: "I would also obey you without displeasure."

Opening the sachet, he took out a papyrus stem baked in the oven, honey and a barley-cake. He ate swiftly, his eyes cheerful. The officer was about to depart when the child cried: "Wait!"

Among servants and followers, Princess Aoura,[17] Thutmose's sister, was seen advancing. Setne wanted to withdraw, but the child seized him by the arm, with strength and determination.

Aoura was already nearby. The young man adopted the pose of a supplicant before the gods, for she too was the daughter of Theban kings and similar to the immortals.

Grave and mild, she listened to the little prince speak to her about his friend, and then turned to Setne and asked: "Where do you come from and what is your birth?"

The chief raised his eyes. He sensed his heart beating like a miner's hammer against the walls of a quarry. He had not seen a more elegant form in the depths of temples and holy necropolises. In the shade of flabella, Aoura's face, powdered with delicate colors, was delimited by a pure and proud line; her eyes concealed the magic of the starry Nile; her bearing had the flexibility of young date-palms in flower, and each of her gestures evoked the delicate frissons of antelopes, reeds and tremulous fountains.

---

[17] This character is fictitious, but Aoura is cited in some nineteenth-century sources as an alternative name for Avaris, the city of the supposed shepherd kings, and Rosny might well have found it there.

"Divine princess," the chief replied, "I am Setne, son of Raneferka, who commanded twelve phalanges in the army of Hatsheput. I count among my ancestors Kheren, to whom King Ousortesen gave one of his daughters. My race long possessed the privilege of living near the throne, but the domination of the Shous debased us. I was born in Tanis."

They looked at one another; the ardent and generous visage that had pleased the child pleased the young woman. Virginal but impure, she was ignorant of nothing of which beautiful, expert and desirable slaves could inform young woman. Only the respect and dread that her brother Thutmose inspired in her had prevented her from delivering herself to men. She sensed her heart indulgent and her flesh sensual before the warrior with eyes of flamboyant shadow. And Setne's soul melted; the earth that bore Aoura appeared as magnificent as the flesh of Nut strewn with stars; he breathed in the incense that the byssus robe exhaled as a navigator breathes in the saffron of an inaccessible coast.

"I will mention your name to the omnipotent lord, your king and that of the Sacred Land" said the princess.

"For having seen your divine eyes," he murmured, "I will not have been engendered in vain by my mother."

Aoura smiled and passed on. For a long time after she had disappeared, he was still shivering, like a date-palm on the hills of Lydia, in the nurturing season when the trees respond to one another across space.

Two images, by turns, made his flesh burn: one with imminent sensuality and the other of anguishing sweetness. The slave and the princess embalmed the beauty of the world for him; they filled it with a mystery more desirable and terrible than the arcana by means of which the priests boasted of enchanting the earth, the sky and the waters.

IV

Setne followed the avenue of sphinxes with profound smiles toward the great temple of Ammon. The sun, already in the middle of its course, was violent and terrible; the sphinxes were slowly extending their violet shadows. After the propylon there was a further avenue of sphinxes, a further extent of silence, enigma and anguish. At the second portal, having spoken to the guard and shown a papyrus, Setne crossed the formidable threshold; he found himself in the hypostyle hall. It was comparable to the temple of the Liban that ancient nature had constructed with cedars six thousand years old, but the trees were made of granite. Countless slaves had hauled them along the river and rolled them over the plaintive ground; subtle and patient artists had eternized therein the impassive figures of gods and pharaohs, or caused their sacred flower to surge firth. The light floated, stirring and cold, mystical, motionless and sacred. A man appeared, as thin as a scarab among fig-trees, and Setne recognized Knoum, son of Seba. His linen garment, dyed crimson, shone between the columns; he advanced with long strides.

"You have come," he said. "May the benediction of Ammon, illuminator of space, destroyer of shadows, cover your heart and your race."

"Priest, equal of the brilliant manes that have triumphed in the Amenti, as knowledgeable as Thoth, the divine scribe, my respect lies before you like the shadow before the palm tree."

Thus they greeted one another, in the fashion of the ancestors, and then the priest, in a familiar tone said: "You shall hear men learned in the secret sciences; you shall see beautiful you women, as befits your sparkling eyes. You may first, if you wish, request the favor of the god; he is more propitious in his temple, the finest that the kings have erected. It pleases him to dwell here and to lend an ear here to the prayers of men."

They approached the sanctuary, but it was only permitted to the young man to perceive the darkness from which the god descended. On the edge of the shadow he said: "Triple sovereign of the world, divine son of your own works, father and mother of the astonishing power sustaining the sky over the nurturing earth, vanquisher of time, space and death, resplendent voyager, issue of Nut, who is reborn every day on the sacred horizon, listen to the cry of my soul, aid me toward the mountains of the eternal life."

He prayed, and the priest listened, with approval.

"My son, you have said the things that it is necessary to say. You may now savor in peace the wine, hydromel and good nourishment that are appropriate to rejoice the heart, and the wise words that fortify the mind."

They went along shady corridors. They passed through pylons, went along the edge of the sacred lake, traversed avenues and reached a house in which human voices could be heard. In a large hall, well guarded against the violence of the daylight, figures could be seen rendered more venerable by large wigs and square beards. Almost all the men wore sacerdotal costume; their mild severity was illuminated by the presence of young women, the brightness of cups, blue tables, enamels and opened stones.

A young priest who had returned from a voyage was recounting the prodigies of the land of Kush.

"Beyond the mountains of Haru there are men with manes. They have the feet of onagers, the strength of a lion and the voice of a buffalo. They nourish themselves on the bark of trees, the fur of bears and black stones as hard as iron. They are afraid of water, which they do not cross; they make alliance with those who know the words that it is necessary to say, which destroy the dragons that no Kushite dares to resist..."

The narration charmed the audience. The naïve face of the young priest increased their credulity. None was desiccated by study, even those who doubted their own science, for the marvel of the world, the unknown of the habitable world, had no precise figure for their imagination.

"Have you seen these dragons, of which it is said that they can strangle a hippopotamus?"

"I have seen a dragon pass by, in a hamlet, in the evening twilight. The howling of the dogs and the fear of the camels had alerted us to its approach. We were enclosed in the chief's house; we perceived the monster through a gap in the wall. It was as stout as a cedar, two hundred cubits long. It walked on a thousand feet and exhaled smoke; its ardent mouth was open; two men could have stood within it. The earth dried up as it passed..."

"The work of Nun is prodigious," remarked an aged priest. "It is said that there is a land of flame beyond the three gulfs. The beasts there are as large as pyramids; they devour the clouds that come from the sea. My father saw a thousand red elephants pass by there, which rose up all the way to the sky.

Knoum spoke in his turn.

"Men only live by the benevolence of the gods. One day, perhaps, when impiety has increased, the monsters will be unleashed and will destroy our descendants.

The old priest went on: "Words are stronger than the monsters. It is by means of the formulae that men enchant the entire earth. With the formulae, one can reach as far as the gods. A few words set an army on the march; others expel the plague or cause the wind to blow over dormant waters. A phrase inscribed by a hierogrammat transmits testimony to posterity. There is an arcanum hidden in the necropolis of Sais; the men who can discover it will know the significance of the sea and the mountains, will command the migratory birds, cause the mysterious beasts to come that dwell in the depths of the abyss. The symbols are full of force and give empire to men who are able to make use of them..."

Everyone looked at him, avidly, for they believed, mutually, that they possessed secret sciences. Apart from legends learned in common, they only set out enigmatic phrases full of ingenious appearances, only bold regarding the news brought by travelers, the reports of men of war and foreigners.

The old priest added: "It is by means of words that the world emerged from Nu, and the power of the gods consists of knowing the language appropriate to all things. All things can be understood. The most immobile and the most inert have an understanding that awakens when one intermingles the figures and the words that correspond to their soul. In the same way that it is sufficient to know the horizon and the signs of the route to direct oneself in the terrible desert, so, in order to secure the obedience of the grass, the furious ocean, the wind burned by the sands, the divine waters that flow from the mountains, ferocious beasts, gulfs and darkness, it is sufficient to know the formula."

Everyone approved. A pale man, whose cheeks were hollow and his ardent eyes red—for he had lost his eyelashes—replied in a dull voice: "Father, equal of the sages who found the art of sculpting stone, your discourse is worthy of your great renown. Nevertheless, is it true that it is speech that is endowed with these great virtues—or, at least, that alone? Does a word have a power of its own, or only a power that has come to it by delegation, like the command delegated by the master to a slave? It is true that a word sets an army on the march, but note that the word in question is Assyrian for a Ninevite, Kushite for a man of Kush. The word, in truth, follows the knowledge, but does not precede it; with the consequence that the arcana for enchanting the ocean, the earth and the mountains can only exist if one knows what the ocean, the earth and the mountains are."

Everyone was astonished by this speech, imagining its mistrust. The old priest replied, severely: "Do you doubt the power of formulae?"

The pale man darted a sharp glance at the assembly. Dread and challenge strayed over the bold mouth. "I venerate the power of formulae; an ignorant man can succeed in doing astonishing things by following a precept that he does not understand. If the gods wish it, they can give us arcana above our intelligence and put in our hands a power whose source is inconceivable to us. But I believe that the gods themselves only create arcana regarding things are first known to them. Given that, it is dangerous to believe that we can find words capable in themselves of governing mystery; it is first necessary to penetrate the mystery. If not, we will speak at hazard."

"Son of Sakar," said the old priest, in a solemn voice, "it is written that the word created the world. If you are raising yourself above the sacred science of the old scribes, who transmitted it for a thousand generations, you are wandering in darkness, like the traveler who penetrates without a torch the land of caverns that is said to open at the sources of the Nile, which descend for ten thousand cubits under the mountains, and where men dwell whose eyes project their own light before them."

"I will be silent if you command it, venerable father, but I cannot believe that speech is the origin of things, any more than that a child is not the issue of a father."

"A father can be engendered by a son. It is sufficient that, in the world of proofs, the shadow of a son returns to incarnation before the shadow of the father."

Setne listened in silence. His mind was no stranger to such things; he had once learned, among the scribes, to savor a subtle reasoning, a tortuous hypothesis and an unexpected argument. But formulae, more often than not, had appeared to him to be empty and tedious. He gazed sympathetically at the priest with the bald eyes.

"In truth," he said, "I believe that speech is only the link to knowledge."

The men nurtured on the wisdom of the temples turned to the stranger; a discreet disdain appeared on their faces. But Heth, the son of Sakar, chagrined not to encounter any soul that wanted to understand him, smiled mildly at the soldier.

The old priest cried: "Chief with the keen eyes, fear speaking lightly about the art of words, fear being similar to the imprudent laborer who claims to be imitating the sculptors in stone."

"I am not entirely a stranger among you, divine sage, for I was nurtured in the sanctuaries, and Kebr, son of Rous, priest of Isis, taught me to trace signs and read secret things. Nevertheless, I incline before your wisdom."

At that moment the slaves brought silver cups, and Setne, turning round, saw a young woman clad in white wool at the back of the room, who was looking at him. Then he breathed more rapidly; he no longer had any difficulty in being silent, having fallen back into the same disturbance that Gaila and the princess of Thebes had thrown into his soul. And while he raised his cup, astonished by the burning softness that enchanted the world for him, he felt a slight frisson run over his skin, and feared being the victim of the gods who sow furious amour and envelop young women in an excessively desirable beauty.

The voice of the son of Sakar interrupted him in his reverie.

"Young chief, I wish you renown and victory! That wish comes at its time, for we know that King Thutmose is about to resume the war against Nineveh."[18]

Setne shivered violently. His soul retraced the awakenings under the tent, the long marches along rivers or in steppes as interminable as the sea, the resonance of trumpets, the noise of dromedaries, and the formidable uncertainty of the morning of battles. He also perceived the bliss of halts, in which fatigue becomes a mildness, the charm of springs and their sensuality, the joyful

---

[18] Thutmose III had a great reputation as a warrior and undertook several campaigns in Mesopotamia, but is not known ever to attacked Nineveh or fought against its army.

howls of victory, the forgetfulness of oneself amid the flight of arrows and the clash of swords.

"Is that true, scribe equal to Thoth? Shall we see the king's enemies fleeing over the resounding plain again?"

"The news will be proclaimed tomorrow in the camps of Thebes, and borne by messengers all the way to the lands of Kush."

Setne rejoiced in his heart; his eyes were resplendent.

"Do you like war, my son?"

"If they had not liked war, would our ancestors not be bending their knees to the Shous? I like wars that disperse those who lie in wait for Egypt and who, without the strength of our hands, would fall upon her like a mongoose on a cobra."

Heth replied: "If you would like to come to my house, I can enable you to read a papyrus on the art of combat; one can take account therein of the character and the armament of various peoples. The man who wrote it, Reben, son of Thouai, was fortunate in his enterprises; he led a fleet on the Red Sea, merited the favor of Hatsheput the Great, and died young without having known defeat. May your fate be similar to his, save for the brevity!"

Setne felt a great desire to see the book; he replied softly: "Your generosity touches my heart. I will rejoice in seeing Reben's book and listening to your words."

At that moment, a shadow slid toward them. Setne saw the young woman clad in white wool. She stared intently at the young man, and disappeared at the back of the room.

"She is as beautiful," said Setne, "as the nascent flower of the nelumbo."

"She is the daughter of a priest of Abydos," Heth replied. "She is knowledgeable, gentle and pious. She lives her beauty!"

His eyes still fixed on the door, Setne was thinking less of war and fearing the departure. Amour resounded within him more loudly than the clamors of battle. He knew the delightful emotion of ambushes, the sensuality of dread expelled by wrath, the frenetic pleasure of all bounding together, with the same courage, toward peril. But he sensed the superior sweetness of confounding himself with women; their beautiful eyes dissolved his strength, he palpitated in the soft pride that they exhale, as agreeable as vanquishing the soldiers of Nineveh.

"If you want to come one day," the priest added, "I will send a slave to fetch you, for the route that leads to my dwelling is tortuous."

Setne accepted. He stayed for a while longer listening to the words of the scribes. Although he was distracted by his memories, he was interested by the discussions, for he had the soul that is often found among conquerors, little made for philosophical invention, but apt to understand many things and to be animated for them.

When he withdrew, the moon had risen over Thebes. It was passing slowly over the temples and obelisks, like a nacreous wheel. Setne's flesh was vibrant with an insupportable desire. Gaila, in particular, excited his senses, for the obstacle that separated him from her was not invincible; but the memory of Aoura added a magical languor to his disturbance.

He was marching impatiently when he heard a clear voice calling to him. At first he only saw a shadow in front of a papyrus hut among the fig-trees. Advancing into the light, however, a young woman appeared, clad in white wool, tightly sculpted by her robe. Her forms

170

were as vibrant as the voice of flutes in the young rice-fields, her hips troubling. A strange smile stimulated the softness of her face, sheltered beneath a diaphanous pshent. Her small feet were shiny, cared for by skillful slaves.

With a tremor, he recognized the daughter of the priest of Abydos.

"Are you calling me?" Setne asked.

"Yes, I called to you," she said, "but don't imagine that it was at hazard; I know you well. Before encountering you among the priests, I saw you commanding your phalanx near the great pylon; I was avoiding the baking sun thereunder. I can invite you into my dwelling without shame. If you're submissive to the laws of Hathor you will want to adore the goddess in her servant. I'm beautiful. My bosom is as soft as a nelumbo flower, my loins very well made, the kiss of my mouth more intoxicating that the wine of Mageddo. Come! You will see me—slowly, if you know the harmony of amour, or springing in a flash from my garments if your ardor is more impetuous than refined. What you do not know yet, I can teach you, and what you know will appear new to you with me. In the temple of Abydos there is an arcanum that teaches the divine caresses; I have seen that arcanum and you will take me for several women. Come in! The night is ardent, the moon amorous!"

He hesitated momentarily, but then he was frightened by his solitary bed and followed the courtesan. She led him silently into the papyrus house. A door opened to an embalmed chamber. A slave lit three lamps. Vases shone like beautiful fish in the moonlight. He perceived, on a table, pots of antimony, powder, henna and perfumes that add the sensuality of plants to that of a woman.

"Would you like fruits, cervoise or my lips?" the woman asked.

She leaned forward. He tasted a young mouth that melted against his own.

"Sit down, if you prefer the spectacle of my person first."

She took off her pschent; her face appeared in the full light, painted with delicacy, the eyes sparkling with kohl, the fresh lips like the roses of fire and water that open in the matinal hills. Then she showed her rounded cleavage and her beautiful arms polished like onyx. Her breasts sprang forth like lovely vases with amber tones.

She fled. "Wait!" she said.

And she reappeared in a tunic of byssus, as transparent as the vapors that descend by night over the Nile. All of the mystery of her body was visible, and yet she remained enigmatic and irritating. She mimed amour in accordance with the rites; she sketched a naïve and tender appeal that went back to the times of King Menkaure.

Desire immediately agitated Setne. Once again he wanted to know the mystery of the woman. Closing his eyes, he held the courtesan against his heart. He thought of Gaila and the sister of Thutmose while the supple body yielded to his embrace.

The caress left him sad.

"There is a shadow over you," said the courtesan.

He admitted that he was troubled by memories.

"I feel sorry for you," she said. "Slavish amour is a miserable malady. It links us to another like a condemned man to the stake. Men who are young and strong, like you, brought up for war, ought to taste all mouths. They are diminished in being fixed. Their desire ought to be as changing as their stride. They should go from woman to woman and live in triumph. And the woman too is wiser who, like me, has known thousands of men...."

"Are you not the slave of the passer-by?"

She began to laugh. "Make no mistake, soldier; I can choose. No man penetrates here who has not excited my desire or my curiosity. My needs accommodate to circumstances. I'm a patient and resolute huntress. If I happen to take an old man or a poorly made man, it's because they have some singularity in them. There are old men whose education is inappreciable, and infirm ones full of the god of sensuality. And besides, it makes me better able to love the encounter of men made in your image."

He was not listening. He was bitter and chagrined. His soul was suspended between war and amour; he was full of fermentations with no outlet, at the moment of existence when strength becomes a torture because it seems futile. Silently, he put a little turquoise on the courtesan's table. She smiled.

"I would have preferred to give you more intoxication and not receive that stone!" she said.

He got up and left. As he drew away into the night she called after him: "Leave the amour that lasts to laborers and merchants. Thutmose will give you women of Syria and Kush in abundance. The man whose heart is not free will be the laughing stock of the enemy."

V

On the three days that followed, Setne fund the son of Thutmose on the drill-field; he taught him again to draw the bow. The child became more adroit; he brought down his repast without difficulty, and took pleasure in aiming at other targets. He became attached to Setne; he waited for him impatiently at the end of the maneuvers; but the Tanite was only thinking about the princess; his ardent eyes were fixed on Thebes, hoping to see a white litter appear, shaded by the flabella with curly fringes.

Aoura did not appear. The chief despaired of seeing her again. He spent entire evenings prowling around the royal gardens and along the river bank, dazed by dreams.

He did not believe that he was in love with the princess. Such a thought had something frightening, mad and criminal about it. In any case, he did not recognize any of the emotions that accompany amour. It was not the possession of the young woman that he seemed to want, but merely her presence. No image of a caress or kiss troubled the desire he had to perceive the small proud silhouette that had appeared before the Theban camp. He was doubtless more likely to believe it a magical influence, the will of a god or a soul, when an amour so foreign to the men of Egypt came, than to attribute it to the divine quality of the descendants of Ahmose.

He found what he experienced for Gaila more explicable; the memory of the feast burned his senses. Each of the slave's attitudes was fixed within him; desire ravaged his flesh and growled in his breast like a malevolent beast.

The greeted the morning of the sale with joy, and the sun was still far from its zenith when he set forth along the Nile. The terrible plain, breathless in the harsh light, seemed condemned to eternal dryness; the implacable sky opened like a devouring maw, and motionless Egypt, durable and sad, awaited the kiss of the solstice, when its cisterns would be delighted and its mud would howl with joy. Then the father of life, the great red Apis, would embrace his conquest, his patrimony attached to the desert, and the shadoofs would precipitate green life all the way to the summits of the hills.

Setne reached Ankhi's dwelling. He went through the pylon briskly, traversed the courtyards, and was received by the hostess. She was not wearing a wig; her head was as bald as an aged she-monkey, but her eyes were still beautiful, soft and despotic.

She smiled at the visitor.

"I would be anxious," she said, "if I were your mother. You put too much ardor into your actions. It is thus that one emerges from one's caste to command men, but it is thus, above all, that one runs toward death."

"I serve Death," said the young man. "I have seen her wings on twenty battlefields. There is nothing redoubtable about her."

"No," replied the hostess, "there is nothing redoubtable about her; she is beautiful and consoling for those who are ready for judgment."

Her gaze, fixed before her, seemed to be seeking the great reaper. She sighed. Like almost all Egyptians, she had a faith so perfect that eve her flesh no longer revolted against death. She glimpsed the divine realm of the soul, the Amenti, the gods of the South and the North, the sources of the Nile, the boat of Osiris; she ornamented with the splendid memories of her youth the land of death.

"You've come to buy your slave?" she said. "Take care! She's proud, mysterious, and too subtle; she'll read your heart, she'll be able to use you if you don't defend yourself." She added: "But she's not ingrate, she knows how to keep her promises; thus, you'll get good or evil out of her, in accordance with your actions. I'm hiding nothing from you. Reflect. And have no fear of offending me by leaving her with me; I won't be embarrassed by her. But if you want her, you must pay her price."

Setne paid little heed to the loquacity of the good hostess. His desire was becoming insupportable. "I want her!" he cried

"I don't know of any flaws in her," the old woman went on. "She's beautiful and strong. She can weave linen and cover it with embroidery; she's skillful in working with gold and silver thread. The men who have known her have taken pleasure in her possession. I can't sell her for less than ten five-year-old oxen."

"That's the price I offered."

"Yes, but you'd been drinking cervoise and wine; your soul was speaking within you. You might have forgotten your offer, for I don't suspect you, son of Raneferka, of being like the merchants of vile caste who take back their word. Since you accept, I'll have Gaila come; it's necessary that you look at her again. We don't sell anything that hasn't been seen by the purchaser."

The hostess gave the order to summon Gaila. Light footsteps were heard; the Bedouin slave showed herself in the doorway. She was not entirely unclad, as on the day of the feast. A narrow linen tunic enveloped her beauty, marking the rhythm of her gestures with a new elegance. Her hair was still thrown back to one side, like the mane of a mare.

She smiled at the Tanite and stood there waiting, full of an enigmatic, disquieting charm.

"Take off your tunic," said the hostess.

Gaila appeared in her magnificent nudity.

Gently, the old woman turned her around, showing off her limbs, her breasts and her shoulders.

"She's perfect, you see. Her flesh is full and firm, her skin fresh and very delicate. Although she has served, no child has deformed her belly or caused her breasts to sag."

The examination made Setne impatient; it displeased him to see the old hands passing over those charming forms. He said: "I recognize that the slave is exempt from flaws. Have the deed of sale written. Don't forget, dear hostess, that you are also ceding me the infant, Gaila's brother, for two oxen. I will bring my witnesses."

"The deed will be ready tomorrow."

He gave her a gold ring as a guarantee; in accordance with custom, the ring would belong to the vendor if the purchaser withdrew from the sale. The Egyptian woman, judging that such a ring was worth several months of a slave's work, allowed Setne to take Gaila away.

He had carried off the slave as a lion carries off a gazelle to its cavern. When he had her alone, he buried himself in her sensuality. He did not see that she remained almost motionless in his arms. The folly of Hathor obscured his soul. But in the end, a pleasant lassitude relaxed him.

The flesh of the charming slave palpitated softly against his own; when he opened his eyes he saw a delightful smile, and the tenebrous gleam of eyes. It was at that moment that she asked him: "Don't you want to tell me your secret?"

He opened his mouth, but could not speak. He was ashamed. Even though she was his slave, it seemed to be insulting her beauty to confess a desire for another woman.

She saw his embarrassment, and said, politely: "Have I not said, my master, that for you I will do everything gladly? My words are not vain. If it is necessary to serve you with regard to another woman, don't hesitate to ask it of me."

The more he heard Gaila, the more he was convinced that he could tell her everything. His tongue was loosened. He told her about the extraordinary amour that was blossoming in his soul.

She listened with a vague smile. Familiarized with every human adventure, nothing had astonished her for a long time. In any case, having fulfilled a chimerical project herself, she was ready to do anything and hope for anything. Nor did she share Setne's respect for a royal person. In her vagabond slavery, she had known the weakness of Egyptian women, and that even priests and monarchs did not escape their treason.

Finally, she responded: "You bear the accomplishment of your desire within you. Are you ready for anything? I'm not speaking about courage, for those eyes answer for that, but the work of patience, of cunning?"

"I'm ready for anything."

"Then you shall know the princess of Egypt," she said, with a long gaze. "I don't know whether you'll have her for an hour, or seasons, but you'll possess her..."

She was speaking at hazard, persuaded that the first condition of success is a violent faith. By virtue of a phenomenon proper to her race, she gave herself the illusion as she prophesied, ready to risk her life in the game, rich in audacity, energy and wily prudence.

She went on: "To begin with, you can do nothing by yourself. It's necessary to obey me with confidence. I know the places where the princess goes, and I'll put you in her passage. You'll have the attitude that I shall indicate to you, and you won't make a gesture without making me party to it very exactly."

She considered him with a kind of malice. And he listened to her, full of a pleasant attention, with such a keen sentiment of feminine subtlety that he came to find his amour less extraordinary. He also sensed that she would be a sincere ally, in spite of her youth, her beauty and her voluptuous flesh.

"And what do you want in exchange for your devotion?" he said, after a long silence. "For the pleasure I obtain with you pays the price of the slavery..."

She raised a hard face. From the depths of her soul, a cry of murder rose. She heard her father roar in the furnace, her sisters howl at the rape of the nomads, her mother uttering a great sinister plaint. She saw herself again, among the yellow reeds, and the soft beasts, holding her silent little brother against her breast, while the blood of warriors streamed over the pasture and a fire of joy rose up before the trembling stars. Then she relived the terrified flight, and the long slavery in which she had submitted to the lust of men, and known all the forms that they give to intercourse.

"After the murder of my family," she said, "I was captured in the desert of Kenner by merchants of the Gulf. I knew the first man by violence and pain. Until then I had only lived in terror and blind hatred. The rape enlightened my soul. I made an oath to reconquer the land of Zoum and to enable my blood to reign over the tribe off the Bene-Asher, now wandering in the land of sand. Death alone will release me from the oath. Now, I have need above all that my brother lives and grows. Without the lust of masters I would have lost him a hundred times; I would like to be sure that he will never be separated from me."

"Your brother will grow in my shadow," he replied, gravely.

She kissed his hand. Then, stirred by hope, and that hope filling him with ardor, he put his mouth once again to the lips of the slave, in which an inexhaustible voluptuousness sparkled.

VI

Aoura was bored. She was no longer interested by the beautiful slaves that King Thutmose had given her, and the amour of the male was still forbidden to her. Her breast rose at the sight of well-constructed men, her nights were stormy. In vain, a Memphite whom she had adored and a daughter of Lydia with the contours of Isis offered her their caresses; she no longer took any pleasure in them.

With a less elevated sentiment of duty she could have seduced one of the young men who served in the court. She respected the gods, the law and custom, and, in sum, she was virtuous; but virtue was still unaware of modesty and chastity. Thirty centuries later, Aoura would have been a chaste young woman. Under the eighteenth dynasty, nothing similar was demanded. On the other hand, duty required royal daughters to obey the Pharaoh and not to know a man without his consent. Religious and loyal, worshipful of the will of her brother Thutmose, Aoura was incapable of transgressing the commandments. She had the merit of that; her curiosity and her desire became insupportable.

That day, she had dispersed her slaves and she was sitting in the shade of a tamarind. Three fountains were falling upon the grass and nourishing a basalt basin in which sacred birds were parading their luminous bodies. The trees, to which the soil of Egypt is harsh, extended their green freshness and their elegant lines everywhere.

There were so many roses that the stones of the palace were impregnated with their perfume.

But Aoura was bored, indifferent to the luxury for which so many men had perished. She remained motionless for an entire hour; she would have fallen asleep with sadness if she had not been due to go to the temple build by Amenemhat III,[19] where she like to pray to the soul of the king and the god of Thebes. She went there often; the place had been more favorable to her wishes than any other. She also liked it because of the route that it was necessary to follow, and for an old sacred lake whose flowers were prodigious.

She called her slaves. The Memphite and the Lydian immediately came running, but she refused their services and sent for her palanquin, her black servants, her porters.

Gaila was waiting on the road to the Amenemhat temple, amid the wild vines, on the edge of the ancient lake where the nelumbos raised their winged corollas. A temple ruined by the Shous was visible, which might have dated back to the days when the Egyptians did not yet make use of metal. It displayed red columns, porticoes of porphyry, whose inscriptions time and the blows of men had not been able to ruin entirely, with the figures of thickset men, and a lion designed by a naïve chisel but very veridical. Trees and flowers grew in the gaps between the columns or on platforms filled with earth, and hardly anyone ever approached the grim place, where reptiles battled with carnivorous birds. Sacred Egypt, rich in symbols and in svelte figures, in simple, proud, eternal lines, was scarcely recognizable in

---

[19] Amenemhat III was a pharaoh of the twelfth dynasty, now thought to have ruled from approximately 1860-1814 B.C.

that dense ancestral work, in which the life of men and beasts seemed too submissive to reality. No one was any longer encountered there but old sorcerers, women who read fortunes or equivocal foreigners.

Gaila waited patiently for the passage of Princess Aoura. Clad in fiery red, with a grasshopper and a serpent made of green stone, in her hair, she was holding a figurine in the shape of a crescent in her hand. By those signs, the prophetic women of the far shore of the Red Gulf were recognizable, to whom the Egyptians—especially Egyptian women—attributed an accurate prevision and the knowledge of redoubtable arcana. Sometimes they were hunted, sometimes they were left some liberty. Thutmose, to whom one of them had made an accurate prediction, was presently covering them with his protection. And Gaila was counting on attracting the attention of the princess, who was due to go, that morning, to the temple of Amenemhat, as she did at the beginning and end of every lunation.

The day was ardent. Herons on one foot, sentinels of melancholy, stood in the shadow of the willows or at the points of creeks of promontories. A phoenix and pink flamingoes rose up lightly toward the sky; the quiet water, full of islets were animals and plants swarmed, filled the profound landscape with life.

Thinking about her native land, Gaila detested that quietude. Her soul rose up rancorously against the tranquil beauty of the land of Egypt. But an interior vision made her smile; she took pleasure in the memory of the master in whom she had put her hope.

She shivered, her penetrating gaze swept the sea and recognized Princess Aoura among her followers and servants. Then the nomad seized a little flute that she had hidden in her robe, and drew faint sounds from it, which sometimes resembled the grating of grasshoppers and sometimes the plaint of a sparrow frightened by a horned viper.

When she was close enough, the princess wanted to know where that voice was coming from. She perceived Gaila costumed as a sorceress, and became excited, for she was credulous and avid to know the future. Even so, she would have passed on her way—but her eyes encountered Gaila's. She was subjected to the fire of seduction that escaped from the nomad. The flute gave voice to its most dolorous cry; the young Bedouin woman marched toward the escort without ceasing to look at the princess. That movement was favorable to her. She appeared with an elegance of rhythm and a mysterious charm that acted on the servants as well as on Aoura.

The latter, raising a nonchalant hand, had the porters halt, and asked, with a hint of suspicion: "What do you want, daughter of the Gulf?"

"Sister of King Thutmose, I posses arcana that can charm men, beasts and the birds of the sky. I know the signs of the night and the desert, and I can punish those who offend me. Above all, I can see into the future as into clear water. But I cannot say everything; the gods would punish me. It belongs to those who have a subtle mind and who are not ignorant of any of the art of good scribes to clarify my words."

She put such a mild gravity into her speech that Aoura, who was not fearful, ceased to be suspicious.

"Tell me, daughter of the Gulf, what I ought to dread and hope…"

"I will trace your fate," said Gaila.

She drew a copper stylus from her bosom and described a complicated figure on the ground, in which eyes, triangles and crescents were perceptible. The she said: It is necessary to put your bracelet, Princess, in a triangle, or on the point of a crescent. Only then will the figures be an arcanum."

The princess got down from her chair and placed a golden bracelet on a crescent, Gaila seemed to be immersed in meditation. Then she made the bracelet leap several times. Her forehead creased, her eyes became fixed, as if elsewhere.

She said, in a somber voice: "You must fear the evils that are in the west, and in everything, avoid the figure of the serpent. It will be harmful to you, if a man who comes from the south and who bears a little of the blood of ancient kings in his blood does not come to your aid before two years have elapsed."

Aoura darted a proud and fearful gaze at the slave. "And how can I avoid the figure of the serpent? It is present everywhere in the palace of Thebes."

"It is only redoubtable in your own rooms and your garden. You should make it disappear or veil it. You should avoid it, above all, in your adornment...."

"By what sign will I recognize the man who ought to come to my aid? Is he a scribe who will give me an arcanum? Is he an enchanter who will render me invulnerable?"

Gaila did not reply immediately. She traced new circles on the ground, murmuring words in the language of her homeland. Then she resumed, in a guttural voice: "The gods do not want to speak more clearly. It seems that the man has encountered you already and will soon encounter you again. That is all I can tell you now, but if you wish, I will wait on the road another day..."

The princess was disturbed. Daughter of a superstitious land, and credulous by temperament, she had no suspicion of the slave from the Gulf. An image that had not displeased her floated before her. She saw the plain of Thebes again, and the chief of the phalanx with sparkling eyes. Desire swelled her young, sighing breast. Noticing then that the seeress had a seductive mouth, she said: "I do not forbid you to wait for me on the road. But fear lying. I know how to attain you!"

She put a piece of silver in Gaila's hand, and said: "Give me a kiss with your mouth, as a sign of sincerity...."

She drew the slave's head toward her and, assuring herself that the red lips were as tender as they were beautiful, she said, with a hint of disturbance: "Yes you should come back. I order you to be here on the eighth day that will follow this one."

But that was not the day that Gaila had chosen. She replied: "I cannot come before the fifteenth day, daughter of Hatsheput; the gods oppose it; we must not disobey them."

Aoura hesitated momentarily, impatient at being opposed in a desire, but her piety and her natural mildness prevailed.

"You will come on the fifteenth day, then. If you are free, you will follow me; if you are not, I will have you bought by King Thutmose for my service."

Gaila watched the princess and her escort disappear into the enclosure of the temple of Amenemhat. She smiled mysteriously, with a sort of indulgence, content to have succeeded in her first attempt. Then, even though she was not jealous, she thought sadly about the beauty of Thutmose's sister. She took out her little copper mirror and looked at herself alternately in the water of the lake and the metal, taking pleasure in her face.

VII

Gaila did not give Setne any account of her conversation with the princess. In disguise, she prowled around Thumose's palace, and succeeded in conversing with royal slaves. She learned a hundred things about Aoura's past from an old Nubian woman, and discovered actions, steps and projects from which she might obtain advantage for her master.

Setne came back one afternoon exhausted by heat and fatigue, for Thutmose, who was planning a war, was keeping his troops breathless throughout the land of Egypt.

The young chief sat down in his garden in the shadow of an awning, in an enclosure of date palms and sycamores. White and pink lotuses raised their delicate heads over the water of a little pool, while a heron, ibises and wild ducks slept in the heat of the day.

Setne was dozing in that fashion when he heard a light footstep on the grass. He raised his eyelids and saw Gaila enveloped in a hyacinth fabric, her hair still damp from the bath. An odor of aromatics floated around her; her eyes distilled a fire, sometimes veiled and sometimes as bright as topaz; her breasts protruded partly from the cloth, pure, ardent and luminous, uplifted by an intoxicating emotion.

The soldier forgot his fatigue then; he forgot his cares and he forgot himself. He wanted to melt into that delicious flesh. He advanced with tender eyes, his mouth tremulous with lust. The slave slipped away from his arms, laughing. With a slight anger, he pursued her, as in Ankhi's gardens. But she, clever and full of a sure instinct, as silent in running as the warriors of her tribe, divined each of the man's movements merely by the sound of his body or his footfalls, and remained invisible. Sometimes he perceived the reflection of the hyacinth robe, sometimes a wave of hair in the penumbra. His desire increasing by the minute, he shouted in a tone of command: "Stop, Gaila!"

But there was silvery laughter among the palms. He shouted louder. She replied: "You're scaring me, Master!"

He said, in a softer voice, but imperiously: "Stop! I wish it."

She sprang abruptly from the foliage. He placed her quivering, upon his breast, and bit her with a devouring kiss. She was no longer laughing. Her large eyes sparkled with audacity and pride.

"Return my kiss," he said. "You're as cold as a granite figure."

She returned the kiss, without ardor. Her body was soft and passive. Carried away by the fore of passion, however, her forgot everything and embraced her violently.

He detached himself from the embrace with a hint of humiliation and asked: "It's quite indifferent to you, then, to be mine?"

"I'm not yours. My will is absent. I lend myself; I don't give myself."

"Why?"

"I only want to give myself by virtue of amour—and I can only love the man who loves me."

"You're very presumptuous! Who can guarantee that they will not love in spite of themselves?"

"Me! Brutal males have taught me my own character. I know of myself that which you must be ignorant of yourself. In any case, no man can know what a woman violated a hundred times can know. There is always a will, however feeble it might be, a desire, however paltry it might be, in your caresses. That blinds you. But a slave delivered to purchasers learns to regard amour as an enslaved miner regards the wall of his prison..."

She changed her tone abruptly. "Why do you care about that petty thing? If the master commands his slaves to turn a water-pump, does he desire that his slaves enjoy it? It is sufficient for him that the water irrigates his land. And if he demands that a slave give him pleasure, what does it matter to him whether the slave shares it? I am your slave, made for your labor and your will."

He did not reply, for that argument seem peremptory to him.

After a long silence, Gaila said: "Listen; I have been laboring for you..."

She twisted her hair, assembled it with copper pins, and full of a languorous softness, considered her master, sprawled on a grassy bank.

"I've seen Princess Aoura. I've spoken to her. I know many things that it's better not to tell you."

He had shuddered. The image of the sister of Thutmose rose up in his soul with a quiver of beauty.

"You're quite mad!" murmured Gaila. "What hope could you have? A man who lives without a goal resembles those gnats that lose themselves in the gulf..."

He was listening impatiently; she started to laugh.

"If you can, tomorrow morning, at the hour of the repast, approach Thutmose's son and talk to him. Ten days later, when the gnomon marks the second hour before sunset, go to visit Heth the priest. From the terrace of his garden one can see the river and the road that leads to the temple built by Amenemhat III. When an escort approaches, conducting the princess, go out on to the road."

"And what should I do?"

"Nothing. Fate, and your slave, will regulate the outcome of these encounters. Are you content?"

"Yes," he said, "and I have confidence in you."

She smiled, with a hint of melancholy. She feared the future. But, shaking her fine, imperious head, she looked her master in the face, tender, malicious and resigned.

"It's in yourself that it's necessary to have confidence. The man who doubts destiny should not emerge from his nome."

VIII

Setne found Heth in the shade of a tamarind, where he was tracing figures on a papyrus.

"Doubtless you're seeking an enchantment or the signs of an arcanum?" the young man said.

The priest looked at him, smiling with a mouth where everything seemed a mystery. He said: "I'm not seeking any enchantment other than that which measures things, for in the time when men can fix exactly the dimensions of round or straight figures, weight the wind that stirs the sea or the springs that descend from the mountains, the arcana will be pale that can only weave words. Little things are made in the image of large things; the man who learns to calculate by a figure the length of a garden or the height of a tree, will one day be able to measure by a figure the height of the mountains of Kush, and that of the moon. Such are the reliable enchantments. For a long time I have seen that I might be able to discover others."

The chief listened with interest. Although he believed in the gods of his homeland, he had an inclination for coherent and clear things. He remembered the ennuis that had once rendered magical science fatiguing for him.

"Our ancestors doubtless possessed more confidence in the gods than we do," he said, "but many of their formulae are obscured."

Irony appeared beneath the priest's eyelids; he replied evasively: "They have transmitted astonishing things to us; many of their words hide a wisdom that eternity will not contradict."

He spoke in a bitter tone, in which some rancor was evident, for he had never been able to discover an important arcanum: neither those that command the lightning, nor those that make shadows appear, not those that stop the course of water or disperse the flight of locusts. Nevertheless, he dared not open his soul to the young man.

"And how can it be," Setne asked, "that one can predict by means of a figure the distance or the height of things?"

The priest did not reply. He went to fetch from an outhouse a long, straight table charged with a box and a slender ruler measuring four cubits. At the ends of the ruler, two smaller rulers were attached, one of which turned on its support, while the other was fixed and perpendicular.

"Would you like to choose an object?" the priest said. With the aid of this ruler, I will measure its distance—or rather, given that I do not know the distance of everything present, go and fix this staff in the ground yourself."

Setne took the staff and went to plant it in the garden some distance away. Then the priest moved the long ruler until the small fixed ruler was directly in line with the target Then he orientated the turning ruler toward the staff, took from the box a system of rulers much smaller than the first, the base of which was proportionally very short and adjusted the small system in the image of the first. Having thus formed a triangle, he measured the length from the base to the summit, multiplied the result by fifty and said: "The staff is eighty-seven cubits away."

They verified the distance together with a stonemason's double cubit and found that the distance was eighty-six cubits and three quarters. Setne was wonderstruck.

"One only has to take lines long enough to measure the distance that separates the banks of the Nile as accurately, or the height of the Moon."

"But…," said Setne, pensively, "it's by magic that you can thus obtain the distance of a figure?"

"By a magic similar to that which permits bronze to be forged, or an ox to be attracted to a cart, or navigation with the aid of sails on a tumultuous sea. It's sufficient to observe that for two similar figures with three sides, if the angles are equal, the lines of the same direction will be the same number of times greater or smaller. So, if in the large figure that you see here the baseline is fifty times greater than that of the small ruler, the side that marks the distance will also be fifty times greater. Practice will show you that it is so, and you can conclude that the longest distances can be measured, provided that one knows a single line and an angle."

Setne did not understand at first, and even when the priest had repeated the explanation, tracing the figures, he could only glimpse a possibility, but it was evident that, with reflection, he would be able to grasp the whole problem.

His admiration for the work of the priest was extreme.

"It seems to me, in truth, my father, that Ammon has made you party to a force capable of penetrating the secret of the world."

The priest's nostrils flared; a vivid flame illuminated his temples and the dry shin that covered his cheekbones, for praise was accorded to him with a frightful parsimony by his contemporaries. Sages were suspicious of him, the multitude believed him to be a pernicious power, He was harshly punished for not being content to know the emptiness of formulae; each of his arguments with his fellows had led to painful aftermaths.

In those ancient times, the work of precursors could surpass their century immensely. The simultaneity of discoveries and their expansion would not even be born with Athens. A priest or isolated dreamer might imagine theorems that were only reinvented a thousand years later, and an infinity of marvelous things were lost in the bosom of civilizations that were beautiful and grave, but inattentive. Many a time, arms and tools were found that, not giving sufficient results immediately, did not emerge from the hands of their inventors. The alarming defeat of Hipparchus is the symbol of the centuries-long gap that then intervened between discoveries.[20] Without a doubt,

---

[20] Hipparchus employed trigonometry to make numerous astronomical discoveries; almost all of his own works were lost, but later astronomers evidently knew about them, preserved his discoveries and built upon them, so the reference is a trifle enigmatic. It might refer to the speculation that he constructed

the ingenious Chaldeans and the patient observers of Egypt found a thousand profound things of which Chaldea and Egypt remained ignorant until their decrepitude.

Heth savored the soldier's praise as a prophet that of his first disciples. He nevertheless had the finesse to understand that it was necessary not to weary the young man's attention. Observing that the violet shadows were elongating before the house, he said: "In a few hours the boat of Osiris will descend into the somber waters, the pernicious abysms. Let us gather our strength to await the decline of day, and, if you wish, tell me what your projects are. I have seen the waters dry up and be reborn more often than you; my advice might be useful to you, as that of a man who has followed the caravans is to someone who has not traveled the confines of the yellow sands.

In a bright room, poor in ornaments, cervoise, barley cakes, dates gilded like honey, cheese from Sais and a wild cock of the cataracts covered a blue table decorated with enamels.

"This is what the river is about to bring down to the fecund earth. The wells announce it; the rats are quitting the lower ground."

They both smiled at the image of good fortune, the memories evoked by the flood, and the great cry of the laborers when the mild world of the waters bathed the bathed the sighing earth.

"The gods only water Egyptian soil thus," observed Setne. "Other peoples must await the waters of heaven; often they do not arrive. This soil is the most beloved by

---

a heliocentric model of the solar system long before Copernicus.

the immortals, the most beautiful of all those that Osiris visits."

"I don't know," Heth replied. "it seems to me that there might be other lands more agreeable, where the summer is cooler and the trees more abundant. Woods grow with difficulty in Egypt and dry out in the wind of the desert."

"I don't like woods," said Setne. "It seems that one lives there in slavery. They're like a sad and gigantic dwelling where nothing remains of fallen walls but the pillars, and where the foliage makes roofs as long as a day's march. Everything there is hidden and perfidious. The plain is clear and free, beneath an uninterrupted sky; it gives confidence to the heart of man."

"Not to mine! I approach the forest like a habitation of the gods, undoubtedly perilous, but hospitable. The desert is no less filled with ambushes, and in addition, hunger and thirst inhabit it eternally. But tell me, has Thutmose similar to Ammon not proclaimed the departure of the troops yet?"

"No," said Setne. "We're awaiting the commands."

"I cannot imagine," said Heth, "since your birth permitted you to choose, why you have preferred the existence of the warrior, and its cruel fatigues, to that of priests; for your mind is not rebellious to knowledge."

"Believe, divine scribe, that it is no less necessary to extend one's mind to surround an enemy troop than to inscribe sentences on papyrus."

"Perhaps you're right," Heth murmured, in whom rancor awoke against the priests who had disappointed him. "The science of scribes is even less certain than that of battles. I will give you the papyrus that I mentioned to you."

He went out and came back with a russet scroll, which he handed to the young chief.

"You will find there," he said, "all the fashions of combat of the Ninevites, the Syrians, the men of Kush, the nomads of the desert and the Sidonians, as well as lists of various weapons, projectiles and animals of war. The book is reliable. Nothing is reported therein that had not been verified."

Setne's eyes lit up with pleasure. He took the papyrus and thanked the priest ardently.

"Be fortunate in your actions," murmured Heth, softly. "In any case, your eyes promise success or death. And death is not redoubtable."

For the tenth time, Setne looked out of the bay at the back of the room, which overlooked the road. He saw a violet litter on the road, still distant.

"If I don't succumb," he said, "I'll bring you back the arcana of Asia. It's said that the Chaldean priests have secret sciences."

Setne marched toward the old temple of Amenemhat. He penetrated into the first enclosure, which was ruined and no longer guarded, in order to wait for the princess. Sphinxes outraged by the Shous extended their pensive menagerie; fallen obelisks could be seen, a pylon of porphyry and the roof of the temple, above a forest of columns. The soldier's breast was tremulous with impatience, dread and amour; but he did not think that his step was extraordinary. Another will reassured his own. He obeyed Gaila with a confidence that was naïve and firm.

The silence was profound, almost terrible. The large sun, very yellow and already declining over the west, was roasting the dry earth. He scarcely passed anything but a scarab, an agile horned viper and a furtive rat. Meanwhile, the violet litter advanced, very slowly. The flabella were agitating on the edge of the enclosure; the slave guards showed themselves first, and then Setne saw the face of Aoura appear. It was as if the earth hollowed out around him; a vertigo seized him; his temples hardened. He felt his hamstrings relaxing like broken bowstrings. He did not move, inclined, his hands slightly extended.

At the sight of him, Aoura had shivered. Gaila's predictions had made her expect the presence of the chief of the phalanx, and gave that presence a troubling significance. She ordered the porters to stop. With a gracious audacity she walked toward Setne. It could not be divined that she was timid, tender and indulgent; in that enclosure, where her ancestor reposed, her young beauty seemed proud; a devouring disdain was marked in her large eyes with shady lashes.

Setne sensed more bitterly, in the obscurity of instinct, the desire to struggle against her and vanquish her. The audacious grace of her hips, the bold virginity of her young breasts, filled him with a disturbance for which he could only find an analogy in the fear of seeing his phalanx flee the clamors of the enemy.

Aoura was covered in light veils, almost entirely transparent in the interstices of the byssus. She raised toward Setne a tranquil gaze in which the certainty showed that she had a world at her service. Deep down, however, she was as troubled as he was, for she believed Gaila's words, and she observed with avidity the man who was to have an influence over her fate.

She spoke in a cold tone. "Is it not you who taught my nephew to use a bow? Tell me your name again. I promised to mention it to Thutmose."

"I am Setne, son of Raneferka…," he replied.

"…And you come from the nome of Tanis," she said. "Did you not tell me also that one of your ancestors descended from the old kings?"

"I did say that. Any of my people will tell you that."

She smiled then; she observed the soldier's face with more complaisance.

"You know," she said, "that the war has been decided. The departure of the troops will be proclaimed in a few days. The commands will be given after Thutmose visits Ammon. Do you like war?"

At that question she advanced her head with a sort of anxiety. Setne, who had been tremulous before her until then, had straightened himself up. A vehement ardor agitated his face.

"I love war!" he said. "My heart becomes as light as a falcon when the battle trumpet resounds."

She shivered at that sonorous voice. Already, young and agile in ideas, she saw him returning from Assyria in triumph. The image of a victorious soldier entering into her life as if into a citadel did not displease her.

"If you love war and if you know how to lead your troops," she said, "Thutmose will be able to discover you and reward you. You know that he protects those who fear him more that death."

"I know that. It is not without reason that his soldiers have more courage than enemy soldiers."

The eyes of the princess, excited with admiration for her brother, shone like the fire of emeralds.

"Your name," she said, "will be found on the royal papyri."

An extraordinary softness passed over the soldier's soul. Aoura did not wait for his response. She made a sign to her porters; she headed slowly toward the second enclosure.

Setne watched the violet chair disappear under the pylon. His heart was more agitated with dreams than the Red Sea by waves. And the ardent boat of Osiris, ever larger and more coppery, descended over the distant desert between two pyramids.

IX

When she emerged from the temple of Amenemhat, Aoura was thinking ardently. For having spoken to Setne, her soul was more impatient, her ennui harsher. She gazed at the plain where the shadows of pyramids were lengthening; she lamented being a daughter of the kings of Thebes, submissive to laws unknown to the women who prowled by night around papyrus cabins. At the memory of the brown face and the broad chest against which it would be pleasant to agitate, she almost wept with the desire to know masculine strength.

Thutmose will know his name! she thought. *I shall make it repeated by the son of Hatsheput.*

She saw Setne victorious, designated to posses her by the king himself. Her loins quivered. Lying on the cushions of her litter, she abandoned herself to a mysterious embrace. Soon that dream rendered reality more morose, and she ordered her porters to walk faster.

At a bend in the road she uttered a cry; between two yellow chimeras she had just perceived the witch of the Gulf. The red garment sparkled in the oblique rays of the sunset. Gaila's eyes seemed to be lost in the slumber of a dream.

"Stop!" said the princes, impatiently.

In her haste to consult fate, she descended from the litter and ran toward the chimeras. After a few paces, however, she blushed at her haste, and waited for Gaila, who advanced nonchalantly and magnificently, with the voluptuous undulation of the beautiful women of her race. They considered one another, each charmed by the other's grace. In Aoura, a little of the emotion induced in her by Setne was transposed to the newcomer.

"Do you know who I have seen?" she said.

"I know," said Gaila softly. "Your eyes say so."

The Egyptian woman smiled. She was confident. She said: "The war is imminent, daughter of the Gulf. Will he escape the enemy? Will he please Thutmose?"

Gaila traced figures on the ground and consulted them in accordance with the rotes. She was emotional herself; she moved the bracelets, the rings and the jade serpent for some time.

"Fate is favorable!" she said. "And you can do much for him, if you make his name known to Thutmose."

"Thutmose will know it," said Aoura. Can you not accompany me to the palace now?"

"No. That would bring us misfortune..."

The princess looked at her with a melancholy chagrin.

"Why are you rejecting me? I would like to take you upon my heart, to kiss your lips a hundred times. The women of Egypt would laugh with joy if I spoke to them thus. You, I sense your coldness..."

Gaila tilted her elegant head. The memory of so many men who had rushed brutally upon her rendered the tenderness of the daughter of kings more charming. It was the fourth time that the two women had met since the day when they had encountered one another beside the lake of Aroë. Every time, the princess showed herself more familiar and affectionate.

Out of gratitude, the slave offered her lips. Aoura threw herself upon her with a cry of joy. Seizing the voluptuous body of the nomad in both hands, she covered her neck and shoulders with kisses.

"Your mouth is fresh, witch; you are a divine fruit. Can you truly not go with me to the palace of Thutmose?" She contemplated the slave with moist eyes.

That desire increased further when Gaila replied: "I cannot go now."

"But the gods do not forbid you to come to me forever? Say that you will find a day!"

"I will find a day," Gaila replied.

Aoura gave her a kiss longer than all the others.

"Will you be here on the day of the full moon?"

"Yes."

"Oh! Try to determine that I can take you then. I would like to make you happy, you see. Adieu, joy of the eyes, sacred flower..." She went on: "Do you truly believe that the Tanite warrior will escape the war? Are you sure of it? I don't want him to perish."

"He will not perish."

The princess returned to her slaves; the litter disappeared around the bend in the road.

Gaila was still emotional. The Egyptian woman's amour touched her, because of its tenderness, and she took some pride in it; but she did not understand it. She could not share it, dominated by the profound instincts of the daughters of her race, who only knew the male. Aoura's generosity penetrated her heart, however. Remembering all the insults that her body had suffered, she was moved to tears.

She lingered for a long time in the same place. The rapid twilight had died over the Nile. The stars of Egypt rose in their glory, and the river, swollen by the waters of Kush, warm, numerous and palpitating, got ready to cover the old fecund earth. It was one of those resplendent nights in which every creature savors the joy of living, and Gaila, sighing prayers, abandoned herself to forgetfulness. She would give herself no rest until had crucified those who had thrown her father into the furnace, and she also wanted, with a good deal of tenderness, the triumph of Setne.

As she was dreaming thus she saw a shadow advancing beneath the luminous dust of the stars. She recognized the rhythm of the stride and placed herself in the middle of the road. "Master!" she cried. "It's me, Gaila."

But he had already recognized her.

"What are you doing to the road at this hour?" he said, with a hint of jealous anxiety.

She replied, gravely: "I'm working for your happiness! I know that you've seen the princess and I've seen her too. Your image is growing within her. It's necessary now to be fortunate in the war, and your destiny will be accomplished."

The slave's voice was low, but very clear.

"You've seen her?" he said, agitatedly.

"I've seen her. I'm guiding her will. If she spoke to you at the temple of Amenemhat, it's because I wished it, my master. Have I not said that a woman can do what would stop men? I've rendered your memory brilliant in that young head..."

The road sloped upwards slightly. They perceived the river, which seemed full of falling stars. A subtle, ashen light wandered over the surface of the ground and faded away amid the violet darkness.

"You've done that?" he said. "How fortunate I am to have bought you, Gaila! And you've talked to her about me again, this evening?"

"About whom do you expect me to talk to her? I traced figures in the sand for her and you; the presages are favorable..."

He extended a grateful hand, but he was intoxicated when it reached the warm and undulating flesh. Drawing the young woman toward him, he kissed her violently on the mouth.

If he knew, thought the slave, *that Aoura's rouge is still there!*

She started to laugh, and did not return the kiss.

"I'd like your amour!" he sighed,

She adopted a mocking tone. "It's necessary not to want everything. It's a madman who covets the lioness and the gazelle at the same time."

"What do you want, Gaila? Make a wish, and I'll grant it!"

"I've made my prayer. You promised me your strength to accomplish it. I don't desire anything *now*. What could you do, in any case, since you're about to leave for Mageddo or Kadesh?"

"I could give you your freedom."

She shuddered. The blood of nomads bounded within her like wild horses on the savannah.

"You could set me free without dread, for the work I want to accomplish for you and the work I want to accomplish by means of you bind me to you. I have made two oaths, from which death alone can release me. Don't render me my liberty before your return. I'll be better shielded being your slave."

He relaxed his grip and said, sadly: "You will love a man of your race."

"The gods alone know! Don't think of it yet, my master. It's necessary to arrange everything for your departure."

"You'll accompany me."

"I will do as you wish, but I don't think that would be wise. Someone is required to speak about you to the princess, and who can do that except me?"

He said, with jealousy: "But you'll be alone. I won't be able to know what you're doing. And I don't want you to belong to other men."

"No force can stop a woman who wants to give her body. Is it possible that you don't know that? Your presence would make no difference. But be reassured: no man will possess me. I swear that on my brother, and you must know that that is my greatest oath. In the war, I would embarrass you; a woman there is useless and dangerous. Here, I shall not cease to work for your fortune. In any case, it's necessary that Aoura does not know that I'm your slave. Can you not lodge me elsewhere than in your house? Eventually, even if I'm better hidden than a viper in the grass, I might be discovered there. I know two old women near the city gates who live on the produce of their garden. They only have one female slave. It would be easy for me to live there on my labor, or at very little expense."

"I don't want you to work for others!" Setne exclaimed. "You'll have what you need to live during my absence."

They walked for some time in silence. Regret as vast and profound as the night enveloped their souls. Setne's desire launched forth, with an equal force, toward the sister of Thutmose and the intoxicating slave. He did not separate them; it seemed to him that all of destiny was confounded within them; and his soul, still half-primitive, carried away by strong sensations, was no longer astonished. Astonishment is the offspring of old civilizations; Setne now found it simple and natural to conquer Aoura. His hope was as young and energetic as his race.

He spoke in an ardent voice. "You have told me, Gaila, that I will succeed. Do you still believe that?"

"You will succeed, my master. All the signs are favorable, and that is why I want to link myself with your destiny." In a low voice, with an emphasis that impressed the young man, she added: "The gods have interlaced our lives. They cannot be separated without misfortune for both of us. Don't forget that."

He felt full of faith in her. And he did not cease thereafter to have the energy that more often than not leads men to a violent end, but which is the only thing that can also lead them to triumph. Destiny is a gamble; the weak play the game with a small stake, but the strong put their lives on the line.

PART TWO

I

The armies of Thutmose were marching westwards. Already the tributary peoples of Nineveh had seen their phalanges dissolve before the genius of Misraim. The king of Thebes imprinted on multitudes the velocity that had signaled great captains since fabulous times.

They had arrived before the forest of Zahal. A horseman could not go around it in eight days. It was sacred, full of terror, unchanged for a hundred centuries. The desert stopped it to the south and the both; marshes putrefied toward the west, and the plain of Hennar, where Thutmose counted on defeating the forces of Nineveh extended to the east. The Egyptian army had a choice of two routes: the forest or the desert of Hamm. But the forest of narrow paths, almost impenetrable for oxen or donkeys, could not be traversed in a lunation, while it would only take thirteen days to reach the Hennar via the plain and Hamm.[21]

There was a third way. It followed the Zahal as far as the extreme south, and then the sands of Nomi. The waters were then crossed at a favorable place, and there was a narrow route, difficult but reliable, through the vast marshes. It opened to the Hennar via a gorge. Its length was ten days; but, practicable for a few hundred

---

[21] The geography of this section is entirely imaginary.

men, it would not have give passage to an army without immense delays.

By means of his runners and the treason of a Kahai chief, Thutmore had a clear vision of those things; only one way was good. But, like all great war chiefs, he liked to throw multitudes forward in a single mass, and trouble the enemy by means of skillful diversions. If he could seize the gorge that opened to the south of the Hennar with a small troop, the Ninevites, in order to recapture it, would doubtless dissipate numerous phalanges there. That attempt was worth risking a thousand men.

Thutmose was thinking about that, at dusk on the thirteenth day of the sixth moon. The fires of his camp were reddening the stars; the king's heart swelled as he contemplated that Egypt living in the bosom of Asia, that great river of men that flowed at his voice, all the way to the horizon. And he said to himself that the rapidity of his march had surely surpassed the previsions of Nineveh. The chiefs of the city of bronze must believe that he was still far from the Zahal, and that they would not reach the hills of Hennar for two weeks.

Pensive, Thutmose stood immobile on the edge of the royal tents; the warriors stood up to see, mingled with the fires, the darkness and the coppery moon, the god of victories who was drawing them along in his violent force.

There was a rumor at the frontier of the camp. Messengers came running. They announced that Setne, son of Raneferka, who had been beating the desert with two hundred men, had brought back captives, oxen and donkeys.

Thutmose wanted to speak to Setne.

The chief appeared when the moon had already passed the height of the hills. He threw himself in the dust and adored Thutmose.

"Get up," said the king, "and reply. Measure your words exactly to the truth."

Setne got up. Thutmose took pleasure in looking at him, for he was a rapid and perspicacious judge of men.

"How many prisoners do you have? Where did you capture them? Are there chiefs among them?"

"I've taken nearly a hundred prisoners, three days from Zahal, to the south. Being small in number and with buffaloes nourished near the lakes, they counted on crossing the waters at the limit of the desert and passing along the narrow route through the marshes to the Hennar. None escaped. Two chiefs are among them."

"Have they talked?"

"They have talked, and I know that along the route that they expected to follow, five hundred auxiliary cavaliers are to pass in order to join the armies of Nineveh. They are carrying tributes in precious stones, silver and embroidered cloth."

"Did those chiefs know of my presence?"

"They were unaware of it. They knew your glory, divine king, but they were unable to divine the rapidity of your march."

"Did they believe that they would reach the Hennar before the Assyrians?"

"Yes. Your enemies do not expect you there before the black moon."

Thutmose remained silent. He looked into himself, his destiny, and that of peoples. His meditations clashed like armies, until his will was fixed. Then, still observing the young chief, he said rapidly: "Can you stop that caravan between the marshes, reach the gorge within ten days and take possession of it?"

Setne replied without delay, for Thutmose did not like slow wills.

"The captives have told me the route, and I will be able choose guides among them who will not deceive me. King similar to Ammon, your orders will be accomplished, or your servant will no longer be of this world."

"I can give you a thousand men. Will you have the strength to lead them?"

"Your gaze cannot be mistaken. I will have the strength, since you do not think me unworthy of it."

"Go, my son," said Thutmose, gravely "my gaze serves me well, undoubtedly, but do not think that I do not know the chiefs of my phalanges; it is not without cause that you have been designated to roam the desert. You have succeeded; you will succeed. Good fortune is with you."

Setne sensed the magical breath of a god and his marvelous ardor pass over him. His soul swelled; it became more powerful. He exclaimed, in the sweetness of the dream and the violence of enthusiasm: "King even greater than your renown, the man who could resist your arms would succumb before your wisdom. You have given me victory; it will not abandon your servant so long as your grace is allied with him."

His voice pleased the king, for it was neither humble not fearful, but worshipful and full of courage. He thought he was hearing one of those men who do more by virtue of amour than servitude; he knew that those are the best warriors, audacious against death and loyal in misfortune. Touching the chief with his scepter, he said: "Let you fate be blessed by your master. May you live a long time, in order to serve me and learn that I recompense with justice those who are devoted to my glory."

II

When Setne returned to his tents he saw that the captives had been parked. All of them seemed to be asleep, as the warriors were also asleep, save for the guards.

The chief contemplated his troop with a secret joy. By the light of the fires, the sentinels, black or red statues, were calling out at intervals, in accordance with the custom established by King Ahmose, vanquisher of the Shous.

Setne made a tour of the camp; he made sure that all was well. Only then did he sit down beside the fire. The odor of roasted meat and papyrus stems delighted his nostrils. He broke his fast, maintained all day, and found life good that gave such a savor to nourishment and enabled him to succeed in his enterprises.

He summoned the centurion of the guard and offered him barley wine. He was a warrior from the nome of Sais, skillful in running the desert and sniffing out the enemy, full of energy, courage and stratagems, but devoid of a taste for pitched battles.

"Habak, son of Takeren," he said to him. "We depart tomorrow for the Hennar. Our march must be rapid. We shall have few donkeys and even fewer cattle; the forest will doubtless be accessible by the southern route of which the captive from Belem spoke. It's necessary to integrate that man."

"Is the army of the king of kings not going to continue its route?" Habak asked.

"Yes, but we will join it beyond the marshes."

Habak approved of the hazard; his long black eyes and his mouth with tanned lips smiled. "I like marching under your orders," he replied. "Ammon protects your enterprises, and danger fears your footsteps. It's agreeable to be in that fortunate shadow."

Setne remembers Thutmose's words and rejoiced in their being confirmed by the centurion's. The future was shining like an enameled cup. "Bring me the captive," he said, in a hollow voice.

While Habak disappeared between the fires, Setne had a vision of the land of Egypt: the image of women passed like the odor of cinnamon and lilies of the valley when the intoxicating hour descends over the delta. It was impregnated with the violence of battles and delicious cries of victory. The slave and the princess mingled in the soul of the chief with the murmur of the reeds of the Nile and the rumor of canals during the flood. And he sensed that the gods were sending him across the expanse a subtle resemblance of his native soil and beloved women.

He took pleasure in that dream for some time and then, with a start, he returned to the Mesopotamian night. The plain of asphodels silvered the perspective all the way to the edge of the firmament. The silence seemed to fall from the stars. Nothing could be heard but the voices of watchmen, at intervals, like the cries of herons on a promontory, the intelligent barking of jackals and the distant roar of a lion. The fires were dying down; the moon, fixed on the waters of the sky, was more clearly visible.

Meanwhile, Habak brought the prisoner. He was a tall chief of the sands, with violent eyes. A long beard grew on his face, and bituminous eyebrows; his terrible mouth seemed made for tearing buffalo apart; with the movement of his lips it glittered like nacre in a seashell. His features were nervous and agile, but he was able to immobilize it like a face of ivory. A black crown, from which two horns seemed to sprout, shadowed his head. The amplitude of his body was increased by garments of linen and camel-hide.

He stopped before Setne with the serenity of a god.

"Chief of the sands," the Egyptian said to him, "you have told me that you are not in the service of Nineveh."

"I told the truth. But I had sworn to protect the caravan."

"The gods are more powerful than your word; you have not failed in your promise. The men of the caravan have become our slaves, their chief has perished; is it not me who has inherited your oath?"

"According to our custom, I no longer owe anything to anyone; the death of the chef and the servitude of the others releases me from my vow."

"Do you not want to engage yourself to your master?"

The chief of the sands turned his gaze away from the plain and fixed it on Setne. The liberty of great wild beasts shone there like the star of Osiris in the well of Syene.

"I cannot have two masters, my oath and you. If you take me as a slave I will obey you as a slave; if you want my oath, I ought only to belong to the oath."

That response did not displease the Egyptian. He linked his gaze with that of the captive.

"Choose your master!"

The hard face quivered and showed its teeth with a violent joy. Mastering his mouth, however, the tall nomad replied: "Intar, son of Zaoud, will be the slave of the oath. His word is as unshakable as the Sineh. You can rely on it."

"You will guide us," said Setne, "to the gorge of Koud, which you claim to know; if you have lied, you will sleep in death."

"So be it! I will guide you."

The Egyptian chief gave Intar cervoise to drink, and while the chariot of Isis inclined, they talked about the forest of Zahal, the unnamed mysteries, the marshes where the last Men of the Waters lived, and the plain of Hennar, where the men armed by Nineveh were to assemble.

III. The Dry Cistern

Sixty hours had passed since Setne had quit Thutmose's camp. It was morning. The sun, already high, appeared over the desert like the round mouth of a furnace. The Egyptians had almost no water, either for the beasts or the men, but the cistern was nearby. They perceived a meager oasis of reddening palm trees and plaintive grass. Setne, Intar, Habak and ten soldiers were heading for it at the gallop of their onagers.

"By Ka." said Habak, "the oasis is poor! It wouldn't give pasture to a dozen donkeys. Are you sure, chief of the sands, that there is enough water there for our men?"

"Nine years out of ten," replied the Bedouin, "There is water there in abundance."

They reached the oasis. Intar pointed to the cistern, where an old split water-skin hung.

"It's here."

He leaned over, his fiery eyes exploring the dark hole. A long shiver agitated his meager body.

"The cistern is empty," he said. "I don't think the skins will encounter a drop of water." He lowered his head again and looked into the utmost depths of the cistern. "It ought not to be like this now," he added. "It only dries up for one season in nine years."

Mastering his annoyance, Setne asked: "How many days are we from the next cistern?"

"There's a well to the west, three days away, and a cistern to the east which we could reach before the end of the day. But that would delay our progress, while the other is on the route."

Setne made no immediate response. He sensed the wing of the black god. His entire destiny was in suspense; and his eyes paused fearfully on the twelve hundred men that King Thutmose had confided to him.

"My soldiers can't wait three days," he said, bitterly. "It will already be hard for them to march until nightfall..."

The chief of the sands and the Egyptian considered one another in silence, with equal sadness, for the soul of Intar had softened. Incapable of transgressing his oath, he had nonetheless hated, at the beginning of the journey, the man who had surprised his vigilance; but Setne's silent confidence had acted upon the nomad's soul. His rancor had diminished by the hour, and he no longer called the wrath of the gods down upon the expedition.

In a hollow voice, he said: "There is another route that would advance the march toward the gorge, but it is terrible. It traverses the desert of dragons, the forest of tigers and the marsh of the Men of the Water. It's an impure land, more ancient than any on earth. You'll lose men in the morning, in the desert of dragons, and in the evening in the forest. The following dawn, you'll see the

Men of the Water. There, your entire army might perish. Such is the frightful route. Our forefathers knew it. Entire tribes were swallowed up there. Only Doud, the son of Schoun, was able to come back with his men, for having pleased the men of the marsh. But he did not transmit his arcanum.

Setne had heard the reports of captives, guides and scouts too often to be credulous. He listened to Intar without saying anything.

"Is it known, at least, that the route leads to the gorge?" he murmured. "Did you know Doud, or have these things been recounted to you?"

"I've seen Doud in his old age, and I've also known Schemel, the runner who approached the desert of dragons by the route we'd have to follow to reach the cistern. He saw the marsh of the Men of the Water to the north. In truth, Schemel was only able to recognize the stumps of the road, but scarcely twelve hours' march separates the limits of those two journeys..."

A shadow fell between the two men. Setne turned and saw Habak. The old centurion's eyes expressed the same fatalistic will that was born in the Tanite's soul.

"We'll go via the desert of dragons and the marsh," said Set. You can abandon us on the threshold if you wish, Intar, for your oath does not condemn you to that ordeal."

Intar smiled with his gleaming teeth. "This dry cistern has changed my oath, since it has changed your route. I will go via the land of the dragons and share the fate of your army."

Those words attached the two men. They sensed it with certainty.

"That is good!" said Setne. "You will follow the oath as you dictate it to yourself. And I shall not forget it."

He emerged from the shade of the palm tree and went to command the departure.

IV. The Dragons and the Forest

On the fourth days after the departure, in the morning, Setne and his soldiers reached an oasis between the hills. Date palms grew on the heights, males to the west and females to the east. A spring poured forth between granite banks.

"We're two hours from the desert of dragons," said Intar. "Let your men drink and fill their water-skins without delay. It's necessary that we pass through the marshes before nightfall."

The army only stayed in the oasis for half an hour. Sitting under a date palm, motionless and mute, Setne passed through one of the great emotions of his life. His soul was convulsed by energy and anxiety. He was about to gamble with destiny. Before the cross of Isis had reached the height of its course, everything would be settled; Thutmose's men would be destroyed, or on their way to the battle.

As he was lost in thought, a hand fell upon his shoulder. He saw the corroded face of Habak, who was smiling at him with humility and courage.

"Habak," he said, "would we have dared to reappear before Thutmose if we had arrived too late to surprise the caravan?"

"No," the centurion replied. "And you did well to turn away from the route that was too slow. Thutmose estimated you better than that, even if we fail." He shook his head slowly, and added: "War is a gamble with death. No one should play it who refuses the stake. And your centurion will pass joyously, this evening, if he must, into profound death."

"It seems that you don't love life," murmured Setne. "No one is as tranquil as you when death flies, with her darts and her trenchant blades!"

"Yes, I love life," said Habak, "but it is my nature to fear nothing before a chief that I love."

Setne looked at him emotionally. Although he could be hard, and even ferocious, for having killed so many men, witnessed so many tortures, treasons and pillages, there was a tenderness in the depths of his being. It was not necessary for him to make a promise or an oath to ally himself with his fellows; and he sensed that he loved that old man.

"Don't forget," said Habak, "to have the livestock and the onagers precede you..."

Setne smiled.

"I don't fear the dragons overmuch, he said, or the tigers...only the men who live on the water. Intar spoke in accordance with his own people. His race exaggerates; they see a people in a tribe, an army in a phalanx. I don't believe that those who have perished in these deserts were in numerous troops. The nomads scarcely assemble more than a hundred when they traverse the sands. Strangers to discipline, acting at hazard, tigers or dragons might easily surprise them, but I have difficulty believing that a single one of our phalanges, if it is marching attentively, cannot traverse these forests full of lions.

Habak listened to him with a slight impatience.

"I know Intar's race well," he said. "It's true that their speech exaggerates; words carry them away more easily than our Egyptians, so their stories are magnificent; they have wings. But a man like Intar knows how to reduce his words during a march and keep his fine stories for late evenings. I don't claim that the peril is invincible, but it's not despicable; Intar's eyes have told me so."

"Be tranquil, Habak. It has never cost me to foresee a peril greater than the reality. Everything will be done as if the dragons and the tigers could annihilate an army. As for the Men of the Water, I fear them veritably. Their marshes render them formidable; we might all perish there. It's a throw of the dice against the night. But who would win a battle if he did not put hazard in his party? Who would even deliver one?"

"The Men of the Waters allowed Doud to complete his journey, after taking him in amity..."

"I have not forgotten that, and we'll talk about it again when we're in sight of the marshes. It's necessary to march, Habak."

The soldiers had drunk and filled their water-skins. Setne had the trumpets sounded. He presented himself at the front of his phalanges, on a mound planted with turpentine trees, and, surrounded by chiefs, he announced that the hour of combats was imminent. He made the simple speech of men of war, full of threats and promises.

"I am alone, with the chief of the sands," he concluded, "in knowing the road and its ambushes. Woe betide those who believe that they can have recourse to flight; water, fire, beasts and men will not take long to annihilate them. They will never see the land of Egypt again, and their shades, expelled from our necropolises, will wander eternally in darkness and fear.

That harangue made its impression. The Egyptians of the powerful epochs, not conceiving of death, could not fear it in itself. The subterranean city, the necropolis, had scarcely any more terrors than the city in the sunlight; everything developed with simplicity, and eternity. And the kings of the eighteenth dynasty remained sheltered in the tomb from cowardly actions or military courage.

Thutmose III, more than any other, had borne the prerogatives of his dynasty into the judgment of souls, and the priests, still full of the memory of the Shous, and dominated by that stubborn, vindictive and generous prince, did nothing to combat the dogma, so Thutmose III's army was the bravest that ever emerged from Egypt.

Setne allowed the dread to expand and increase in the multitude, and then he went on: "I will keep a book of your actions. No one will be forgotten. Those whose death will have been the most beautiful will return to Egypt to receive the great embalming there. Those who survive after strong acts of war will receive a command and a considerable part of the spoils. Cowards will be prey to filthy beasts; living, they will be nailed to the trunks of trees; dead, the jackals and the vultures will receive their cadavers as offerings."

The soldiers saluted their young chief with long cries; the trumpets sounded the departure, and the great desert and the great terrible sky reappeared as they emerged from the oasis.

The army marched until midday; then granite cliffs appeared, where a creeping brushwood grew. The firmament seemed harsher there; a russet light wandered between the fissures. Something false, like an eternal ambush, made the silence savage.

Intar, who was in the lead with the beasts of burden, examined the cliffs for a long time. Then he came to say to Setne: "It's through the gorge on the right that it's necessary to enter the land…"

"Send the bulls through first," replied Setne. "Choose from among the least docile. The iron phalanx will follow them. It's necessary that the initial peril be swiftly averted."

The bulls passed through, and then the iron phalanx and then the entire army, without anything stirring in front of them. Setne saw a mild and sinister country of yellow beaches, putrescent waters, and plaintive vegetation full of rust, mildews and necroses. An insipid odor rose with the vapor of pools; moist beasts swarmed on the promontories, darting immobile gazes over the expanse or devouring one another in silence. Extraordinary birds could be seen, with immense feet the color of flesh, which alighted on the islets or rose like arrows into the sky, and an unnamable beast in the form of a lizard with scaly wings, which fluttered heavily at the level of the mangroves and tamarisks.

The army marched swiftly. It had to cross a muddy causeway; afterwards it skirted large stones in which vague muzzles could be seen, sculpted by vanished humans. Then more marshes surged forth, with bright ashen colors. The bulls bellowed; colossal forms undulated between the mangroves; a mysterious terror spread from man to man and rendered flesh tremulous.

Setne went forward to assist in the attack. The bulls had fallen upon monsters; others recoiled with profound clamors. Long bodies were seen coiling around breasts and heads. The iron phalanx did not budge, fascinated; Intar incited them, his blade raised. It was the minute when panic takes possession of men. Rapidly, Setne observed the scintillating beasts, thirty cubits long, with cold eyes and frothing mouths; he only counted ten.

It's necessary to kill a dragon! he thought. *Otherwise, these faint hearts will be chilled by fear*.

He drew his sword with a trenchant blade; he considered a great bull that was struggling in the formidable grip, and launched himself forward with a bound. He sliced the dragon through the middle. The severed sections writhed horribly.

Setne shouted: "What are you afraid of, faint hearts? Does not each of you have a well tempered sword?"

Intar had already imitated the chief's example. He succeeded in cleaving a dragon, but only half way through; a blow from the tail threw him to the ground. Hesitation returned to the hearts of the warriors, until the chief of the sands had got up and seized his blade again.

Only then did the phalanx advance, launching its darts and striking with lances. Men fell, but also dragons; the victory was not in doubt for long. The hideous beasts lay on the ground, amid warriors and bloody bulls.

That triumph filled Setne with joy, not because he misunderstood its scant importance, but because it destroyed in minds the apprehension of something prodigious or magical. He had the cadavers collected and gave them a warrior sepulcher, which was done in accordance with a simpler rite than on the soil of the homeland, but with a mysterious promise of return; the god Horus, after a few generations, would recover the bodies thus abandoned from the foreign soil and bring them back to the holy necropolises.

Setne pronounced the speech of judgment. He spoke about the imperishable cycle, Ammon-Osiris, glorious day spring from fecund night, the scintillating boat in the full waters of darkness and impure spirits, the resurrection in the bright waters of the firmament. He announced the bliss, in the light of the Amenti, of warriors died without weakness. Then he reserved the cadaver of the bravest warrior, which would be embalmed during the evening halt, and given recompenses.

That first contact with peril was good for him. It pleased his men and made them redoubtable; his sword, his speech and his actions seemed full of force. When he gave the signal to depart they were no longer following an unknown leader; a new energy was born in them, obedient and warm: faith.

The army marched for an hour without encountering any obstacle. Then it traversed a crepuscular terrain. Plants the color of ash grew on the edges of coppery pools; limp and sad trees whose bark was coming away in scales agitated sparse spiral foliage as dry as tinder. Black snakes fled; moist creatures plunged into bloody waters; bald vultures rose up at the summits of rocks, which screeched as they soared over the men.

Finally, the dragons reappeared, more numerous, on sand the color of charcoal. Setne raced forward; he cried to the phalanx of the advance guard: "Close ranks, and receive them on your lances! They won't be able to reach you..."

The warriors obeyed. The attack of the dragons ran into a quadruple harrow of iron, while the archers on the flanks launched a rain of arrows. The beasts persisted; the instinct of victory was in them; of so many millennia when everything had succumbed to their strength on that residual terrain of fabulous times. Blood and flesh made horrible pools; a few men were carried off in the impetuous attack, but the phalanx triumphed. Nothing remained but writhing stumps and scattered heads biting the void or devouring one another, red water and sticky foam.

That victory filled the Egyptians with a joy more violent than the first. It gave them the sentiment that the era of the beasts was over, that they would always be vanquished by an army in battle. What wild beasts could be more terrible than those dragons, which fought together, and each one of which could have vanquished a lion?

Now, in those times, the Beast was still terrible; it was only braved in the past. Its mystery, its strength and its hordes, surging from the Unknown, were feared; human legend was filled with its malice; Egypt rendered it a worship that, for all that it was indirect and increasingly symbolic, was still divided between gratitude and terror.

The shadows extended over the desert; the furnace of Ka was sinking toward the hills. The army had surpassed the land of the dragons; immense marshes extended to the left. It reached the edge of a forest. Setne ordered a halt. He said to the chief of the sands: "Thus far, the stories of your people have been in conformity with the truth. We still have three hours of daylight. Do you think that is sufficient to traverse the forest?"

"According to Doud's account, it requires a quarter of a spring day, if one escapes the tigers. Then one enters a regions where the soil is red; trees and bushes are sparse there, and until the marshes of the Men of the Water it is similar. Now you know all that I know myself. If you have the time, perhaps it would be better to traverse the forest in the morning; the wild beasts will be sated then, and we'll have less to fear from a surprise attack by the Men of the Water."

"But I don't have the time, Intar. It's necessary to cross the forest before dark, or, at least, arrive close to the far edge. I don't fear the tigers; they can't be more redoubtable than the dragons."

"They're quicker, and almost ungraspable. Doud recounted that those in this forest don't hesitate, even when solitary, to seize a man from the midst of a hundred other, with the speed of a dart and the strength of an elephant. They spring out of the shadows without anything allowing them to be anticipated. It isn't possible to calculate the wound that one inflicts on them with an ax, an arrow or a lance, so disconcerting is their suppleness. Scarcely have they appeared that they're under cover, ready to recommence the attack and vanquish again. In truth, Lord, I believe them to be more terrible than the dragons. They will surely carry off a considerable number of men, and spread terror, if you have the imprudence to disdain them."

"Thank you," said Setne, "but even if the danger were less redoubtable, I would not disdain it."

"It is pride that dooms the lion," said Intar, gravely.

Setne distributed throughout his troop the men who held lances and long darts. Those weapons, alternately inclined to the right and the left, bristled from the army and defended it against the sudden bounds of wild beasts. He did not leave the men ignorant of the peril.

"The coward will be punished by himself, for in the forest, the sole refuge is in courage. Whoever emerges from the ranks will fall under a mortal claw."

Intar had found the pass; it was like a strip of red desert, scarcely interrupted by a little brushwood, between two millennial forests. The phalanges penetrated into it silently.

"One might think," said Habak, "that a river of death had passed, like the sea that killed the cities of Kenen."

They perceived trees so high that they seemed to be touching the waters of the sky, some of which must have been fifty centuries old. The warriors contemplated them with suspicion. They sensed a force so old that nothing in the Delta or the land of Kush approached it. Here, man was not yet present; it was the soil of legend, full of secret and formidable forces. Extraordinary things, ancient nature unvanquished, were growing there, perhaps sufficient to annihilate all the toil of nations, all the genius of armies.

For a long time the forest remained silent. Scarcely a few subtle breaths passed, which went from leaf to leaf and suddenly died, like an interrupted speech. Sometimes, there was an agile flight, the flash of a snake, the tawny body of a deer, the leap of a monkey or a bird in the branches, and then once again the immense lake of trees, grass and beasts hid its profound life. But the sun tinted it red; its brazier was seen swelling behind giant columns, and the cry of the evening rose up, little flutes piping on the edges of nests, nervous monkeys, herbivores trembling at the arrival of the devouring night. There was still a truce, however. Only a few hungry beasts were waiting in ambush. The great royal beasts, the living sepulchers, were asleep in their ossuaries.

The sun was going down rapidly, from branch to branch. It appeared to be holding the occident of the forest in its round maw. It finally sank, and the noise of furious beasts was magnified, drawing ever closer, like the resonant waves of the sea.

"Can you see any sign announcing the end of the forest?" Setne asked Intar. "We've been marching for three hours..."

"None. Doud mentioned a great clearing that was an hour from the edge. We haven't reached that clearing yet..."

"It's necessary to reach it and camp there," said Setne, "for we can't traverse a hour of forest, perhaps more, in profound darkness. The moon is dead at the commencement of the evening..."

Darkness dominated the coppery light; forms became vague; the space was populated by fabulous things; anguish hovered over the phalanges. Suddenly, an enormous beast crossed the hedge of lances. A cry of death was heard, and then the beast reappeared, with a man in its jaws. It disappeared between the trees.

Setne had shivered. He sensed the terror siding into souls and chilling limbs.

"In truth," he murmured, "those are more terrible than the dragons!"

Immense roars filled the air. The entire forest was nothing but an immense clamor. In spite of their number, in spite of the order and their pointed weapons, the men no longer believed in their strength. The same distress reigned that kept the Kushite sheltered in his cavern. And again, the beast surged forth. Forms as rapid as lightning bounded in the penumbra, crossing the line of lances and carrying men away. One tiger passed within six cubits of Setne, Intar and Habak, and disappeared before they could launch a dart or lift a sword.

"We haven't been able to stop one of them!" Setne cried, angrily.

Another cry of agony, and then another; the weapons of bewildered warriors clashed; a sigh of fear rose up from a thousand breasts. The shadow thickened; they could no longer see further than a few cubits; the reflection of weapons added to the horror of darkness.

Humiliation filled the soul of the Egyptian chief. Suddenly, he found himself under the beast. A warm and powerful weight had rolled over his breath; a fetid mouth blew in his face, and he saw fiery eyes and sparkling teeth descending. He thought he was doomed; he struck at hazard with his sword. Already, Intar and Habak had fallen upon the tiger, but it carried off its victim. Habak discharged a blow of his ax at the head, Intar's sword plunged, and Setne found himself on his feet again. His sword had pierced the tiger's heart. The monster died, with a great scream.

"Are you wounded, my Lord?" cried Habak.

Setne had a torn shoulder and a bloody breast, but no deep wound. The tiger had seized him by his garments. He placed his hand on Habak's head and looked at Intar in silence. Both were as close to his heart as if one mother had engendered them. But the cries of fear did not cease resounding along the sinister route. Always the same drama, more hideous than the increased darkness, always the light and formidable bounds before which the multitude of armed men remained as impotent as a herd of deer or gazelles. At each attack of the wild beasts a soldier disappeared into the night and death.

Setne hastened the march, and with twenty warriors armed with pikes he presented himself successively at the front of the phalanges, encouraging the crowd with strong words. No one was listening to him; an immense terror was making the soldiers totter; some, seized by madness, ran into the carnivorous forest.

Then Setne became desperate. He sensed his weakness and the weakness of man Ancient nature weighed upon his soul as it weighed upon feeble populations in fabulous times. He believed that that frightful terrain would be his sepulcher,

Instar's voice pulled him out of his discouragement. "The clearing!"

The open strip in which the army was marching broadened out. A vast triangular area appeared, confusedly strewn with vegetation. The sky cast a meager starlight there, which gradually increased in the light of the nascent moon. Then Setne, encouraging his men with a loud voice, caused the long Theban trumpets to resound.

Before the open extent, however, the phalanges broke up. Everyone raced forward in a vertigo of terror and hope. Tigers bounded through that disorder, ad Setne, devoured by rage, feared the supreme panic. His voice and Habak's summoned the iron phalanx. That elite troop deployed around the leader, organized in the red light of the rising moon. The trumpets, with increased energy, sounded the rallying cry.

At that moment, two tigers glided toward Setne. In response to a curt order, the pikes were raised. The audacious beasts pounced. One of them fell on the points. Pierced through, it writhed, with a long roar so formidable that the pikemen dropped their weapons. But already, Intar's and Setne's swords had pierced it with twenty thrusts. It rolled over in the middle of the phalanx and lay still. A long cry of triumph, prolonged through the clearing, reanimated the crowd.

The other tiger had seized a prey and carried it away. Armed with a short sword, the victim struck relentlessly, frantically. A fortunate thrust stopped the wild beast in its tracks, Intar, Habak and several soldiers raced forward, but the tiger bounded outside the circle of lances and swords three times. Its immense claws tore

227

muscles, pectorals and entire shoulders. Finally, its entrails sprang forth. A sword punctured its eyes, and ten javelins nailed the beast to the ground. It stayed there, panting, for a long time; the soldiers, exulting in its agony, delivered thrusts at intervals that awoke it with a start and drew long howls from it.

Then a fanfare sounded the triumph; confidence was reborn in the bewildered souls; the phalanges reformed. In the broadening clearing, weapons plied by firmer hands regained the advantage over the monsters.

Setne commanded that large fires be lit and took a roll call of the troops.

He found that he had lost fifty men; that loss seemed small, and in the depths of his soul he rejoiced. But, hiding his joy, he went from fire to fire, insulting his troops, denouncing their cowardice and depicting the torture of those who had fled into the forest.

He added: "Take care that you are in the hands of the gods! Bravery alone can save you, and will save you. Those who attempt to escape by flight will only serve to assuage the hunger of beasts. If I had not succeeded in reforming your ranks, only a few would still be prowling around this clearing and in the forest. The majority would have perished."

The Egyptians listened to their chief with humility. They recognized that his energy had saved them; they obtained a more profound confidence in his resources.

"I shall not seek this evening to discover the most cowardly," Setne cried, "but no peril must any longer surprise you! I am taking my precautions; I will know those who quit the ranks; I will be pitiless!"

"No one will quit the ranks again," said an old Memphite. "We shall be in your hands, like your sword and your staff of command."

And the clamors of the phalanges rose up, amid the smoke and the flames, above the carnivorous forest.

V. The Queen of the Waters

"Let's climb that hill," said Intar. "We'll be able to see the land of the marshes better from there."

Setne climbed, and observed the motionless waters for a long time. They were heavy, leaden and equivocal, interrupted by vegetal islands; they extended all the way to the horizon. A natural causeway traversed them, which swelled into peninsulas.

"It requires three hours of marching to emerge from the peril," said the nomad, "the marshes will not be ended yet, even then; they divide; some stretch southwards, the others northwards. The Men of the Waters do not venture on to solid ground, however, and one can reach the gorge to the Hennar without difficulty."

"Do they fight hand-to-hand, Intar?"

"Yes, after having harassed the enemy. They remain invisible for a long time; their arrows seem to emerge from the waters."

"Do you believe that their bows have a longer range than our Egyptian bows?"

"Their range, according to the accounts, seem to equal the range of my tribe's bows. Yours shoot further, Lord."

Setne considered the causeway again.

"We'll send messengers of peace," he said. "If they don't consent to our passage, I'll occupy that first peninsula; I'll calculate the resistance of the enemy thus."

He summoned Habak with the phalanx chief Bitiu, and ordered them to prepared four hundred men. Then he put on a helmet and a breastplate, took a large buckler and, accompanied by Intar and ten warriors, protected like him against arrows, he headed rapidly for the marshes.

When he approached the edge, he raised his voice to call to the Men of the Waters. At first, nothing budged. The heavy waters seemed dead, as thick as the waves of the sea where two cities lie in eternal sleep. No plant quivered on the sinister extent; the pale nympheas resembled flowers of enamel.

Then the leaves of the nenuphars stirred, and heads surged firth. Extraordinary, with long violet hair that railed like algae, their eyes emerald, their skin blue on their faces and breasts, the beings appeared to be more different from the men of Egypt than the negroes of Libya, the red-haired Scythians, the yellow people or the men the color of ash who lived in caverns. They were not ugly. One of them had a strange, disconcerting beauty, with a tint of nacreous azure, a moist gleam in the eyes, and luminous teeth, not like pearls but opals.

They all remained motionless for some time, listening to the speech of the Egyptian chief. Abruptly, they dived. Their blue bodies disappeared like steaks of light.

"That's not a good augury," said Intar.

He had scarcely finished speaking when twenty arrows emerged from between the broad leaves of the nenuphars. They collided with the Egyptians' solid bucklers

"It's war!" murmured Setne. "Let's go prepare for it."

The little embassy went back up toward the phalanges, and Setne gave his instructions to the attack column.

"You'll march between two rows of bucklers, constantly turned toward the waters. In the center, you'll imbricate the bucklers in a roof. The archers and the slingshot wielders will only launch projectiles on command.

The phalanges, divided into four centuries, set off on the march, heavily. With their carapaces of bucklers, inflamed by the reflection of swords, lances, axes, helmets and belts, they resembled four enormous beasts of flesh, leather, metal and fire. They occupied the granitic causeway without encountering any opposition. Nothing appeared on the melancholy marshes. Only a few shadowy beasts, glaucous serpents and lizards fled and dived.

That immobility troubled Setne; he ordered a hundred well-covered archers to march toward the bank in order to guard against a surprise. There was still no response. On the causeway, the columns marched faster.

They were no more than three hundred cubits from the peninsula when the attack was launched, sudden and formidable, from all directions. An innumerable host of arrows emerged from the water from the flanks and behind the phalanges, while a multitude of blue men sprang on to the peninsula and, hidden among the rocks and the brushwood, awaited the approach of the Egyptians.

The phalanges stopped. Between the crenellations of the bucklers, the skillful archers of Thebes, Abydos and Memphis, took aim at the pale bodies visible close to the surface of the water, or at the heads partly emerging among the reeds and the nympheas. The range of the Egyptian bows, keeping the aggressors at a distance, warded off the catastrophe. The losses of the phalanges were limited to a few wounded, whereas the waters of the aquatic foliage had been seen to turn red twenty times already. Immense cries, in which were mingled human voices and some unusual clamors, were prolonged over the vast liquid surfaces.

Meanwhile, Setne prepared for a further attack. He made the archers advance together toward the bank. They deployed rapidly toward a point on the causeway whether the scarcity of the nympheas and reeds did not permit any ambush. There, less than two hundred cubits from the rearguard of Habak and Bitiu, they prevented the first column from being completely surrounded. The Men of the Waters tried to dislodge them. A swarming mass agitated the marsh. Archers appeared and disappeared with a prodigious speed, harassing the Egyptian archers. The attack had little effect. The Egyptians responded with a volley so murderous that the enemy could not maintain themselves in the open water. The aquatic warriors withdrew beyond bowshot, and, almost at the same time, the attack against Habak and Bitiu was suspended.

Setne followed the phases of the singular battle anxiously. As long as the numerical superiority of the Men of the Waters was not excessive, the Egyptians, with better armaments, could force a passage. However, against ten thousand or fifteen thousand enemies, the struggle would become impossible. Even then, they would have had a chance in direct combat—but the adversaries, taking advantage of the admirable resources of their element, would slip away.

Habak and Bitiu had resumed their forward march. They had almost reached the peninsula when, from all directions, with an extreme impetuosity, the Men of the Waters launched a new attack. They were seen everywhere bounding on to the causeway or the peninsula, armed with lances of a sort with points of shell. There were a good five thousand. Within a few moments they had separated the phalanges of the advance guard from the reinforcement of the archers. The maneuver cost them dear; hundreds of blue bodies bloodied the waters or lay on the ground when the hand-to-hand combat began, initially favorable to the Egyptians. The lances and swords of iron or bronze, and clubs bristling with spikes, were formidable against the weapons of wood and shell; but the fury of the Men of the Waters increased with their losses, and the battle became terrible.

Setne launched reinforcements, of which he took command himself. He fell upon a host of enemies who were assailing the archers from the rear, and smashed through them. It was a massacre. Frenetic clamors spread all the way to the distant islands of the marsh; new swarms appeared among the nenuphars and the reeds.

Setne saw that a decisive action was about to be engaged. He tried to evaluate the number of the antagonists; he judged that there were at least seven thousand, three thousand of whom had completely surrounded the column of Habak and Bitiu. The Egyptian chief thought he had to make a decision. He had the Theban trumpets sound; he occupied the space that separated him from the archers and then, with seven hundred men, he awaited the assault.

A high-pitched, bizarre and melancholy music rose up over the waves. Long red flutes were seen to emerge two bowshots away. They surrounded the upper body of a woman, toward whom all the Men of the Waters turned momentarily, with an evident fervor. The woman drew a little nearer to the causeway and Setne, surprised considered her.

Long hyacinth-colored hair flowed around her and could have enveloped he blue upper body. Her eyes were glinting like torches with green flames; her body had very pure forms and admirable movements. She made a grand gesture and uttered a loud cry. Immediately, the waters swarmed around her; bodies and heads emerged like salmon in the spawning season; an enormous multitude swam toward Setne's soldiers.

To begin with, the young woman remained motionless, out of range of arrows. When she saw the carnage that the Egyptian archers had wrought among her own people, she summoned a few gigantic men and was borne toward the causeway. Her arrival frightened the assailants. They precipitated themselves against the Egyptians with terrible clamors; but Setne caused the phalanges to bristle. The forest of points, to which the soldiers imparted rapid movements, received all the blows and broke their impetus. Soon, the cadavers and the wounded were a thick barrier, which stopped the arrows of the Men of the Waters, while the Theban archers took aim at their leisure and struck with every shot.

But it was only a respite. Setne sensed defeat approaching. Already his advance guard was giving way; furious masses were penetrating the lines of iron and bronze. The attack was reaching its full force when the Queen of the Waters stood up on the promontory. She raised her arms in a cross and gave the signal for a supreme effort. Everything broke. The dislocation of the phalanges happened with cracking sounds, as if the bones of a colossal beast had been broken.

Meanwhile, the resistance had reached its limit. Arrows, stones from slings, clubs, lances and swords never ceased striking the naked bodies of the Men of the Waters, but in vain: the voids were immediately filled by new troops.

Thutmose will never see his phalanges again, Setne said to himself, bitterly.

The images of Gaila and Aoura floated through the tumult of the battle. The Tanite sensed the awful weight of death upon his breast. Full of determination to make a supreme effort, he darted a long glance at his soldiers. Thirty cubits away, the Queen of the Waters was advancing triumphantly. The guards, with great sinister cries, were driving the Egyptians back. Setne conceived the project of capturing her, He assembled a nucleus of men chosen from the iron phalanx, hid them behind a curtain of willows, and waited.

The battle flowed back toward him. Memphite archers fled toward the shore. Then, raising his sword Setne gave the signal for a desperate attack. His men launched forward. Their surge crossed fifteen cubits, irresistibly. The Queen of the Waters found herself surrounded. A gigantic Theban soldier armed with a spiked club felled an enemy with every gesture. He cleared a passage all the way to the Queen, seized her and carried her away. Weapons were raised against her; but Setne had bounded forward. He deflected the swords with murderous points and, seizing the young woman, he carried her away in the midst of his men.

Meanwhile, the Men of the Waters could no longer see their sovereign. Their sinister voices called out without receiving any response. At first their impetus seemed to increase further, but then a vast lamentation rose up, and the attack faltered on all sides.

The phalanges reformed, and regained the upper hand. After a few moments of hesitation, the Men of the Waters returned to the marsh. But the danger had not disappeared; the causeway and the peninsula were still surrounded by invisible enemies who would want to avenge their queen once the first discouragement had passed.

Time went by. The great waters remained mute and motionless, as if nothing inhabited them but the snakes, fish, lizards and turtles that appeared at intervals in their crystal turbulence. Long red steaks and motionless bodies, however, betrayed the struggle, and on the causeway, the Egyptians were piling up their dead and their wounded.

After a rapid roll call, Setne returned to the Queen. She was sprawled on the ground, indifferent to the soldiers who were guarding her. Among those brown men she seemed even more extraordinary, with her hyacinth hair, her blue skin and her immense eyes of smoky flame. When the chief arrived, she stood up and looked at him. Anger and despair quivered in her face. Her lips, tremulous over the opal teeth, displayed hatred for the victor.

Setne spoke to her in a soft voice. At first she did not listen. Her gaze was fixed on the lake, vague and terrible. At intervals, she had fits of violent fury, which caused her long hair to undulate. Then there was a sort of relaxation. The eyes brightened; they had the gleam of beautiful moist stars when a fine vapor rises into the firmament. The impetuous soul that they revealed appeared to undergo an abrupt revolution.

The Queen of the Waters put both hands over her breast. Designating Setne, she pronounced a few incomprehensible words in a voice that was a trifle hoarse, but as gentle as the voice of fountains. Then she made a sign that all the others should draw back.

"I think she wants to make an alliance with you," said Intar. "And it's necessary to erect a tent, Lord, for she doubtless desires to be hidden.

Setne had his tent brought and erected in the middle of the peninsula. A sudden lightness on the part of the young woman testified that she had been understood correctly. When the tent was set up, she went into it first. Setne accompanied her, curious as to what would follow. He had heard mention of strange peoples who drank blood to cement amity, and he expected some ceremony of that nature, resolved to submit to it.

When the flap of the tent had closed, they stood still for a moment, considering one another. A strange mildness animated the Queen's face. Alone with her, Setne saw more clearly that the strange blue body had a seductive form and that no woman could have more beautiful eyes. Even the opal teeth, glinting in the penumbra like changing clouds at sunrise, were not without charm.

She approached him and took his hand. In that gesture, a long hank of hyacinth hair streamed over the soldier's forearm. It was cool, light, and quivering with a personal life. The hand was also cool, melting, smoother than the nascent petals of a nelumbo. A slight disturbance caused a frisson to run along the chief's spine.

The young woman spoke in a voice as musical as a fountain; the emerald gaze never ceased to contemplate Setne. Then, still uncertain as to what she wanted, he advanced his free hand and placed it on the Queen's shoulder. She made a rapid movement; their breasts touched. He knew what the pledge of union demanded of him was...

He forgot the combats, the fatigues, the rude and precarious life, and, drawing the young woman against him, the strangest of those he had encountered, he made an alliance with her...

Outside, the wounded were moaning; the phalanges were completing their preparations for new battles; the cries of subaltern commanders could be heard, the clash of weapons. Then the extraordinary clamor of the Men of the Waters announced an imminent attack. Heads and blue bodies were seen emerging *en masse* from the marsh.

But the flap of the tent was suddenly raised. The Queen appeared, her face softened by a charming lassitude. Her emerald eyes blinked in the light. She raised her hands, pronounced slow words, and the war between the Egyptians and the Men of the Waters was over.

VI

It was the seventh day of the journey. The previous day, Setne had reached the gorge to the Hennar where he wanted to take the Ninevite caravan by surprise. He chose the location of the ambush in the morning.

The route narrowed at first between two lines of red rocks, then widened into a semicircle, and then narrowed again. An insipid breath blew over the plants; meager beasts ran over the warm stone; reptiles paraded their long bodies and vitreous eyes, and carrion birds rise up on trenchant wings.

Setne examined the sad place. There was none better for the ambush. As soon as the caravan came into the semi-circle, its forward progress and its retreat could both be cut off, while, launching their arrows from the height of the rocks of charging unexpectedly, the Egyptians could sow panic among the men of the escort.

The young chief meditated for some time. He was approaching the outcome that ought to give him the favor or attract the scorn of Thutmose, and he did not want to leave anything to chance. Full of anxiety and hope, he gave his orders. Six hundred men were hidden in coverts in the rock or the brushwood, two hundred were ready to cut off the retreat and two hundred more to bar the route to the Hennar. No one was to budge before the trumpets had sounded the attack.

Thus, the pass was ready to welcome the caravan, and Setne, sitting in the shadow of a rock, was eating smoked meat and lotus beans. His emotion had passed. He was entirely focused on the action. He saw his centurions coming, gave them precise orders, and only kept Habak and Intar beside him. Then he sent new scouts along the route.

The day advanced and the sun was a quarter of the way through its route when scouts arrived, out of breath.

"The Assyrians are coming. There are many beasts of burden: donkeys, mules, horses and dromedaries..."

"And warriors?"

"There are several hundred..."

"As many as us?"

"No, a little more than half."

"Are they marching rapidly?"

"They were five thousand cubits away. We've marched three times faster than them."

Setne made a last inspection of his men. He saw that all was well, and stationed himself, with Habak and Intar, at an intermediate height, behind a clump of bushes. The landscape seemed solitary: the meager animals, the reptiles, the vultures and the scrub gave no indication of the presence of humans.

Meanwhile, in the distance, men became visible, and then donkeys, horses and dromedaries. Weapons glittered in the sunlight. That advance guard moved forward slowly and cautiously. The scouts stopped in order to observe the circle of red rocks; but their suspicion did not last long. Well-armed and numerous, they had no fear of the small bandit hordes that sometimes lay in wait for caravans on the route, and did not even think that the Egyptians could have reached the place. The entire company resumed its march. Other animals appeared, slaves, merchants and stewards attached to the Ninevite army, and then women, some carried by donkeys and camels, others on foot, enveloped in white wool.

Soon the area was invaded. It was like a population, a tribe in search of new pastures. The footfalls of the animals and the cries and murmurs of the men reverberated from the rocks; a donkey began braying; men agitated in the midst of nervous horses; jewels and weapons glinted as the caravan moved. Brown men of the desert were most frequently recognizable, along with merchants from Assyria and Persians with bright faces, red-haired barbarians brandishing large bows the color of blood, and negroes with an oscillating gait.

Eventually, the advance guard approached the exit from the circus. Setne gave the signal. The Egyptian trumpets resounded on the rocks. With a ferocious clamor, the archers unleashed their arrows. A homicidal rain fell. The slaves, the women and the merchants tried to flee, at hazard, bewildered. The soldiers spun around, waving their weapons, while those at the front and the rear attempted to reach the passes. But the clamor of the Egyptians resounded more loudly; the trumpets vibrated relentlessly; the arrows felled men and women.

It was evident that retreat was cut off in all directions. The crowd began milling madly, a melee of the soldiers that prevented them from mounting any defense. Only one group of Ninevite veterans was able to assume battle order. They were about two hundred men, tempered by a hundred battles, hard, cold and grim, about half of whom were armed with bows. They responded to the attack. Rapid arrows collided with rocks, ineffective-ly.

Setne saw that if that elite force was vanquished, the caravan was captured. He shouted loudly, ordering half his archers only to aim at the veterans. The storm of arrows swelled, and the Ninevite soldiers, with cries of rage, fell upon one another in a red, greasy, seething pool. When their ranks had thinned and their quivers were almost empty, Setne decided to charge them; he got his reserves ready.

The trumpets fell silent. With two hundred of his best men, Setne turned around the foot of the rocks and the phalange suddenly raced forward, lances bristling, large bucklers extended before every rank, like a fortress of leather and bronze. For ten minutes the Ninevites were seen to fight with all their courage, trying their swords and axes against the forest of sharp lances, but with an irresistible movement, the phalanx felled or drove back the men. Soon, the Ninevites were backed up against the rock, and collapsing on top of one another. Wading in bloody mud, out of breath, they asked to surrender.

It was the end; the caravan was taken.

The massacre continued for some time. Egyptian soldiers were seen nailing Ninevites to the ground, cutting off heads, opening bellies or smashing fugitives against the rocks. Cries of agony filled the air; the wounded were crawling under the feet of beasts of terri-fied beasts of burden, which trampled their plaintive bodies. Prostrate merchants were still begging for mercy when blades or javelins entered their throats. A negro, his woolly hair red with blood, with two darts lodged in his torso and a gaping wound in his back was still trying to climb the rocks.

Setne was finally able to recall his troops; the slaughter ceased, but not the screams, prayers and moans.

In the final count, only a hundred Ninevite soldiers, a few merchants, a few women and a few slaves were killed. Three hundred soldiers were prisoners and there was an enormous booty: wheat and barley for an army, countless beasts of burden, cartloads of weapons, crates of jewels and precious fabrics, leather, garments ad fermented beverages.

Setne contemplated his work with pride. Thinking about the important figure of Thutmose, he felt that he was in an atmosphere of glory. His breast swelled; a keen and strong blood surged in his heart. He believed in the future and saw the divine face of Princess Aoura closer to him than when he had spoken to her in the enclosure of the temple of Amenemhat.

Extracting himself from his magnificent dream, however, he turned to the centurion Habak, who was waiting, ready to receive his orders.

"You'll supervise the division of the spoils," he said. The weapons, the wheat, the beasts of burden, the crates and baskets will be reserved for the king and his army. As for the objects of gold and silver, and the precious stones and fabrics, they belong to our phalanges, to wit: a tenth for me, a tenth to be divided between the chiefs of the phalanges, another tenth for the centurions and the subaltern commanders, the rest for the soldiers. But before then, I'll make the choice of my booty. I'll also distribute the women and the slaves. Have we dead?"

"Yes, Lord. Three dead and five wounded. The enemy has more than a hundred dead."

"We'll make a halt, and do for our dead what is pre-scribed. Go, Habak."

Then he heard the grave voice of Intar: "Is my Lord not wounded?"

He shivered; he smiled at the nomad chief. Thinking of all that had come from him, and the triumph itself, he placed his hand on his head tenderly.

"I will share my booty with you!"

Habak came back with two old centurions. Wounded men were still moaning; a few would moan all day and all night. Nevertheless, tranquility had returned; the women were standing in troops, the more anxious the less pretty they were; the merchants were maintaining an imploring attitude; the Ninevite soldiers were awaiting massacre or slavery, somberly.

"Your orders will be carried out," said Habak, "but the soldiers would like to drink the Ninevites' wine."

"A measure will be given to them this evening. During the day, wine makes the body heavy, and we still have a stage to cover."

Habak, who liked wine and cervoise, showed a re-signed expression. Then he said: "Don't you want us to bring you the women, Lord?"

"Bring the women."

The captives were brought before Setne. In general, the soldiers had not despoiled them, for they had been captured under the eyes of the chief. Several were beautiful, destined for the sars of the Ninevite army. Those wore Babylonian embroideries, transparent byssus and Sidonian crimson. They scintillated with the flames of rubies, aquamarines and carbuncles or the soft gleam of pearls, seashells and turquoise. They shook little silver moons. Gold and ivory figurines, amulets and corals. A few, already visited by the soldiers, no longer had anything but torn garments; blood was trickling from their ears and nostrils, brutally stripped.

Setne distributed the beauties to the centurions and the others to those who had captured them, but he had the jewels and precious fabrics retained in order to make a just division later. For himself he kept a Persian with blue eyes, gleaming skin and coppery hair. She astonished him. He spoke to her in Assyrian without her appearing to understand him. She stood in front of him, silent, sad and proud. He desired her all the more for it, and was drawing her toward his tent when he saw Intar, who was gazing at her with a desperate covetousness. He hesitated. A voluptuous and jealous flux surged in his veins, but with a great effort of will he turned to the nomad and said: "Would you like to possess her?"

In a breathless voice, Intar replied: "I've never admired a woman so much."

"She's yours."

The chief of the sands uttered a hoarse sigh. Seizing his prey with an ardent tenderness, he carried her away. She smiled, with the imperious malice of a woman who senses a great amour descending upon her. Melancholy at first, Setne shook his head and had no regrets.

Two days later, Setne's phalanges reached the exit from the gorge. It was a narrow and tortuous passage, protected by natural forts of porphyry where a thousand archers could be garrisoned without having to fear ten times that number of enemies. It opened on to an immense plain interrupted by three hills toward the south, where the armies of Nineveh and Egypt had already fought violent battles several times, with various fortunes. It was deserted.

Setne sent skilful scouts in all directions. In the evening, they announced that no allied or enemy troop was yet visible.

The chief spent two days fortifying the place. He armed it with blocks of granite to roll down on assailants. He planted hedges of spikes in accessible places under masses of plants, and dug traps everywhere. Thanks to the slaves and the Assyrian prisoners, the work was done quickly; the gorge became inaccessible.

When the place was ready, emissaries returned one after another to announce the approach of the Ninevites from the north and the Egyptians from the south.

Then Setne was gripped by a great agitation. The defense of his fortress seemed to him to be assured. It would be glorious, but it could not give a vast hope, like a command on the battlefield. He asked old Habak's advice, who replied: "Send a messenger to beg Thutmose to let you fight with his army. Bitiu is skillful and obedient. He will be able to defend the gorge, which you have rendered inaccessible.

Setne did as the old man said. He announced to his master the capture of the caravan and the works he had accomplished for the defense of the pass.

The messenger came back after two hours, when Thutmose's advance guard was already perceptible on the hills. The king authorized Setne to rejoin the army and give command to the phalanges to Bitiu.

Setne set forth, only accompanied by Habak, Intar and twenty archers. The plain was still deserted to the north. No Ninevite runner was furrowing it as yet.

The young Tanite chief appeared before Thutmose at dusk. The king did not speak to him at first. Standing on the highest hill, he was casting a final glance over his camp. Four army corps were visible, over a breadth of three thousand cubits, and a double depth. The advance guard occupied the three hills; it was mainly composed of archers. Pyres were already being built, but Thutmore had forbidden lighting them until the last moment, for fear of a surprise attack by the Ninevites.

When Thutmose had gazed for some time and seen that all was well, he turned toward the Tanite. His face was grave but his eyes were cheerful. Everything had gone as he had wished and augured well for the imminent battle.

"Be welcome," he said to Setne, putting his ivory staff on his shoulder. "The servant who has accomplished the work conceived by his master will be recompensed. You have been able to command a thousand men across the desert; you will command ten phalanges against the Ninevites on the day of the battle."

Setne uttered a cry of joy and prostrated himself before Thutmose.

"Who would not die for you, master of the world!" he murmured.

The king was pleased by that joy. He liked all conquests, and there were none more agreeable to him than those the hearts of his soldiers gave him.

"Get up," he said. "Recount your journey to me, briefly."

Setne spoke briefly, but when he spoke about the dragons, the tigers and the Men of the Waters, the king became animated and wanted to know everything. Then a doubt passed through him.

"Be careful," he said. "I don't want anyone to tell me more than the truth. Have you seen these things?"

"I have taken twenty men from my phalanges, King of Thebes. Interrogate them..."

Thutmose wanted him to finish his story.

When Setne had depicted the capture of the caravan and the works carried out in the gorge of the Hennar, he said: "That's good! Everything has been accomplished as it ought to be. My gaze will follow you during the battle, Setne, son of Raneferka, and you will receive in accordance with your merit."

And. dismissing the chief with a slow gesture, he remained alone before the rapid dusk

PART THREE

I

For a long time, a slave massaged Aoura's body, still warm from the bath, with balms from Araby that were incorporated into the skin, and light Syrian perfumes that recalled the enchanted breezes of the Liban at every movement.

Aoura contemplated herself in a large silver mirror that Thutmose had sent her from Asia. Her torso had grown; she was almost perfect, and her breasts, delicate and round, with their little pink fruits, were connected in a charming fashion to the tender neck, the voluptuous nape and the beautiful, well polished shoulders. She loved herself. Braced in front of the bright mirror, she tried the innumerable play of attitudes, sometimes raising her arms, curious about the shadow of the armpits, sometimes flexed for the caress, sometimes full of emotion in contemplating the mystery of life and imagining the happiness of the man who would be designated by her brother Thutmose to know her.

Once she had dreamed that the king himself might be her first lover. That would not displease her, although she was fearful of displeasing her sister Hatsheput, who was jealous. But that dream no longer visited her. Her choice was fixed; among all men, only one veritably attracted her flesh.

Twelve months, however, had passed since she had spoken to him in the enclosure of the old temple of

Amenemhat. She ought to have forgotten him, and, in fact, she could no longer form an exact image of his bearing or his face; nothing remained but an impression of tall stature, supple forms and bold eyes. Alone, perhaps she would have let the memory fade, but she saw Gaila every day. The two of them stimulated the flame. Thus, far from decreasing, the amour of the Princes of Thebes increased with absence; she could no longer compose a legend of happiness without binding Setne tightly within it.

When the slave had finished infusing her with balms and sprinkling her with perfumes, Aoura dressed in a swathe of byssus and went on to the terrace. Thebes was scintillating in the strong morning light. The new temple built by Thutmose was growing among those of the ancestors. The city of the hundred gates was more populated with sphinxes than the Libyan desert with lions, buffaloes and elephants; columns and obelisks sprouted like an immense forest of stone, enameled walls sparkled like immense gems. The Theban people could be seen swarming in the squares, on the steps, in the narrow streets, outside houses on mud and papyrus, and in boats floating on the Nile all the way to the horizon of the plains, pyramids and pullulating cities.

But Aoura, sated by that spectacle, did not pay much attention to it. She agitated in the shade of the tamarinds; like a great mobile flower, she embalmed the air with each of her gestures. Joyful at first, impatience slowly took possession of her. Gaila was late. For the slave had been able to remain free to come and go at her caprice, by virtue of the tender generosity of the princess of Thebes and the enigmatic reasons she gave for her conduct.

"She promised to come!" said Aoura, nervously.

She knew full well that the promise of the daughter of the Gulf had not been categorical, but in her chagrin she did not want to admit that to herself.

"I want her to obey me!"

It was the thousandth time that she had proposed to herself forcing the will of the mysterious Bedouin. Fundamentally quick tempered, but not tyrannical, the princess did not dislike Gaila's capricious tendencies; it was a more complex attraction, which gave an extraordinary price to the strange young woman's submissions.

Suddenly, a smile brought Aoura's eyelids closer together. A red silhouette appeared down below, among the sycamores. The princess would have recognized that stride in a hundred thousand, which sowed rhythm and sensuality.

When Gaila had climbed the steps of the terrace, Aoura said, coldly: "You're late!"

"No," replied the slave. "I hadn't promised anything."

She stood before Aoura, serious, mild and firm. The princess, her eyes lowered, saw the small feet enveloped in ribbons, a delicate ankle, scarcely burnished, quivering. The spectacle softened her. She raised her head, and saw Gaila's magnificent lips, where the redness of the flesh took on the charming tones of petals and moist seashells. Then she smiled, and, kissing the slave's eyes tenderly, said; "Oh, you're indifferent! Don't you know the impatience with which I await your coming? You make me suffer."

"I can't do otherwise. And I'm not indifferent. I think about your happiness day and night."

"But you don't experience any impatience. Here you are before me like a submissive slave. That's not what I want, Gaila."

The Bedouin woman smile enigmatically. Her large eyes stared at Thebes, full of dreams.

"Have I not said that the daughters of my race are simple?" she replied. "They are only able to love the amour of a man. But their amity is as faithful as their hatred. Now, I would die for you, daughter of Ahmose, as I would die for my vengeance; why desire anything else? As well ask a lioness to engender monkeys, or a vine to produce dates."

Chagrined, Aoura exclaimed: "I'm beautiful, though..."

"You are the most beautiful of all women, Mistress. From the Red Gulf to Syria, no daughter of men is comparable to you."

The princess smiled, drew Gaila to the silver mirror and, contemplating their delicious images complaisantly, she said: "Witch, the man who possessed us both would be more fortunate than the gods."

Those words troubled the slave. "But you would not permit," she said, "a man to love both of us?"

"Why not?" said Aoura, tenderly.

"Would your pride not revolt, or would you not be jealous?"

Aoura started laughing. "No, Gaila, I would not be jealous, I would be glad. The man who loved you would appear more beautiful to me if he loved me too. I would find that very pleasant. And, then, he would no longer be able to think of any other woman. We would be able to render him faithful!"

Gaila contemplated the princess with a shiver of joy. "You merit that someone would die for you!" she said. "Nevertheless, consider that I am only a wanderer, a thousand times outraged."

"One does not lose the force of the blood! Have you not told me that your brother commanded a large tribe of the Gulf? Thutmose esteems the chiefs of your race; Thutmose knows me well."

The nomad's face was covered with darkness. "My father is not avenged," she said, "nor my mother, nor my brothers. Those who seized our pastures live in peace and abundance. The first virtue is hatred."

Her eyes darted a red flame. Aoura sensed clearly that her companion possessed the first virtue of vigorous races fully. She had the same maxims, albeit more tenderly.

"Do you believe that one of Thutmose's phalanges could get rid of your enemies?" she said.

"No. The men of Daour have a thousand warriors in the vigor of age, and as many old men and boys capable of handling a sword. Ten phalanges would not be sufficient to envelop them, for the chiefs must not flee. It is necessary that they perish, buried up to the neck, or roasted in the furnace, that their women are raped and their entrails thrown to the jackals. Only thus will justice be satisfied."

Aoura listened to the nomad with admiration. She liked strength. Pensively, she said: "Would your tribe consent to pay tribute to Thutmose? The king is not avid. A few beasts of burden would acquit your debt."

"We would no longer be free," said Gaila, bitterly.

"Oh, yes! You would be the king's allies; no tribe could attack you without igniting his anger."

They fell silent. Then Aoura sighed. "Who can tell where Thutmose's warriors are fighting now?"

Gaila smiled. That morning, she had seen one of the men of the desert, who, invariably outdistancing the king's couriers, was spreading among the lower orders the news that was as yet unknown to the upper castes.

"Thutmose is victorious," she said. "He has defeated his enemies in a great plain one day's journey from the Euphrates."

"How do you know?" cried the princess of Thebes, trembling with pleasure. "Why are you talking today, having kept silent on other days?"

"Have I not told you that the arcana are not always efficacious?"

"Is the news certain?"

"Unless an evil god..."

Aoura interrupted, impatiently: "And what do you know of Setne?"

Gaila hesitated, because she knew nothing about her master. But she only dared hide that partially.

"I have seen that he has fought gloriously, then the signs became obscure. Nevertheless, it seems that he had gained the king's favor..."

She stopped. Trumpets sounded at the great pylon. A courier appeared, thin and black, followed by servants who were crying: "Thutmose has slain twenty thousand men, and Setne has felled ten thousand!"

The young women had raced on to the terrace; they were pale with joy. Aoura, kissing the face of the slave passionately, cried: "I believe in you, witch!"

II

The courier appeared before Queen Hatsheput, the elder sister of Thutmose III.[22] Tall and massively propor-

---

[22] The author inserts a note here to specify that this is not Hatsheput the Great, who was the sister, guardian and wife of

tioned and benevolent appearance, with the eyes of a heifer, misty and slow, she was jealous, imperious and vindictive. She did not look at the man blackened by the deserts, desiccated by hunger, tanned as if with dust, who had thrown himself on the ground. She remained as motionless and dormant as the statues of temples, but, as no one could speak before her without her having permitted it, she finally said: "King Thumtmose has sent you?"

"The king of kings has sent me," the man replied, "with five other runners, by the Syrian route. Three of my companions fell, of malady and lassitude. The other two perished under the swords of nomads. There were also runners on other roads. If any of them have arrived before me, daughter of Ahmose, I am only bringing you dead news."

"No one has preceded you," said the queen, coldly. "Speak."

And the courier spoke, his face to the ground.

"Three months after the battle of the Hennar, Thutmose encountered the enemy again, in greater number, in the plain of Sades, near the Euphrates. Ten sars have crawled at his feet; thirty others have lost their breath. In the evening, the count was made of twenty thousand hands, cut from the dead. And there is an innumerable booty of gold, silver, precious stones, amulets, beasts and weapons. All of Assyria fled before the face of the king and that of his servant Setne."

Thutmose II. Thutmose III had at least three wives, including Merytre-Hatsheput, the mother of his successor, Amenhotep II, but she is not thought to have been Thutmose's sister. It is thought that one of his wives might have been his half-sister Neferure, but that is disputed.

"Who is that man?" said the queen, with a cold curiosity.

"He is the right arm of Thutmose, terrible in battle, full of cunning. The king wants him to march after him in the command and in the council."

"His name has never been mentioned to me."

"He comes from Tanis," said the courier. "At the beginning of the war he commanded a phalanx, but Thutmose, having recognized that he was successful in his enterprises, sent him with a thousand men to the gorge of the Hennar, where Setne surprised a caravan. Then he commanded the right wing in the battle; he overturned five thousand Ninevites. Afterwards, at Sades, he enveloped a third of the Assyrian army. That is why our lord has raised him above the other chiefs of war."

After a pause, the courier added: "Admirable Queen, the king will follow his couriers at a distance of four months."

"Withdraw," said the queen. And she added, for she was not miserly: "You have served well. You will be given three four-year-old oxen; the protection of your masters will extend over you and your race."

When the courier had left the room, Hatsheput summoned her sister and communicated the news to her. Then she said: "Have you ever heard any mention of this young Tanite warrior?"

Aoura blushed. "Yes," she replied. "Have I not spoken about him? He is the man I saw teaching your son Amenhotep the use of the bow. His family, it is said, was allied to the old kings."

"Perhaps Thutmose will finally allow you to know a man," said Hatsheput, with a sort of vivacity, for she feared that the king might keep that charming sister for himself. "Would you like that chief?"

Divining her sister's desire, Aoura replied without hesitation: "I would like him."

Hatsheput's features relaxed. "Then I will speak in favor of that marriage," she said.

She dismissed her sister. Aoura fled joyfully and went to find the nomad. She reported the queen's words to Gaila, who listened with pleasure, and then with pity; she saw that the fate of the princess was now settled.

But a shadow of death, of the jealousy of the queen, hovered over her.

III

At the end of the first moon of Autumn, the rumor spread through the valley of the Nile that the army of Thutmose was approaching the isthmus. Thin and rapid men ran from city to city announcing the great news.

Among the boats of the Nile, the swarming cities, and all the way to the smallest clusters of huts constructed of dry wood and papyrus, Egypt entire soon knew that his army was bringing back an enormous booty, ten thousand captives, horses, donkeys and singular beasts. At the new moon, the standards of the advance guard appeared before Thebes; then the sand was seen rising all the way to the horizon. The soldiers arrived, black, savage, fleshless and indefatigable in tattered, dirty or absent garments. But the weapons were still shining, and the satisfaction of a great booty rendered the faces dignified.

At the gates of Thebes the trumpets sounded. Closer and closer, the fanfares followed one another along the dusty roads. Then the light Theban drums rattled like an innumerable army of cicadas. The carts jolted along the road, sparkling with scythes, harrows and sharp lances.

The phalanges massed, slow and formidable, bristling with points and shadowed by great bucklers. They seemed heavy by comparison with the archers, sling-wielders and swordsmen, but those who carried clubs were marching like stone statues.

The army was not to enter Thebes. It dispersed around it and chose its encampments, while three elite phalanges, which guarded Thutmose, presented themselves before the great pylon.

In a fulgurant cedar-wood chariot, encrusted with suns and moons, the king was standing, covered with a garment as coarse as those of his soldiers, his head shaded by a light woolen pschent. Other chariots followed in which chiefs were seen flamboyant with sardonyxes, beryls or sapphires, with multicolored baldrics, bucklers laminated with gold and silver; for Thutmose, sober, simple and almost a stranger to any sensory joy, showed a disdainful indifference for his person. By contrast, he rejoiced in seeing a magnificent luxury streaming around him in his companions. In order not to displease him, Setne had put on embroidered garments and ardent jewelry.

The first phalanx of guards was engulfed within the pylon, amid the savage clamors of the Thebans.

A frightening crowd expanded, like a foam of faces, a swell of brown bodies, with long waves of violet, crimson, white, green or saffron fabrics, and cries, reinforced by sudden surges of enthusiasm or weakened by long refluxes of curiosity, imitated all the noises of a tempest against rocks and among great trees.

Then, as the king passed by, there was a long silence, of which the density of beings made something strangely material. The simplicity of the formidable master disconcerted the people every time. They searched therein for a symbol, a myth, a mystery, experiencing at first an obscure disappointment, but very rapidly, a reaction as violent as thunder rumbled in their souls, and then, immense, frantic and irresistible, the entire adoration of a people for the victorious chief, all the confused life of a crowd sensing its unity, all the passionate servitude of a nation that can only exist by virtue of a powerful authority, agitated that great human flood, drawing inexhaustible cries therefrom.

Thutmose traversed that hurricane of emotion with a visage as hard as granite; but a gleam of arrogant joy filtered into his gaze. The guards drove back the audacious. One man, mad with enthusiasm, succeeded in getting through the hedge of lances and threw himself upon the king's chariot with a savage affection. It would be his death if he touched Thutmose, but a glorious death, which entailed, for those who believed themselves in a state to appear before the infernal judges, exemption from several ordeals.

The king, annoyed, gestured to the fanatic to withdraw. The other took no account of the order. With an extraordinary leap he reached the platform of the chariot. There, prostrate, holding the master's feet, he requested with loud cries that his life be cut short by the royal sword. Already, soldiers were about to seize the man. Thutmose, no longer able to save him without falling in the eyes of the Thebans, drew his weapon with a smile and plunged it into the heart of the supplicant. Roars of joy saluted that execution; a long tempest of enthusiasm rose from the depths of the multitude, and a thousand furious creatures rushed forward to touch the bloody dust.

The escort reached the palace. Thutmose entered it with the ten great chiefs of his army. The queen was waiting in a hall strewn with herbs, roses and lotuses, with cut palm leaves, myrtles and great Nile seeds. Hatsheput displayed herself on red petals, with pale rubies and beryls in her hair, stout and heavy, her eyes enveloped by thick lids, and Thutmose, who had loved her dearly, found her still desirable.

"Here you are, finally," she said, "conqueror of the vast earth. Egypt was sad and miserable during your absence. But like the beneficent Nile, your return makes your people cry out with joy."

Less inclined than her to emphasis, he replied: "I've brought you a thousand slaves, coffers full of embroidered cloth, gold and silver jewelry, fiery stones, enamels, precious leather and perfumes without number..."

His gaze, moving sideways, encountered the elegant body of Aoura. She was standing on herbs mingled with young nelumbos, so tightly clad in gold and hyacinth cloth that every contour was perceptible. Her black hair was a night constellated with amber stars; her proud eyes, soft and more changeable than the evening sky, astonished Thutmose.

"How beautiful you are, my sister!" he said. "There is nothing about you that is not delightful to see." His nostrils flared; a heavy frisson of lust ran through the entire body of the man, sensible to the beauty of women.

Hatsheput went pale, her slow soul filled with murder, while Aoura, charmed at first and then anxious, turned her eyes toward Setne, standing at the back of the room in front of the other war chiefs.

Already, the king, an energetic master of his will, had postponed his desire until later. He went on, gravely: "For you also, Aoura, I have brought slaves, precious stones, gold, silver, and the perfumes of the Euphrates and Syria."

Then he made a sign to Setne, who advanced and prostrated himself before the queen.

"This," said the king, "is my beloved servant. His strength has been half of my strength, his arm has brought victory everywhere. I want him to have the first place after the king and the queen, and let everyone incline to his commands."

He placed his hand gently on Setne's head, and declared: "You have not asked me for anything yet. I would like to do for you whatever you desire."

"The king has heaped me with benefits," replied the Tanite. "He has recompensed me a thousand times."

"But you have not asked me for anything," repeated Thutmose. "Let me know your desire."

Setne darted his gaze at Aoura. She went pale; their faces confessed then that they loved one another, but they understood immediately that the time had not come, and Setne said: "My lord will permit me to wait for a few days. I am not yet ready to express a desire."

"Very well," said Thutmose, with a smile. "I will wait until the day of Osiris."

He raised Setne up himself, and sent out all the chiefs. And while he sat down beside the queen, he was still considering her younger sister with an ardent covetousness.

Thutmose spent the night with Hatsheput and rendered his duty to her. He took scarcely any pleasure in it.

The queen, anxious and vindictive, knew that her brother desired another woman. She would have passed over a slave carelessly, or even a free daughter of Thebes, but she could not suffer the idea of sharing with

260

her sister. Only Aoura, in Egypt or in the lands conquered by Thutmose, was her equal, and against her
alone. Hatsheput experienced an insupportable jealousy.

The king got up early in the morning, dressed with
his usual simplicity, and then, having made a meal of
fish and papyrus stems, he picked up an ivory staff in
order to go out.

"Where is my lord going?" asked Hatsheput, softly.

Thutmose never lied to his family, his servants or
his soldiers. He only masked the truth with enemies.
Above all, he had never hidden anything from his wife.
This time he hesitated, imperceptibly, for he was not
unaware of Hatsheput's jealousy.

"I'm going to visit the gardens and the works," he
said. "I shall also go to see our sister Aoura."

She could not contain herself. She demanded: "And
what do you want with our sister?"

Thutmose no longer hesitated. His sovereign will
did not want to fear obstacles. "It is time," he said, "that
she knew a man."

"And who will you give her?" said Hatsheput, very
pale.

"She will have the same master as you."

Although, in the reign of Thutmose III, everything
bowed down before royal authority, even the formidable
power of the priests, the legitimate wife retained almost
intact the prerogatives that would be successively weakened thereafter.

Hatsheput rebelled. "I do not want to have a rival!"
she cried. "Take any other, and I will say nothing. But
for her, Thutmose, it is necessary to give her a husband."

"No will can rise above mine!" said the king, forcefully. "You will not have a rival. Only you will be my

wife. But it is good that our sister has children of the blood of Ahmose. Ours might perish."

She replied vehemently: "Why give vain reasons? You are only thinking of your desire; that is unworthy of you. No king of our dynasty has coveted more than one of his sisters, and all of them, however, have counted them in great number. Such was the will of Ahmose. Be careful, in defying it, of attracting the anger of Ammon and ending your magnificent reign in defeat or shame!"

"I have done as much as Ahmose," he said, angrily. "Why should I not have a will equal to his?"

She feigned a profound dejection. "Woe betide whoever scorns the ancestral law! Thutmose, are you forgetting that that man founded our dynasty? Are you forgetting that he labored for our glory, that he delivered us from filthy slavery?"

"I'm forgetting nothing!" he replied, with a more violent anger. "I shall erect a new temple to the sacred memory of Ahmose, and our royalty, magnified by my hands, will accept a few new customs, without the souls of the ancestors being offended..."

She was about to reply, but he did not want to listen any longer; he disappeared into the gardens without her daring to follow him.

IV

Setne, trembling with amour and dread, had retired to his house. He knew that he was loved by Aoura, but he carried away, like a wound, the covetous gaze that the king had cast upon his sister. He wanted to see Gaila very quickly, thirsty for her face, her body and her advice.

262

An old slave had opened the door. Setne listened distractedly to his salutations. He marched through the rooms and the garden, impatient to see the woman he desired appear. He came to the enclosure of date palms and sycamores where he loved to repose. The water, faint and fresh, was murmuring very softly; memories rose up in the young man, abundant, luminous and so precise that his heart groaned with lust. He thought he could see once again, on the grassy banks, in the penumbra constellated with rays of amber and amethyst, the delightful form of his slave. Everything that she had predicted had been accomplished on the battlefields of Mesopotamia, as in the palace of Thebes; but had she foreseen Thutmose's desire?

He stamped his feet, impatiently, while the sun began to decline from the zenith. He had been careful to send a soldier with a message to the house of the old women where Gaila was living. Perhaps the nomad had been absent or the soldier had fulfilled his mission poorly? The idea came to him abruptly that she had quit Egypt, weary of such a long wait. He glimpsed the agile form gliding through the cities and solitary lances, prey to need, giving her body to men in exchange for nourishment or shelter.

That imagination, by torturing him with fury and jealousy, made him understand more fully how much he loved his slave. He could not remain in the dwelling any longer, and he was already heading toward the pylon when he heard youthful and silvery laughter, which he recognized as easily as if he had seen a face.

"Gaila!" he cried.

And, turning round, he saw the beautiful black fire of her pupils and the Bedouin's red lips. Then he forgot his dread; King Thutmose ceased to dominate his soul like a menacing shadow. Nothing remained but that delectable flesh. With a cry of joy he drew Gaila to his heart...

He got up again with the melancholy that the slave's indifference left him, but he did not express it. He said: "Your predictions are realized, Gaila. I have triumphed over enemies, gained the favor of the Thutmose, and..."

"And the love of Aoura!" she interrupted, with a smile. "Yes, the signs did not lie."

He took the young woman's hand with a joyful ardor. "But it's by you that I knew the signs, and you've aided me so well! My strength belongs to you, daughter of the Gulf."

"Keep your word and we'll go on to the end!"

He considered her with an eye suddenly filled with anxiety.

"Are you sure of that? This morning, I perceived an obstacle that might become insurmountable..."

She remained silent, full of shadows; her eyelids fluttered at intervals. He respected her silence, because he believed that she was consulting her mysterious science.

"Yes," she replied, "the danger is great, my master, if you intend to have Aoura for your wife. But remember that I haven't promised you that. I said that you would know her. Perhaps it will only be after Thutmose. Perhaps also, the king, his desire slaked, will give her to you without difficulty, for he does not love the same woman for long, and he will yield quickly to the anger of Hatsheput. You're not jealous of your king?"

That question embarrassed Setne. Any other sentiment than the dread and love of Thutmose seemed sacrilegious to him; and yet, an obscure bitterness swelled in his breast.

"How could I be jealous of the king?" he exclaimed, finally. "He sanctifies everything he touches. I only fear that he will not want to give me Aoura."

She feared that too. In truth, Thutmose was scarcely occupied with women. He knew few caprices, and all were brief; but how much more seductive might the princess of Thebes, his sister, seen to him than all the daughters of Asia, Egypt and Kush?

Gaila's will had a brief weakness. She sensed against her the star of the man who overturned empires. Then, her Bedouin temerity returned, and enabled hope, and she said: "Let us rest, my master. Thutmose will do nothing before the coming night has passed. Any action would be futile."

"Can you not interrogate your signs?" he said, with anguish.

"I have interrogated them. They are obscure. They will not speak before tomorrow."

He resigned himself. Momentarily, he saw again all the perils that he had traversed and vanquished, the favor of Thutmose conquered, the amour surprised in Aoura's eyes; then, fatalistically, he abandoned himself to destiny, and, turning his eyes toward his beautiful slave, he became disinterested again in everything but touching her red lips.

V

Thutmose spent more than an hour walking through the gardens. He stopped several times beside artisans and questioned them, for the king, curious about everything that men do, took almost as much interest in the works of the sculptor, the mason and the laborer as in his soldiers. Hard and just, he liked to punish by surprise, or recompense abruptly, but that morning he forgot to do either. The image of Aoura persisted in tormenting him. It had been presented to him at the precise moment when, weary of triumphs and voyages, weary of war itself, which had become too facile, Thutmose was prepared to welcome some new form of desire or domination. The only thing that gave him pause, more acutely than he would have thought, was the tradition of Ahmose. On the other hand, the jealousy of Hatsheput drove him to infringe the custom, not because he had the intention of sacrificing his wife, but because hers was the only will that could contest his, the only one before which he had sometimes yielded.

When he had made a tour of the gardens and court-yards, he headed toward the building where the princess lived. His hesitation had disappeared; at least, he believed so. He went up the steps of the terrace without stopping. He passed through the prostrate slaves and, going through the colonnade, he opened the door and went in. The first room was deserted. Thutmose headed toward the chamber where his sister slept.

When he went into it, he perceived a young woman clad in red who watched him come in.

Among the innumerable captives brought on the eve of battles or after the capture of cities, the king could not remember ever having seen eyes of such mysterious beauty, variable at every movement of the eyelids, combined with a more enveloping and profound life. The mouth too was surprising, an admirable flower of red flesh in which, dazzling and soft, the white gleam of the teeth appeared, and whose vague, curious, sensual half-smile astonished the conqueror of the Ninevites.

Motionless at first, she took a step; that simple movement revealed the ardent harmony of her body. Then, bowing, she waited in silence for Thutmose to speak.

"Who are you?" said the king. "You resemble the daughters of the Gulf who read destiny..."

"I am Gaila," she replied, "daughter of Rub, chief of the Bene-Asher, who reigned over great pastures. And I have received the gift of seeing the future. Before your messengers had arrived in Thebes, I had announced your victories in the Hennar and the Euphrates. I also know, king of kings, what projects are brooding in your heart, and the dangers that they will make you run."

He considered her with anxiety, suspicion and admiration.

"What are these dangers?" he said, abruptly.

She met the king's eyes, and did not turn her own away.

"Those that threaten rebel sons."

The king's suspicions increased; his face was covered with anger. "Is it to Queen Hatsheput that you announced my victories?" he cried, in a menacing voice.

But she responded without disturbance: "The queen does not know me."

"It's necessary to swear it!" he said harshly. "Those of your race swear on the heads of their fathers."

"By my father, dead in the furnace, and by my vengeance, to which I have consecrated my life, I swear, King of Thebes, that I have never spoken to Queen Hatsheput."

He calmed down. His doubts vanished. He knew that Hatsheput was too proud to deign to act directly against a rival, and he had no suspicion of the obscure link that united Aoura and Setne.

"Why have you come?" he said. "And where is my sister Aoura?"

"I've come for love of her. My life belongs to her. The dangers you run, she is running with you; and in saving you, it is her that I am saving."

He did not detest those words; he was pleased to believe that this charming creature had a free and voluntary soul. As the conversation went on, he discovered a beauty more numerous in her, a life more extraordinary, a rare and doubtless unique quality.

Already, the caprice that he had experienced for his sister was partly displaced toward the witch; he softened to the new desire. He did not struggle against that desire. The shade of Ahmose, which he venerated and feared in the same measure as the great gods, twice evoked, troubled him obscurely.

In a low voice he said: "You have not said what perils I am running."

"The alliance of all your enemies and the arrival of barbarian peoples similar to the Shous, who live far beyond Nineveh, Ecbatana and Syria...armies ten times more numerous than those you have fought."

The king's visage palpitated with warrior ardor. "I do not fear all the peoples of the world."

"No, but your lieutenants surrounded, a wound that renders you incapable of command, and, in sum, the will of the gods?"

She was speaking quietly, in a grave, soft and mysterious tone. The king sensed the unknown forces passing over him that caused conquerors to bow down. "And if I yield to your advice?" he asked.

"The gods will disunite your enemies. Each will want to fight on his own account; you will crush them one after another."

268

They had drawn closer together. Thutmose's hand had encountered the slave's arm. At that contact, he shivered all the way to the ankles.

"Tell me what it is necessary to do," he murmured.

"It is necessary to search for the man who ought to know Aoura. Consult the will of your sister; name the best of your warriors to her, in order that she should choose. For your other actions, events will guide you. It is not good that a man should know in advance all that he must do. Fortune too soon predicted becomes insipid, and in any case, a king such as Thutmose, when the will of the gods is not too strong, can even vanquish fate itself."

Those last words pleased the king violently. His hand pressed more tenderly on the round arm of the slave.

"Very well!" he said. "Aoura will designate her husband, and you will pay the ransom!"

He had seized her; their breasts touched; the king's desire was entirely detached from Aoura. Understanding that it was necessary to wait, however, in order to give the full price to the ransom, and also—she proudly insisted—in order that Thutmose should retain a finer memory, she said in a low voice: "Go now, king of kings. Give me two days to submit. Thus you will please the gods…"

She interrupted herself, with a faint smile, and added, in an even lower voice: "And you will also please your servant more…"

He hesitated, palpitating with lust, but Gaila's profound eyes, with an infinite softness, dissolved his will. He also sensed, confusedly, that he would have a strange pleasure himself in obeying and waiting. He yielded.

"Have Aoura summoned," he said.

VI

It was the day of Osiris. Setne was inspecting troops in the camp of Thebes, but he was scarcely putting any ardor into it. He had not seen Gaila again for three days. He had searched for her in vain throughout the city, and returned in vain ten times to the house of the old women where she had lived while he was at war in Asia.

A papyrus, brought by a man of the people the days before, had predicted a great happiness for him. At first he had been certain that the message came from Gaila, and then he had began to doubt. And he lived uncertain and miserable in the dread of having lost his slave, despairing of the future, no longer believing in Aoura's amour. Even the favor of Thutmose seemed precarious to him. The king remained enclosed in his palace, neglecting his war chiefs. Setne believed that he divined the cause of that; every time he thought about it, he felt full of a disgust for life.

The sun reached the highest point of the sky. The city and the camp were asleep; only Setne was walking among the barracks, tracked by anxiety. He came to his old phalanx. It was camped almost in the same spot where, in the spring of the preceding year, he had encountered young Prince Amenhotep. His heart beat faster with astonishment and emotion.

Immense periods seemed to have gone by, so prodigious had life been. Everything that the slave had predicted in Ankhi's gardens and the little house in Thebes had been realized. The favor of the formidable king had descended upon the obscure chief, the vast army of Thebes recognized, after that of Thutmose, the authority of Setne, son of Raneferka.

Like a brilliant painting on the wall of a temple, the Tanite saw once again the desert of Nomi, the land of the dragons, the night of the tigers, the strange People of the Waters and the extraordinary queen who had trembled against his breast. Was it possible? Had those things really happened to the man who, such a short time before, had been exercising two hundred men in the camp of Thebes?

He had a great quiver of pride and strength, and he braved destiny. He could die; he had undertaken a career as vast as if he had lived for a hundred years. And while he contemplated Thebes, motionless in the dazzling light, the sacred Nile, the land of Egypt flourishing in the concluding flood, and the sleeping phalanx with which his glory had commenced, the faces of Aoura and the nomad rose up, so clearly that he made a gesture of seizing them.

His soul weakened. It wanted ardently still to savor the joy of living, it was roaring with lust and amour. The past joy rendered the dread of the future more frightful. He uttered a hoarse sigh, and turned his gaze toward the pale palace that rose up between two temples, in a forest of columns, over a lake of trees and flowers. His entire being convulsed with desire and fear.

An agile troop passed over the plain. Setne recognized the nomad auxiliaries. He had recruited them himself, at the hazard of skirmishes, and had obtained that Intar would be their chief. The sight of them made him shiver. Marching toward then, he made them stop with a sign. Intar advanced toward the Tanite, laughing; his violent eyes, his white pointed teeth and his face the color of old leather—the entire being that hatred or sadness rendered sinister—was now illuminated by joy.

"Are you happy, Intar?" the Egyptian asked.

"You have made me happy," the nomad relied, ardently.

His gaze wandered over the troop, then, with an ecstatic tenderness, over a veiled palanquin carried by six eunuchs. A curtain lifted. Setne saw a milky face, coppery hair, and the bright eyes of the Persian woman who had been captured in the gorge of the Hennar with the Ninevite caravan.

"For the gift that you have made me of that woman," Intar murmured, "I will be your slave eternally."

When the nomads departed again, Setne felt his heart even heavier. The sun was declining; the shadows of the tents and barracks began to extend over the plain. A slight breeze rippled the Nile. Already, the army was waking up.

Then, from the northern pylon of Thebes, three heralds of Thutmose appeared, clad in red, preceded by a fanfare. They advanced slowly. Their arrival announced a grave event; the military chiefs got up as they approached, attentively. For a long time they remained silent, and then the trumpets fell silent. The oldest cried, in a voice that could be heard two thousand cubits away: "King Thutmose, king of kings, summons his servant Setne!"

Setne advanced, full of anxiety, uncertain whether he was to receive a new favor of whether Thutmose, having discovered Aoura's secret, wanted to exile a rival. He followed the heralds without saying anything, impatient with their slowness, but it was necessary not to think of making them walk any faster.

They reached the palace; the king was in the enameled hall that had served, since Ahmose for judging powerful chiefs and monarchs, or for decreeing great recompenses.

Thutmose was seated on a cedar chair encrusted with ivory and silver. Queen Hatsheput was sitting beside him. They were alone; only a few servants could be seen prostrate at their feet, faces to the ground.

"Approach, my servant," said the king. "Today is the day of Osiris. You promised me to ask me a great favor. What shall I give to the conqueror of the Euphrates?"

In spite of his anxiety, those words transported Setne, for he adored his master. Tremulously, he said: "You have heaped me with favors, King of Thebes. I have searched in vain for another that I might desire. No one is as able as you to recompense his servants."

Thutmose smiled. He believed in the Tanite's sincerity.

"What can we do for Setne?" he asked, turning to the queen.

Hatshetput fixed her bovine eyes on the chief and said, in her heavy voice: "What would you prefer, chief of great courage: all the taxes of the nome of Tanis, for your entire life, or to mingle your race with that of your kings?"

He went very pale, and trembled on his legs. His thought escaped him, vertiginously. For a minute, he was unable to respond.

"You're hesitating?" said Hatsheput.

"Oh no!" he cried, impetuously. "I'm not hesitating. What are all the tributes of all the people of the earth compared with a union with the race of Ahmose, Thutmose and Hatsheput? But your words fill me with astonishment and dread!"

Then Thutmose, leaning his ivory staff on the young man's shoulder, said: "Go and seek the consent of Aoura. Afterwards, we shall fix the day of your union..."

A slave conducted Setne. He reached the raised terrace that preceded the princess's apartments. There he felt a kind of weakness. Prodigious as his good fortune appeared to him, everything seemed pale compared with this supreme victory. Undoubtedly, he had audaciously coveted the daughter of kings, he had trusted in Gaila's prediction and his fortune to be accomplished in accordance with his wish, but in the depths of that prodigious adventure, everything had seemed shadows, dreams, moving and delicious visions, not realities, whereas now he was marching toward Aoura as his phalanges had to encounter the Ninevites.

He took a few paces more. A door opened of its own accord; he saw the young princess, in the midst of her maidservants. She was clad in the same garment of gold and hyacinth as on the day of Thutmose's arrival. Her breasts stood forth as proudly as if they were naked; her small white feet reposed on a carpet of acacia flowers; her legs were scintillatingly clad, tapering, round, delicate and quivering on the saffron wool of her chair.

She got up as Setne approached.

"The king has sent me, holy princess…to ask you whether you will consent to unite yourself with your servant."

She was slightly troubled. A charming languor appeared in her beautiful eyes; she dispersed her slaves with a gesture.

"It is the will of the gods…," she said, in a low voice.

They were very close to one another, Setne half-prostrate before her. He straightened up when she had spoken.

Their bodies touched; an equal intoxication hastened their respiration.

Setne felt on his mouth the sacred and magnificent mouth of the daughter of kings.

VII

The king of Egypt remained Gaila's lover for six months. She was Thutmose's only veritable amour, the only one of whom he retained a delicious memory through his life of a great conqueror. Neither the jealousy of Hatsheput, who was discontented with the perseverance of that liaison, nor the revolts in Syria, could separate him at first from the daughter of the Gulf. She was faithful to him. She paid loyally for the marriage of Aoura and the vengeance against the despoilers of the Bene-Asher.

The heart of Setne bled because of the absence of the woman who had been his slave. He could not destroy his love for her; he hid in Thutmose's gardens in order to see her pass by; Aoura's caresses could not charm his pain.

In the sixth month, however, the imminent war occupied Thutmose. The nomad took advantage of it. She made him know the future. He knew that the gods ordered their separation. As that prediction coincided with others that the famous scribes had made to him, he believed in it. Nevertheless, he resisted. A hot ember of passion persisted in his heart. Moreover, he experienced for Gaila an attachment more durable than amour. She inspired a superior confidence in him, and her prophesies seemed to him the most valid of all.

One day, he said to her: "I want to obey the gods, Gaila, but they have not ordered me to forget you, nor to neglect your science…and how will I be able to consult you if you depart?"

"I can live with your sister Aoura, my Lord. She desires that; I would be happy with her."

"It will be as you request. You shall have riches at your desire. I have also prepared the vengeance against your enemies. The best of my chiefs will retake the pastures of your ancestors from the men of Daour."

He looked at her tenderly. Like a country one is abandoning after long days of joy, he saw her in all her beauty, and was profoundly saddened. But he never went back on his word. She had already raised an insurmountable mountain between them.

He said then: "Daughter of the Gulf, Thutmose does not forget! I have known very sweet pleasures through you, which I will regret for a long time. In any case, my shadow will extend over you to protect you, and I want you to retain, for as long as you live, a little of my power. You will possess the land of Sikeren, two thousand oxen, a thousand donkeys, five thousand sheep, five hundred slaves and authority over the ten towns that depend on that land."

The next day, Setne received the order to mobilize ten thousand men. First he was to retake the patrimony of the Bene-Asher, and then dissipate the coalitions of nomad tribes that had formed to the east of the Red Gulf, while Thutmose would march against the Syrians.

In four days, the Tanite had finished his preparations. Aoura had obtained permission to accompany her husband; Gaila brought her infant brother, in order to have him recognized by the tribe of his fathers.

The expedition's march was rapid. Setne had agile troops under his orders, hardened to marching, among whom were Intar's nomads and the troops that had followed him to the land of the Men of the Waters. Gaila's presence rejoiced his heart, but, as if still enveloped by the amour of Thutmose, she inspired a kind of dread in him. She seemed renewed. The caresses of the king of Thebes had effaced the memory of all the violences suffered by the slave, and even her union with Setne, so that he spoke to her as if she were, like Aoura, the daughter of a royal race.

One evening, when they were no more than eight days from the pastures of Daour, the fires of the camp were reddening the plain and the hill, and the desert extended its profound frissons, its asphodels, its harsh grass, its rare islets of date palms and cacti and its prodigious lakes of stars, Aoura said to her husband: "Why are you hiding yourself from me?"

He was mute with shock. She smiled, gentle and mocking.

"I penetrated your heart a long time ago. I know who it is for whom you agitate by night on your couch, and on whom your gaze is fixed during the marches, with so much trouble and chagrin. I don't experience any astonishment in consequence. Her beauty has already troubled my soul; even my brother Thutmose, who had laughed at amour, was unable to escape her. There is no woman who is comparable to her."

"Oh yes!" cried Setne, vehemently. "The one who reposes by night against my bosom cannot be surpassed by any other: I would die if she were to be taken away from me!"

They were the words she desired to hear. She replied: "I believe in your love, Setne, but I would be surer of keeping it forever if Gaila remained with us..."

They fell silent. Setne, moved by gratitude, kissed Aoura's little foot. Nothing could he beard but the cries of the sentinels calling to one another at intervals, the yapping of jackals and, occasionally, the thunderous clamor of a lion.

The hills were well-guarded; the Egyptian phalanges sheltered from any surprise. And the chief, indifferent to the nomads that were prowling around his army, was only anxious about the obscure tent where the woman he had possessed as a slave, and perhaps would never possess again, was asleep.

That was because she seemed, in fact, to have forgotten the old days. She did not flee Setne, but she greeted him with a strange gravity, and as she never quit her young brother, Eloh, any intimate conversation became impossible. Heaped by Thutmose with slaves and wealth, she marched in the midst of troops like a queen. And she lived as naturally in command as she once had in slavery. Her attitude, without her being severe, dominated the servants, the soldiers, and the chiefs. Even Setne was submissive to that elegant and strong majesty, which excited his passion to the point of delirium.

One morning when she had come to see Aoura, he waited on her route. Eloh was not with her. Only two slaves accompanied her. Then he approached her and said, in an imploring voice: "Have you forgotten me, Gaila?"

She looked at him seriously. "I have not forgotten anything. Have I not accomplished all that I announced to you?"

"Yes," he said, with a tremor of his entire body, "you have accomplished more than I dared to wish. But you have withdrawn from me, Gaila, and you know that I love you."

"I belonged to the King of Thebes."

"You're free now..."

"I will not be free until the vengeance is accomplished and Eloh is recognized by the chiefs of the Bene-Asher."

Every day, Intar and his nomads brought back Bene-Asher dispersed in small groups in the solitudes. Since the conquest of their pastures by the warriors of Daour, they had wandered, poor and starving, in the plains where grass in sparse and in marshy lands. Fallen, they scarcely lived, on the milk of their thin cattle, the paltry plants that grow in the desert, hunting wild beasts, and booty captured from their enemies when they could surprise them in small numbers.

They retained the memory of their beautiful pastures bitterly; stubborn in faith, like all those of their race, they were awaiting the hour of vengeance. So, Intar found them credulous to the great news that he had announced to them secretly. They arrived among the Egyptians clad only in rough hides—for they had no longer woven wool or flax for some time—with large black horns on their heads, emaciated to the point that Thutmose's soldiers, hardened to all miseries, were disgusted by them. They prostrated themselves before Gaila, swore obedience to Eloh, son of Rub, in whom they recognized not only the descendant of great chiefs but also the elect of prophecies, for whom the phalanges of the terrible King of Thebes were marching.

Meanwhile, Setne divided up his troops. Intar, with a thousand nomads, supported by twelve hundred light infantrymen, headed southwards by roundabout routes; they were to bar the way to fugitives. Eight phalanges veered to the south-east in echelons. Setne intended to lead the attack from the north himself. For several days the Daourites had been agitated. They knew that an Egyptian army was advancing toward their pastures, but, especially because of the size of the contingents, they could not believe that it had been raised against them. Even when they learned that a large number of the Bene-Asher had joined the arriving forces, they did not conceive any great anxiety, for the idea never occurred to them that King Thutmose would want to avenge a paltry tribe dispersed in the desert.

When Setne was no more than half a day's march away, however, the rumor went around that he was bringing back Gaila, daughter of Rub, with her brother Eloh. Nevertheless, no one was certain of that, for Setne and Intar had sown contradictory stories among their own soldiers, and the Bene-Asher, alerted, did not betray the secret.

The Daourites sent messengers. They offered their alliance, and they came to ask the Egyptian chief whether he intended to pass through their lands. Setne did not want to receive them.

The nomads realized that it was war. Assembling their tents and flocks in haste, they commenced the exodus. Setne had hastened the march of his light troops. They reached the rearguard of the enemy, encumbered by cattle, cats and sheep. The rearguard prepared for battle, in order to protect the flight of the bulk of the army. The terrain was favorable to them, marshy and strewn with brushwood.

Sheltered, the Daourites seemed redoubtable. A frontal assault by the old Theban phalanges might have succeeded, at the price of immense sacrifices. Setne contented himself with a violent skirmish of archers and sling-wielders. In the meantime, the bulk of his forces moved up stealthily, some distance away, behind the dunes.

The nomads, defending themselves doggedly against what they believed to be the principal attack, did not perceive them at first. When they understood, the flanking movement was pronounced. Egyptian lances and bucklers glittered to their right. At the same time. Setne launched a new frontal assault.

Abruptly, the Bedouins decided to retreat, inasmuch as their center and their advance guard, with the women and children, ought to be safe. But they were unable to withdraw in order; many were obstinate in wanting to save the livestock; they were seen driving oxen and sheep. Their cries, mingled with the bellowing, disrupted them spontaneously. The long Theban trumpets sounded the charge. The phalanges closed up like immense pincers.

Only two or three hundred Daourites escaped. The rest fought energetically at first, but could not hold firm against the forests of lances. The indecisive lines collapsed; the bravest persisted vainly in hurling themselves against the wall of bucklers bristling with iron. Then, sensing their weakness, they threw away their weapons and begged the victors for mercy. One of their chiefs cried: "What have we done, men of Egypt? We live in peace with King Thutmose and we would not have refused to pay him tribute..."

But the others, their expressions bleak, were not astonished. They had never known anything but the war of tribes falling upon one another unexpectedly and snatching land and flocks at hazard. Vanquished, they no longer hoped for life.

Setne was having the weapons collected and the captives penned when great rumors and clouds of dust rose up. It was the Daourites' center and advance guard returning; to the south, they had been driven back by Intar's warriors; to the west they had encountered phalanges placed in echelons. Their rout was complete. They were fleeing in panic, seeking an issue among the brushwood and the dunes, careless of the fate of the women and children.

Very few broke the line of investment; it was sufficient for Setne to launch his reserves to terminate the battle. Almost the entire tribe was captive. In that quivering mass, parked between the marshes and the hills, the plaints of the wounded mingled with the shrill cries of women and children. Sometimes, moved by a sudden revolt or a vertigo of terror, a man launched himself against the guards; lances and swords nailed him to the ground. But almost all the warriors awaited destiny without a movement or a word.

Setne occupied himself with gathering the chiefs. He found nearly sixty of them, who were to appear before Gaila and Eloh. An hour before dusk, they were taken to a pasture where the Bene-Asher were assembled. Gaila and her brother were standing on a high platform hung with violent cloths. The vanquished chiefs understood their fate. Only one prostrated himself to beg for mercy. The others stamped their feet scornfully. The daughter of Rub had the oldest brought forward, and spoke to him in a soft voice.

"Do you remember, chiefs of the Daour? Ten years have passed since the night when you surprised our people. For ten generations our forefathers nourished their flocks on these plains. But you came; the night was not finished and our chiefs were dead. Five hundred warriors lay on the ground, my father perished by fire after his entrails had been spread, and my mother had succumbed to your outrages. Now, it is said: Vengeance is holy; death will pay for death; torture will be the price of torture. Chiefs of the Daour, it will be done to you as you have done to ours; you will perish in the furnace, your warriors will be sold in the slave markets, your wives, after being raped, will be subjected to the same fate. Let anyone among you who believes that is not just raise his voice."

The chiefs did not protest in the name of justice. They too knew that vengeance is holy. But they proffered threats. A giant whose eyes were blazing like carbuncles in the light of a torch cried: "Our race is not dead. Those who have escaped will roam the desert in their turn, until strength returns to them. The tree of the Daourites will be verdant again. Our sons will multiply like the fish of the Gulf. We will take back our pastures again. Your chiefs will be roasted in the furnace, your women raped, your warriors sold in the markets of cities!"

"It will be thus!" cried the others.

Gaila listened to them without anger. Now that she held them at her feet, her hatred had disappeared; she admired their courage.

"Bene-Asher," she said. "Do to these men as they did to yours."

With a roar of joy, the ragged multitude of the Bene-Asher fell upon the Daourite chiefs. It seemed that the massacre was about to commence. By means of their insults, the vanquished tried to summon a rapid death. But a strange order succeeded the initial fury. The convulsed faces resumed an apparent impassiveness, the clamors died down; of so many armed hands raised to strike, not one fell. The torture was organized.

Like good workmen, taciturn and laborious, men lit fires around the Daourites, while others built pyres on the plain. After sunset, those great sinister fires illuminated the slow and measured torture of the chiefs. They eyelids or their lips were cut off, or their teeth were broken, one by one, with a hammer. Sometimes their fingernails were torn out or their nipples burned. One eye was punctured, while their wives and daughters were raped in front of them. Only toward the middle of the night did they begin to perish. The entrails were withdrawn from some, but slowly, in order that they would not perish prematurely; others had their feet roasted first and firebrands were drawn over their bellies. Some were sprinkled with boiling water. Two old men, buried up to the neck on a mound that the fires rendered ardent, screamed like onagers.

Gaila had withdrawn. Her pious work was completed; the dead were no longer crying out for vengeance. As she was no longer taking pleasure in the suffering or the cries of agony she had had her tent and Eloh's moved to behind the dunes, where the earth was silent.

The night was pure; the star of Isis had an extraordinary glare. It was blue, it seemed to be leaping, paling the little constellations around it. Gaila lingered there, considering it. That was the star chosen by Setne, and its brightness, on that evening of triumph, troubled the nomad. She sighed. Now that everything was done in accordance with her will, she felt a violent desire for happiness, which filled her with dread.

Her guards lit large fires. At times, the star of Isis became imprecise in the smoke or was confounded with the rapid edge of a flame. The breeze, curt and abrupt, stimulated or suppressed the red gleams. It brought the

rumors of the camp and the field of tortures, but attenu-
ated and murmurous.

Gaila sensed, confusedly, that for her, the time had
come to live. Her gaze, surpassing the zone of the fires,
strove to catch sight of Setne; for she knew that he
would come. Every evening, after having checked the
vigilance of the sentinels, he passed close to the nomad's
tent.

Finally, she perceived him. He advanced slowly,
before his attentive escort. A dip in the terrain hid him,
and then he reappeared between two fires, as visible as
in broad daylight. He saw Gaila standing in front of her
tent, and dread paled his face. She made him a sign to
advance.

"Are you satisfied with your vengeance, Gaila?" he
asked.

"Yes," she replied, "you have done as I desired in
capturing the chiefs. The blood of my people is no longer crying out to the heavens. And my last servitude is
over. From this evening only, I am free.

And it seemed that she had changed again. The
slave and the king's concubine had disappeared. Something soft and indomitable shone in her splendid face, as
if Gaila had never quit that naïve soil, and she was a new
young woman, awaiting the caresses of a man. Then
Setne realized that she was the foremost among all
women; he prostrated himself before her.

"Do you remember," he said, "that I loved you
when you were a slave, and that your liberty never depended on anyone but yourself?"

"I remember. Then, again, I was not your slave any
more than I was Ankhi's or the others. I could have run
away; I could have rejoined my vanquished tribe. Then
vengeance would have escaped me. Only Egypt could

give it to me, and the evening when you chose me, I read in your face that we ought to unite our stars. And see, we are victorious."

"Gaila," he said, in a low voice, "ought they not remain united?"

"They ought never to cease to be."

He seized the nomad's hand and tried to draw her toward him.

Gaila pushed him away gently. "But it is not indispensable that my body be given to you, Setne..."

"Is it forbidden?" he murmured, in a hoarse voice. "Gaila, my star cannot shine without you. If I have known you only to lose you, victory becomes odious and fortune miserable. You are destroying your work."

"Let me look at your star," she said, maliciously.

The breeze languishing, the flames of the pyres rose straight and bright. The star of Isis vibrated higher and brighter.

"Come," said the nomad.

They found themselves in the shadow of the tent.

Then a small flexible hand seized Setne's hand; he felt cool and amorous lips against his mouth; and in the profound tremor of his being, he knew that it was the supreme moment of his happiness.

SF & FANTASY

Adolphe Alhaiza. *Cybele*
Alphonse Allais. *The Adventures of Captain Cap*
Henri Allorge. *The Great Cataclysm*
Guy d'Armen. *Doc Ardan: The City of Gold and Lepers; The Troglodytes of Mount Everest/The Giants of Black Lake; The Abominable Snowman*
G.-J. Arnaud. *The Ice Company*
André Arnyvelde. *The Ark; The Mutilated Bacchus*
Charles Asselineau. *The Double Life*
Henri Austruy. *The Eupantophone; The Olotelepan; The Petitpaon Era*
Barillet-Lagargousse. *The Final War*
Barbot de Villeneuve.*The Naiads/Beauty & The Beast*
Cyprien Bérard. *The Vampire Lord Ruthwen*
S. Henry Berthoud. *Martyrs of Science; The Angel Asrael*
Aloysius Bertrand. *Gaspard de la Nuit*
Richard Bessière. *The Gardens of the Apocalypse; The Masters of Silence*
Chevalier de Béthune. *The World of Mercury*
Albert Bleunard. *Ever Smaller*
Félix Bodin. *The Novel of the Future*
Pierre Boitard. *Journey to the Sun*
Louis Boussenard. *Monsieur Synthesis*
Alphonse Brown. *City of Glass; The Conquest of the Air*
Émile Calvet. *In a Thousand Years*
André Caroff. *The Terror of Madame Atomos; Miss Atomos; The Return of Madame Atomos; The Mistake of Madame Atomos; The Monsters of Madame Atomos; The Revenge of Madame Atomos; The Resurrection of Madame Atomos; The Mark of Madame Atomos; The Spheres of Madame Atomos; The Wrath of Madame Atomos* (w/M. & Sylvie Stéphan); *The Sins of Madame Atomos* (w/M. & Sylvie Stéphan)
Jean Carrère. *The End of Atlantis*

Félicien Champsaur. *Homo-Deus; The Human Arrow; Nora, The Ape-Woman; Ouha, King of the Apes; Pharaoh's Wife*
Didier de Chousy. *Ignis*
Jules Clarétie. *Obsession*
Jacques Collin de Plancy. *Voyage to the Center of the Earth*
Michel Corday. *The Eternal Flame; The Lynx* (w/André Couvreur)
André Couvreur. *Caresco, Superman; The Exploits of Professor Tornada* (3 vols.); *The Necessary Evil*
Gaston Danville. *The Perfume of Lust*
Camille Debans. *The Misfortunes of John Bull*
Captain Danrit. *Undersea Odyssey*
C. I. Defontenay. *Star (Psi Cassiopeia)*
Charles Derennes. *The People of the Pole*
Georges Dodds (anthologist). *The Missing Link*
Charles Dodeman. *The Silent Bomb*
Harry Dickson. *The Heir of Dracula; Harry Dickson vs. The Spider*
Jules Dornay. *Lord Ruthven Begins*
Alfred Driou. *The Adventures of a Parisian Aeronaut*
Odette Dulac. *The War of the Sexes*
Alexandre Dumas. *The Return of Lord Ruthven; The Man who Married a Mermaid* (w/P. Lacroix)
Renée Dunan. *Baal; The Ultimate Pleasure*
J.-C. Dunyach. *The Night Orchid; The Thieves of Silence*
Henri Duvernois. *The Man Who Found Himself*
Achille Eyraud. *Voyage to Venus*
Henri Falk. *The Age of Lead*
Paul Féval. *Anne of the Isles; Knightshade; Revenants; Vampire City; The Vampire Countess; The Wandering Jew's Daughter*
Paul Féval, *fils. Felifax, the Tiger-Man*
Charles de Fieux. *Lamékis*
Fernand Fleuret. *Jim Click*
Charles-Marie Flor O'Squarr. *Phantoms*
Louis Forest. *Someone is Stealing Children in Paris*

Arnould Galopin. *Doctor Omega*; *Doctor Omega and the Shadowmen* (anthology)
Judith Gautier. *Isoline and the Serpent-Flower*
H. Gayar. *The Marvelous Adventures of Serge Myrandhal on Mars*
Louis Geoffroy. *The Apocryphal Napoleon*
G.L. Gick. *Harry Dickson and the Werewolf of Rutherford Grange*
Raoul Gineste. *The Second Life of Doctor Albin*
Delphine de Girardin. *Balzac's Cane*
Emmanuel Gorlier. *The Nyctalope and the Tower of Babel*
Léon Gozlan. *The Vampire of the Val-de-Grâce*
Jules Gros. *The Fossil Man*
Jimmy Guieu. *The Polarian-Denebian War* (2 vols.)
Edmond Haraucourt. *Daah, the First Human; Illusions of Immortality*
Nathalie Henneberg. *The Green Gods*
Eugène Hennebert. *The Enchanted City*
Jules Hoche. *The Maker of Men and His Formula*
V. Hugo, P. Foucher & P. Meurice. *The Hunchback of Notre-Dame*
Romain d'Huissier. *Hexagon: Dark Matter*
Jules Janin. *The Magnetized Corpse*
Gustave Kahn. *The Tale of Gold and Silence*
Gérard Klein. *The Mote in Time's Eye; Starmasters*
Fernand Kolney. *Love in 5000 Years*
Paul Lacroix. *Danse Macabre; The Man who Married a Mermaid* (w/Alexandre Dumas)
Louis-Guillaume de La Follie. *The Unpretentious Philosopher*
Jean de La Hire. *The Fiery Wheel; Enter the Nyctalope; The Nyctalope on Mars; The Nyctalope vs. Lucifer; The Nyctalope Steps In; Night of the Nyctalope; Return of the Nyctalope; The Nyctalope and the Tower of Babel*
Etienne-Léon de Lamothe-Langon. *The Virgin Vampire*
André Laurie. *Spiridon*
Gabriel de Lautrec. *The Vengeance of the Oval Portrait*
Alain le Drimeur. *The Future City*

Georges Le Faure & Henri de Graffigny. *The Extraordinary Adventures of a Russian Scientist Across the Solar System* (2 vols.)

Gustave Le Rouge. *The Dominion of the World* (w/G. Guitton) (4 vols.); *The Mysterious Doctor Cornelius* (3 vols.); *The Vampires of Mars*

Jules Lermina. *The Battle of Strasbourg; Mysteryville; Panic in Paris; The Secret of Zippelius; To-Ho and the Gold Destroyers*

Maurice Level. *The Gates of Hell*

M.-J. L'Héritier de Villandon. *The Robe of Sincerity*

André Lichtenberger. *The Centaurs; The Children of the Crab*

Maurice Limat. *Mephista*

Listonai. *The Philosophical Voyager*

Jean-Marc & Randy Lofficier. *Edgar Allan Poe on Mars; The Katrina Protocol; Pacifica 1, 2; Robonocchio; Return of the Nyctalope;* (anthologists) *Tales of the Shadowmen 1-14; The Vampire Almanac* (2 vols.)

Ch. Lomon & P.-B. Gheuzi. *The Last Days of Atlantis*

Charles Malato. *Lost!*

Maurice Magre. *The Marvelous Story of Claire d'Amour; The Call of the Beast; Priscilla of Alexandria; The Angel of Lust; The Mystery of the Tiger; The Poison of Goa; Lucifer; The Blood of Toulouse; The Albigensian Treasure; Jean de Fodoas; Melusine; The Brothers of the Virgin Gold*

Victor Margueritte. *The Bacheloress; The Companion; The Couple*

Camille Mauclair. *The Virgin Orient*

Xavier Mauméjean. *The League of Heroes*

Joseph Méry. *The Tower of Destiny*

Hippolyte Mettais. *Paris Before the Deluge; The Year 5865*

Louise Michel. *The Human Microbes; The New World*

Tony Moilin. *Paris in the Year 2000*

Michael Moorcock's *Legends of the Multiverse*

José Moselli. *Illa's End*

John-Antoine Nau. *Enemy Force*

Marie Nizet. *Captain Vampire*

Frank Schildiner. *The Quest of Frankenstein; The Triumph of Frankenstein; Napoleon's Vampire Hunters*

Nicolas Ségur. *The Human Paradise; Penelope's Secret*

Pierre de Selenes: *An Unknown World*

Norbert Sevestre. *Sâr Dubnotal: Vs. Jack the Ripper; The Astral Trail*

Angelo de Sorr. *The Vampires of London*

Brian Stableford. *The Empire of the Necromancers (1. The Shadow of Frankenstein; 2. Frankenstein and the Vampire Countess; 3. Frankenstein in London); The Wayward Muse; Eurydice's Lament; The Mirror of Dionysius; The Pool of Mnemosyne; The New Faust at the Tragicomique; Sherlock Holmes and The Vampires of Eternity; The Stones of Camelot* (anthologist) *News from the Moon; The Germans on Venus; The Supreme Progress; The World Above the World; Nemoville; Investigations of the Future; The Conqueror of Death; The Revolt of the Machines; The Man With the Blue Face; The Aerial Valley; The New Moon; The Nickel Man; On the Brink of the World's End; The Mirror of Present Events; The Humanisphere*

Jacques Spitz. *The Eye of Purgatory*

Kurt Steiner. *Ortog*

Michel & Sylvie Stéphan. *The Wrath of Madame Atomos* (w/André Caroff); *The Sins of Madame Atomos* (w/André Caroff)

Eugène Thébault. *Radio-Terror*

Edmond Thiaudière. *Singular amours*

C.-F. Tiphaigne de La Roche. *Amilec*

Simon Tyssot de Patot. *The Strange Voyages of Jacques Massé and Pierre de Mésange*

Louis Ulbach. *Prince Bonifacio*

Théo Varlet. *The Castaways of Eros; The Golden Rock.; The Martian Epic* (w/Octave Joncquel); *Timeslip Troopers* (w/André Blandin); *The Xenobiotic Invasion*

Pierre Véron. *The Merchants of Health*

Paul Vibert. *The Mysterious Fluid*

Villiers de l'Isle-Adam. *The Scaffold; The Vampire Soul*

Gaston de Wailly. *The Murderer of the World*
Philippe Ward. *Artahe; Manhattan Ghost* (w/Mickael Laguerre); *The Song of Montségur* (w/Sylvie Miller)

www.ingramcontent.com/pod-product-compliance
Lightning Source LLC
Chambersburg PA
CBHW060433030726
47495CB00003B/858